Flight 

Sunsinger Books

Illinois Short Fiction

A list of books in the series appears at the end of this book.

Flights in the Heavenlies

Stories by

Ernest J. Finney

University of Illinois Press
Urbana and Chicago

Manufactured in the United States of America
P 5 4 3 2 1

This book is printed on acid-free paper.

"Agents of Grace," *Sewanee Review,* Spring 1994
"Double Smart," *Puerto Del Sol,* Winter 1993
"Flights in the Heavenlies," *Greensboro Review,* Spring 1990
"The Money Tree," *Sewanee Review,* Winter 1990
"Stepsister," *Sewanee Review,* Winter 1992
A portion of "Talus," *Kenyon Review,* Summer 1987

Library of Congress Cataloging-in-Publication Data
Finney, Ernest J.
Flights in the heavenlies : stories / by Ernest J. Finney.
p. cm.—(Sunsinger Books/Illinois short fiction)
ISBN 0-252-06480-1 (pbk. : alk. paper)
I. Title. II. Series.
3556.I499F57 1996
813'.54—dc20 95-32472
CIP

For the San Bruno Public Library,
and for all the librarians there and afterward
who handed me books and gave me the world.

Contents

Flights in the Heavenlies

"How many fingers am I holding up?" the TV interviewer asked, putting her left hand behind her back. She'd introduced herself as Jane Colby; her hair was the right pale yellow for the name.

Cissy didn't know what to answer. The interview area where they sat looked like a dentist's office: small, a few comfortable chairs, flowered wallpaper. Except for the camera, intense lights, and people wandering through, this could be where she got her teeth cleaned. "I really don't know," she said. Jane's smirk cut across her heavy makeup as if it were soft cheese. "I can't even find my purse sometimes." She thought that might be funny, but Jane didn't change expression.

"Well . . ." Jane looked furtively, unsuccessfully, down at a card, then continued, "How did you locate those bonds, then?" The woman couldn't remember her name, Cissy realized. She noticed herself on the monitor; the screen seemed a yard wide. She was startled by her image. Placid, she decided. Bovine? No. Plain? Lined? She was too thin, too tall, her face was pinched, and she dressed like an old woman.

"It was just a feeling," she said. Did she care what Jane thought? She herself didn't watch this channel. Half of her wanted to be sitting right here where she was. In the limelight? She wondered where that word came from. The other half wanted to be somewhere else. Anywhere.

She had been able to walk into the kitchen for the first time and point. "There," she said. Since their grandfather had died five days before, the bereaved family had been searching the old house for eleven thousand dollars in negotiable bonds. One of the sons got down on his knees and with a yellow broom handle started working things out from under the hot water heater. Old clots of dust, marbles and indistinguishable bits of debris, one unbroken graham cracker. "They'd burn up down there," someone said. The son scooted out an El Primo cigar box, dust thick as fur. Before he reached for a rag to wipe off the dust, the son glanced toward her and asked, "How did you know?"

"I just knew," she'd said. The bonds had only got the doves to coo.

Margaret had not come into the studio; she was waiting outside in her car, doing a crossword puzzle, using the steering wheel for a table. For all her bluster, Margaret had fits of shyness where she wouldn't talk to people, or go in with her on assignments. She'd been acting like that since before the bonds were found under the water heater last week. Cissy knew even less about her daughter than she did about herself. But Margaret was her impresario, her contractor. Margaret got her what she sometimes liked to think of as her tasks or assignments. She liked the schoolroom sound of that.

Cissy got into the car. Margaret finished the word she was printing and put the newspaper down. Started the engine. Everything deliberate, precise, as if someone were watching her. "Mother, did that family ever send you anything, like they said? Where you found the bonds?" Cissy shook her head. "I'll have to phone again," Margaret said. "People forget pretty easily, don't they?" With Margaret, everything had two meanings. Forgetting and obligations were themes she hit on often. Cissy's connection to Margaret. To the car. She had no transportation of her own. She had no one else but Margaret.

Margaret slowed down, turned into a residential street, looked at the clipboard where she listed addresses. Began checking house numbers. Cissy didn't help. This was Margaret's part.

"You're sure this is it?" she asked, when they stopped in front of a house with an unkempt lawn. Weathered rolled-up newspapers were scattered over the roof like misshapen bananas. It had never happened, but she always had the fear she'd ring and it would be the wrong house. It was bad enough as it was.

"This is it," Margaret said. "They're waiting." Cissy took her time, on the chance that Margaret, exasperated, would come with her. But Margaret picked up her folded section of newspaper and started in on her crossword puzzle again.

Cissy rang the bell. "I think you've been expecting me," she said when the door was opened by a woman her age. The woman looked puzzled. "I retrieve things." It sounded like she was a dog. She would like to sound like a doctor, "I make you feel better," but that wasn't always true. She'd read in the paper that the family she'd found the bonds for had had an argument over the division. Two had been cited for battery.

She was led into the living room. She should try to make it look harder than it was, try to insert some excitement, she thought. But it wouldn't make any difference: the doves wouldn't fly for this; they shifted their feet as she strode over to the green drapes and turned back one side, then reached up to unfasten a diamond earring.

"I know who put it there," the woman said as she got her purse and handed over the right amount. Cissy thanked her, moving toward the door. "I have been looking for this for two months," the woman said, weighing the earring in her palm.

The next was just what she needed: a young mother who'd lost her $906 tax return check. It had been used for a bookmark and was under the guest room bed in a volume of the *Encyclopedia Americana, Desert–Egret*. Her two kids had helped Cissy retrieve the check, crawling under the bed to get the book. The young woman paid Cissy, then added, "I can't find the key to my freezer. It's locked. I haven't been able to open it for a week." This happened sometimes. Unexpectedly, Cissy felt a coo: the sound carried through her body as if her bones were the pipes of an organ. Sweetness, happiness, and goodness flowed over her. Her body rocked. Her eyes closed. One of the children pulled on her skirt. Their mother was looking at her in alarm. Cissy quickly rolled up her sleeve and plunged her arm into the fish tank. Picked the key out of the pink gravel on the bottom. "One of the kids," she said, her arm dripping. "Is there anything else?"

The mother stepped back and hurried to open the door.

She didn't know where the ability came from. It wasn't easy, finding other people's things that were misplaced or lost. Disappeared or just gone. If there could be a date affixed to a beginning, a recognition, it would be sometime after Lyle died. He had been out on a job, crawled under a house, and somehow touched a live two-hundred-volt wire.

At that time she began to hear the sounds but was unable to identify them; it was just grief, she thought during those months. But Lyle's death, she decided later, had begun something, just as their marriage had. They'd met when a new wing of classrooms was added to the school where she taught. Lyle was the electrical contractor. She had quit teaching after they got married. His partner bought her half of the business after Lyle died and made prompt monthly payments for ten years. She lived on that, with Social Security benefits for Margaret. When it was time to go back to teaching, she convinced herself that too many things had changed; she wouldn't be able to fit in anymore. She got by. Babysitting. Cutting out coupons. The last of her savings. Margaret won every scholarship in the district and went off to college.

It was Margaret who first noticed. Who put a name to it. A friend had lost her high school ring. "My mother will find it for you," she heard Margaret say. "She's good."

She went outside when she was called. Just walked over across the lawn and dug the gold and green-glass ring out with her forefinger. Then a neighbor lost his car keys and another his insurance policy. At first she didn't always find what was lost. Time didn't matter. She found a book that had been missing for thirty years. But she had to be in close proximity to the lost object to hear the doves.

Margaret spent nine years, off and on, going to college. She had been a secretary, had worked for the forestry department, then owned her own answering service. She hadn't lived at home for years. Now they both lived on the proceeds of Cissy's assignments. They met only when they had business. Margaret liked mystery too much. She hadn't found out Margaret had gotten married until she got divorced, five months later; that's when Cissy saw it in the local paper under "Vital Statistics." "You *would* read that," Margaret had said when she asked. She decided then that if Margaret couldn't bother to let her know about her marriage, that was enough. She didn't have to worry about her anymore, and she didn't. It made her life so much easier. It was an arrangement between them now.

❦

The phone rang at 3:20 A.M. exactly. She woke up and looked over at the clock as if she had expected the call. "Mrs. Evans, I've been thinking about you." Cissy listened, fully awake. "I saw you on the eleven o'clock news."

"Thank you." She wondered why in the world she'd said that.

"For sixty years, three generations, my family has been looking for something." The woman paused, trying to find another word, but couldn't. "We're not even sure what it is," she went on.

Cissy sat up, her back against the headboard of the bed. In spite of herself, it did something to her when she heard *lost*. She could feel her heart slip into another gear, go faster, as if it were a motor. This time the sound alerted the doves. She'd had that feeling too when she was a young girl: not the doves, of course, but that release, the severing of the connections between herself and her body. When she rode the pony on her grandparents' farm. She'd spent the summers there, helping her grandmother can asparagus and tomatoes and make chutney. Detasseling corn. Riding the pony. When she got a little older she was allowed to ride one of the horses. It caught her by surprise, the first time her grandfather's mare broke into a gallop: she nearly bounced out of the saddle. She'd urged the horse after that to go faster and faster, lying low against the neck, the mane whipping across her face, whispering, "Runaway, run away with me," looking back, watching the dirt fly like dark sparks as May's hooves left the ground. When the mare fell, broke her two front legs, and she came down hard against the pasture grass, it was such a surprise, the sudden shock of stopping, of the flight suspended, that she felt no pain, even though her collarbone and right arm were broken. They shot the horse. No one blamed her. But she never went back to the farm.

"I'll send the car for you," the caller said. "It's not too early? Will a half hour give you enough time to get ready? I just had this idea and couldn't sleep because of it." Cissy noticed it was almost four-thirty; the woman had been talking for over an hour.

She was ready, waiting by the door when she heard the car turn into her driveway. *Is this some ruse?* she thought, going down the walk. *Someone to murder me? Who would take the time?* she wondered. Not the elderly driver who opened the door for her.

It was a mansion. Tree-lined drive. She hadn't thought any of these places were left. She'd thought the rich all lived on the fortieth floors of skyscrapers, under guard. The woman tried to put her at her ease: "Call me Gloria," she said. "I feel sure you can help. I don't know where to start. There's supposed to be something valuable in the house." Suddenly she started weeping. "We need the money; that's why I called. You're our last hope."

Cissy concentrated. "Did he leave any hints?"

"No, nothing. I don't remember him, of course. It's been a family tradition, the story. It's my last resort." The woman tried to compose herself, pulled a handkerchief out of her sleeve, and blew her nose.

"Would you show me around, Gloria?" she asked. The woman was older than she was. Early sixties. At 5 A.M. she was dressed simply but still looked elegant. Didn't try to get rid of her wrinkles or liver spots. Exercised. Tanned. They hadn't walked fifty feet when it happened. It was so sudden she was caught unaware. She thought her feet were going to leave the floor, as if the doves were in full flight. The wing-tip feathers were brushing her insides. She concentrated on moving past the open doorway. "What was that room?" she asked. Had she given herself away? Her knees had almost buckled. Did Gloria notice, understand it was in that room?

"The solarium. Would you like to go inside?"

"Later," she said. "Let me see the rest of the house." It was probably the strongest reaction she'd ever had. There was no explaining. She had tried that with Mr. Raymond, the pastor at her church. He had listened to everything. She'd been going to St. James for years. Margaret had sung in the choir. It was just down the street from her house. When she'd finished, he started. "I must speak my mind, Mrs. Evans." He was rolling a red pencil back and forth between his thumb and forefinger. "We neither speak in tongues," he said with a smile, "nor see our statues shed tears. We're Lutheran." He went on patronizing her. Called Margaret later and said her mother needed estrogen supplements and should see a doctor. She decided what was happening wasn't spiritual. But she didn't go to a doctor.

They had tea in the solarium, and strips of toast with melted butter. A silver service. She had toured the whole house, thirteen bedrooms.

She had herself under control now. The doves were pleasantly cooing back and forth; she felt like she was glowing brighter and brighter from the sounds.

Gloria walked her to the front door: it was after eleven. "Oh dear, it wasn't meant to be," Gloria said. "Would you like to stay for lunch?"

"I can't; I have an appointment, but I'd like to come back again, if I may. I'm not finished by any means."

"You're welcome at any time. Phone first, of course, to see if I'll be home. I don't know your methods or understand your abilities, but I find you to be a most interesting person."

"Why, thank you," Cissy said, amused, enjoying the slight change in Gloria's tone now that she hadn't found anything. Would Gloria offer her a ride home, summon the chauffeur, or direct her to the nearest bus stop?

Whizzing along. She couldn't think of any better word, sitting in the back of the sleek dark blue limousine with windows she could see out of, though no one could see in. She would phone Gloria in a few days, go back. Show her where. She had no idea what it could be. Was that accurate? She wouldn't think about it now. Gloria was going to be good luck for her.

❦

Margaret had three "small" jobs, as she put it, for her that afternoon. "Where have you been? I've been trying to get you all morning," she said when she phoned.

"Busy. I've been busy."

"Well, get your glad rags on. We've got places to go."

The first was finding a safe-deposit box key a neighbor of Margaret's had misplaced. The second was an engagement ring. The third was a surprise, a lost three-year-old girl who'd been missing for fifteen hours. Margaret drove them out to the area, sparsely developed, with a lot of open fields left. Grass covered big mounds of dirt that had been dumped and never spread out. Kids had made bike runs up and over the tops.

"You phoned these people?"

"No, I heard about it on the radio." She had parked the car by dozens of others. Police. Sheriffs. She could see troops of Boy Scouts in their uniforms and men with dogs on leashes. "This is where she was last seen," Margaret said. "And before I forget, here's your share." She counted out bills. Half of thirty and half of five dollars. "I'll owe you the fifty cents," she said. Cissy took the money; there was no use arguing about it. "I get the payments up front now," Margaret said. Cissy wasn't going to say anything about that either, although she had stood like a dummy at both places waiting for the people to pay her, not asking, but not wanting to return to Margaret without the money. The key had fallen through a hole in the lining seam of the woman's purse, and the ring had been in the bottom of the bathtub soap dish.

Cissy put the money in her purse. She didn't feel well. Didn't know what it was; probably from not getting any sleep the night before. Not her stomach but her head. That was unusual; she never got headaches. She put her hand to the back of her head and it was sore to the touch.

No one asked them what they were doing. The new grass, only a few inches high, showed like green felt through last year's gray and tangled weeds. She couldn't help herself; she started walking faster, feeling things getting into her good shoes, tearing her stockings. There was no cooing, only the pain in her head, as if some imaginary bird, yellow, she colored it, with a long orange beak, was pecking at her. It was unbearable; she put both hands crossed over the back of her head, but it didn't help. She kept going, staggering; the yellow bird was pecking right through her skull. And then she fell.

"My mother's found her. Over here. Here!" Margaret yelled.

She could not recall anything about that afternoon. Margaret had insisted on reading the newspaper story to her over the phone the next morning: "Psychic finds . . ." She jerked the phone away from her ear as if the receiver were ready to burst into flames and hung up. The real pain had gone away, but for days later her head felt like it was bruised, tender, shouldn't be touched. She didn't comb her hair for a week. Sat in the front room drinking cup after cup of tea, drapes drawn, only the small lamp on. Didn't dare turn on the TV.

Margaret came over and Cissy was short with her when she tried to hand her part of the reward money. "First, when did we determine we should divide the money equally?" That had always bothered her.

"It was my idea," Margaret said.

She forgot what she was going to say and yelled, "I don't like your ideas. And specifically, I don't want that money. And more importantly, I don't want to ever do that again. I don't care what the circumstances are."

Margaret turned docile, didn't say much. Was certainly glad to take the money. Tried to kiss her good-bye, but Cissy turned away. She had never spoken to anyone like that before. It had never been necessary with Lyle; he was as gentle as a willow. What kind of thought was that? It should be gentle as a lamb. A willow tree? Since that day—that's how she chose to refer to it—there had been a kind of short circuit in her head. She reached for a slice of bread and ended up with a pot holder in her hand. Had she had a stroke? At fifty-one? She wasn't going to a doctor.

She still couldn't sleep well. Lay there, her body dead, her mind racing. What had Lyle felt when he grabbed the uninsulated wire? Would she know him when she caught up with him? She thought of Gloria: it was 2:56 A.M. She waited, watching the big hand. At 3:20 she phoned. It had been almost a month.

"Who? Cissy?"

"Cissy Evans."

"Oh yes, how are you?"

"Send your car; I've been thinking about your problem. Make some coffee too, Gloria." She was brazen.

A half hour later they were sitting in the solarium, waiting for the sun to come through the green hanging plants. She belonged here, she thought. Gloria had been sound asleep; there were pillow wrinkles across her right cheek. She was feeling better by the minute. It was amazing. "What if there is a treasure or something? What will you do?" She had to hurry, get some kind of promise.

"I was a little overemotional, I think, the last time you were here," Gloria said. "I had heard from my investment counselor, then my broker: both had bad news for me. But now it's not so dreadful."

Cissy felt the smooth, smooth before the goodness. But more words came out to intrude. "Then you don't want me to find your grandfather's hoard?" Gloria laughed and she tried to join her. Who was speaking? "What would your response be to me? To Cecilia Evans?"

"I'd be very, very grateful," Gloria said. There was a half smile imprinted on one side of her mouth, as if they were sharing a joke.

Cissy didn't care if the very, very was all she would get. She was being transported. Not by the usual five or six doves but by flocks: she was going to rise. There were flights in her fingers, inside her nose and toes, carrying her away. She leaped up, turned, and pointed at the wall of the house. There had been a window there, covered over when the solarium had been added on. She rushed over and started pounding on the boards with the sides of her fists, shouting, "There. There. Get a hammer." Gloria was looking alarmed: she left the solarium in a hurry. Cissy couldn't stop herself; she tried to pry the board off with a butter knife. That bent back, and so did the two spoons she tried before Gloria came back with the hammer and the chauffeur. *I'm frantic,* she thought. *I'm frantic.*

She grabbed the hammer out of Gloria's hand, put the claw under the edge of the board, and using the handle like a lever, pulled down with all her strength. The board cracked up the middle and half came off, the nails squeaking until the last. She was panting, but she didn't need air to breathe, she needed light. "Get a flashlight," she called back to Gloria. She felt around with her arm in the space. Felt the sash weight that raised and lowered the forgotten window. With the flashlight she saw the metal tube and reached in and pulled it up. It was attached by one twist of rusty wire. She yanked it free and the wall shook.

Her hands were all dirty. She was wet from the exertion. But the doves were cooing and in their places. She felt powerful. Gloria dismissed the chauffeur before she unscrewed the top to the tube. "Looks like what my father used to put his fishing rods in, years ago," she said. Cissy sat down. There was a half cup of coffee left in the pot, and she poured it out for herself. Her hand was shaking.

There was a roll of dirty oilcloth in the tube. Gloria unrolled it. "My," she exclaimed. Cissy didn't listen. She had landed but she still felt wonderful.

She must have dozed because Gloria was trying to get her up out of the chair. "Come on, come on." They got into the car. She closed her eyes for a minute, and Gloria was pulling at her again. They were parked by a door that said MUSEUM STAFF ONLY.

The museum director and two of his assistants had come in early to meet with Gloria, who was telling them about her grandfather.

"May I wash my hands?" Cissy interrupted. They were so dirty they were making her uncomfortable. The director pointed to a door. She made sure they were clean, squirting her cupped palms half full of pink soap.

ꕤ

When she finally got home, it was time for bed again. After ten. Gloria hadn't wanted her to go. She kicked off her shoes and started toward the bathroom to brush her teeth. The front doorbell chimed. It startled her. She wasn't going to answer, but then there were more dingdongs. Through the peephole she saw a woman. A man. Then Margaret, standing behind them. She might have known. She opened the door.

"Mother," Margaret said, "these are Mr. and Mrs. Rhaba. They don't speak much English."

Cissy tried to smile at them, but they didn't make any acknowledgment, just stared back, as if they were afraid of her. "Mr. Rhaba's mother is missing. She's an older woman. She wandered off this afternoon."

As Margaret talked, Cissy decided she wasn't going to do it. This was ridiculous. Margaret's head was between Mr. and Mrs. Rhaba, where they couldn't see, and she winked.

"I'm sorry," Cissy started out.

Margaret interrupted. "Mother, it's going to be cold tonight. She'll be out there all by herself in just her robe." Mrs. Rhaba bent over, to tie her shoe, Cissy thought, but she knelt on the porch and grasped Cissy by the legs: she could feel the woman's face against her knees and warm tears running down her shins. Mr. Rhaba tried to tell her something, but she couldn't understand him.

She rode with Margaret; they had come in two cars. She didn't speak until they were parked in front of the Rhabas' house. She felt the dread. "Margaret, don't do this to me again, because I won't cooperate. I don't know who you take after, but you're the greediest person I've ever known." She opened the door to get out.

"But you have a gift," Margaret said, as if she were disputing with her. Cissy didn't answer.

The house fronted on a golf course fairway. The owners could go out their back gate and play a round at their own private club. She was ushered into the house. There was a police officer, not in uniform, his badge attached to his coat jacket. She was introduced. "The voodoo lady," he said.

"I don't think that's funny," she answered and walked away. Margaret followed, trying to take her arm. She was led by Mr. Rhaba through the house into the backyard. It was dark once they were past the lighted swimming pool. "How large is the golf course?" she asked Mr. Rhaba. He said something that she couldn't quite comprehend.

"About a hundred sixty acres." It was the policeman who answered. "Would you like a light?" he added.

She realized he was trying to be nice. "If you like," she said. She was becoming more apprehensive. She could feel it already. Not the doves inside but the demon. The orange-beaked bird.

"How do you want to proceed?" She looked at him closer. "How do you want to work it?" he said.

"What's your name?"

"Phil," he said.

"I'd like just for the two of us to take a walk. Would you agree to that, Phil?"

"Of course."

She started off. Margaret didn't dare try to follow. Phil came behind, flashlight held high. Its oblong of yellow preceded her. She didn't need the light; she knew where she was going.

"Ma'am, if you don't mind me saying . . ."

"Cissy. Call me Cissy."

"Cissy, we aren't supposed to search until twenty-four hours after, unless there are children involved, or a felony. Because most people turn up. Stopped for a beer. Got to talking to someone. Meeting someone on the sly and forgot the time. That kind of thing. But since she's an older lady and missing since three, we can make an exception."

"What's your wife's name?" she interrupted.

"She's not lost, Cissy."

"What's her name?"

"Louise."

"She's going to be the first woman president in the U.S.A. That's my first and only political prediction." She was beginning to feel hysterical. The sound was coming in waves, *ah boom ah boom ah boom,* against the side of her head with each peck. It was past pain. Her toenails ached.

"I'll tell her that," Phil said. "She'll be amused. But what I'm trying to say is we covered this part of the country club. I had uniformed officers going over this already. Some of the gardeners checked the bushes along the fairways, and they know the layout."

She couldn't listen. Bone and hair were flying from her skull. Her brain was breached, breached. She saw the water and walked right into the pond and reached down for the dead hair of the lost woman.

Before she opened her eyes she knew she was in a hospital. Strangely enough, it was Gloria who was holding her hand. "You're going to be fine," she said in her gentle voice. She would like to be like Gloria, that courteous manner, unsurprised by anything. She could hear a robin sing or the whistle of a siren with the same look of equanimity. "I met Margaret; she's just left to go home. An energetic woman, I must say."

"Gloria, I want to hide somewhere."

She didn't blanch. "We can arrange that. You can come and stay with me."

"I mean forever. I want to disappear."

Gloria didn't have a chance to answer. Phil walked into the room. She recalled him without difficulty. "Good morning, ladies."

He was going to amuse them. She got in first, "His wife, Louise, is going to be our forty-fourth president."

"How nice for the country," Gloria said.

"I haven't had a chance to tell her yet," Phil said. "I've been busy." He held up an armful of green folders. "You made me a believer. I pulled all the current missing persons files. You could be a big help to us."

She never heard it herself, but she must have started shrieking. People came running; she could see them. She watched as her body convulsed and they plunged a syringe into her arm and it was dark again.

❦

She couldn't read minds, but when this doctor came in, she knew it wasn't the usual visit. Not the how-do-you-feel-today kind. He didn't have a white jacket on, either.

"You're not a psychiatrist?" she asked.

"No, a neurologist. I'd like to examine you."

"No," she said. "If there's a reason, I don't want to know."

"That's one way to look at the problem."

"It's not a problem."

"Then why are you in the hospital?" When she didn't respond, he went on. "Whatever the reason for your abilities, we should find out, see if we can find a physical cause. I can't guarantee—"

She interrupted. "You'll end up saying I'm hysterical or menopausal."

"I might," he said. "But I might not." They both laughed. He came back the same day with a pot of white mums. "I always wanted to bring flowers to someone in a hospital, but no one in my family ever gets sick."

He tickled her feet with a feather and stuck pins in her legs. She spent three days in the X-ray room. Other doctors came in, friends of his. Dr. Slade was more Margaret's age than hers, but he could get her to laugh, and she looked forward to his visits. She would have told him about the doves, but he never asked. Didn't seem interested in what had happened to her, or what she had done.

He came in late on a Friday; the nurses were just changing shifts. Sat down on the bed. She would have liked him to take her hand like he usually did when he came to talk, but he didn't. "We didn't find anything," he said. He seemed disappointed. "You had all the criteria. I was almost sure you were the one."

She didn't know what he was talking about. "There is nothing wrong with me," she said, sitting up, frightened now.

"There has to be some kind of an implant, a transformer device that they direct you with. We couldn't find one. Probably with exploratory surgery . . ." His pure blue eyes looked her over as his voice trailed off. She jumped out of the other side of the bed and ran until she reached the nurses' station.

❦

She still didn't feel entirely herself. Gloria had taken her in after her frantic phone call, and somehow Gloria had dealt with Margaret. She hadn't heard from her the whole week she'd been here. Every morning they had breakfast in the solarium, spent hours reading the morning papers as the sun grew warmer and warmer. In the afternoons they took drives through the hills or along the coast, both sitting back, watching the scenery slide by, speaking now and then.

"How have you held off Margaret? I didn't think it could be done."

"I bribed her."

Cissy was embarrassed. There was a glass panel between them and the driver. She heard herself telling Gloria what it was like when she found dead people. "I can't take another," she said. "It's too awful. It's like being split open. Like the doves will get out."

"But finding things, articles, doesn't bother you?"

"No, it's a wonderful feeling."

"Have you ever found anyone alive? I hope you don't mind me discussing this: I was just waiting for you to bring it up. Because, frankly, I find the whole affair fascinating. When you found that painting I heard the angels singing, I swear I did."

Cissy could smile at that. "I've never found a living person. I don't think I could."

"That's unfortunate, isn't it."

"I want to stop everything. I just don't want to do it anymore. I want to get away."

"You mentioned that before," Gloria said. "It's possible, but I'm not sure how it can be done. You're not aware, but you've become a supermarket star. A tabloid journalist's dream material. I read that somewhere too, about you. And to tell you the truth, a few people do know where you are and need your help. Important people." She went on, not waiting for a reaction. "Do you think it would make you feel better if you accepted a few requests? There's one I think is interesting. We—my late husband and I—set up a trust . . ."

Cissy watched Gloria. She had the same look as Margaret. There had to be a way out. Not just an evasion, but an escape. A new identity. *What good is there left to find anyhow?* she wondered.

❦

Gloria had gotten out of the car, and now the chauffeur was holding her door open. She got out too. There were only a few other people on the yacht, and they didn't come near her. Prearranged, possibly. There were several divers in wet suits. It was like a nature movie.

Gloria had deposited an enormous amount of money in a special account in her name. That was for finding the oil painting. But did that give Gloria the right to ask her to do this one? And she was going on and on. "The funds from the sale of these articles will be given to the library to build the new children's annex. If the stories are true about the ingots and the coins, there will be more than enough for the annex and maybe even another branch."

"Life isn't fair, Gloria," she said. "Not always good. Not always bad. But it absolutely isn't fair." She had been thinking that, so she said it aloud. It silenced Gloria. She withdrew into her rich-lady-taken-aback demeanor.

The boat was still in sight of land, but it started to swing around in a wide turn. The divers were looking at her expectantly. The boat slowed and went into another turn. She realized they were making a big circle in the smooth surface of the bay. *Sea breezes,* she thought. *How far do they travel inland before they lose this fine odor of brine?* She almost asked aloud how long it took to get a passport. But Gloria couldn't be trusted.

They had lunch: all the things she had come to like. She couldn't get enough caviar. The first bite was always such a pleasant surprise. She had wondered why in the movies rich people always ate little fish eggs. Because they were delicious, that's why. All especially for her. It was nice to have the kind of power that made people want to please you. But that wasn't good. Gloria was watching her apprehensively. Was she going to let down her friend? "What religion are you, Gloria?" she asked her.

"Well, I started out a Congregationalist and became a Quaker because my husband was one. And now, since I met you, I'm undecided." Gloria wasn't eating; she spoke looking out toward the land.

"I used to be a Lutheran. I used to believe in the possibility of a God; that's all I ever hoped for. But our new minister said I was sick, when I described the goodness I felt when I found something that would make someone feel happy."

"What do you feel now?" Gloria asked, trying to sound calm. "I'm sorry, Cissy; I had no right to do this. Forgive me."

"I feel the doves adjusting their feet on their perch. Stretching out their wings with a flutter or two. We've passed over your treasure several times now. We should come by again in another little bit." She was watching Gloria. "I should be more precise, shouldn't I?"

She was trembling so much she didn't know if she could get to the rail. She saw Gloria raise her arm, and the boat slowed. Slower and slower. She kept nodding, her eyes closed. Pretty. Pretty. And she brought her hands together with a clap and the doves rose up.

"Stop!" Gloria yelled in a surprisingly loud voice.

The boat reversed and Cissy heard the splash of the divers.

❦

"You're sure you want to come back here?" They were parked in front of Cissy's house. Yellow dandelions by the hundreds had come up. No one had mowed.

"I'm sure," she said. The chauffeur was getting out of his door.

"Cissy." Gloria had taken her hand. "We're not sure of the extent of the find, but we thought you might like to have the annex named after you."

"No, that's kind of you, but it's not necessary." She was talking like her now, Cissy thought. Gloria finally let go of her hand and she got out of the car. She was back where she'd started from.

She got busy, put a load of wash in the machine, and filled the dishwasher. It had been a month since she'd walked out of the place. Plugged in the phone. Found a number in the yellow pages. She could get a passport in less than twenty-four hours. "I don't know if I can be ready by that time," she told the clerk, laughing, "but I'll try." It felt comforting to hear herself so cheerful.

She kept busy packing, phoning. Someone to take care of the lawn. To turn off the gas and the electricity. She was surprised when the telephone rang and glad it wasn't Margaret when she picked it up.

"Mrs. Evans? Do you remember me? I've been trying to get hold of you for over a month. Phoned three or four times a day, always no answer, until now."

"Who are you?"

"I interviewed you for Channel 3. Jane Colby."

"I remember you, the cheese woman."

"Well, as you know, you're news. Big news. Mrs. Evans, are you still there?"

"Call me Cissy."

"We should meet again, Cissy."

"I can't"—she hesitated for the right word—"do that anymore."

"You can't, or you won't?"

She didn't answer.

"You have an obligation, Mrs. Evans, not to me or to Channel 3 but to the people that you could help. How many persons can do what you do? It's a marvel, that's what it is."

She wasn't tempted. Give in to it, become rich and famous? Be selective this time. Just feed the doves. Avoid the demons. She had asked, pleaded with the doves to leave, be silent, never fly again. "I've given up," she said. "I can't guess things anymore."

"That's hard to believe."

"You'll have to take my word for it."

"Viewers have been writing, phoning in. We've never had such a response, every time we play your interview. There was a man who lost—"

She hung up. She was going to have to hurry. She stopped cleaning and just packed. She was taking too much, but she didn't know where she was going, if it would be hot or cold. She would take a cab to the airport and decide there. She let in the man who was going to change the locks. There was so much noise outside: the gardener had come and was mowing the lawn. The phone rang again and she picked it up automatically.

"Mother, is that you? I just happened to call and here you are. What luck. Do you know what that friend of yours told me? That I had to leave you alone. You needed your rest. I'm her daughter, I told her."

"What is it, Margaret? I'm really busy."

"What's all that noise?"

"Gardener doing the lawn."

"I could have done that."

"Well, why didn't you?"

"Because I've been busy. You don't know what it's been like for me. I have a twenty-page list. Telegrams. One from the Department of Defense. A secretary phoned: the president's wife wants to meet you."

"Margaret, I'm taking a trip. I won't be able to attend to any of those requests. So don't make any promises."

"Where are you going?"

"I haven't decided. I'll write." She put down the phone.

Where was her suede belt to go with the brown dress she was folding? She looked in the drawer again and found it. When the passport office phoned she was ready, and she called for a cab. She had to wait at the office while they took and developed her photo, but then she was on her way again by bus.

The airport was too big. Travelers rushing around. Long lines at every counter. Announcements you couldn't understand over loudspeakers. She put her suitcase in a locker and wandered. There were too many different airlines. It was like a shopping mall. It was impossible to commit yourself to just one company.

She watched a big board up near the ceiling where places and times appeared like magic in foot-high letters. She read, as it appeared, FLIGHT 305, HALIFAX. There was no line at this airline counter, and she went up and asked the clerk, "Do they speak English in Halifax?" She would like to be able to converse with the residents if she could. She knew it was north.

"It's in Canada," the clerk said, amused.

"I'll take a ticket, one-way," she said. She'd try a foreign place next time, she told herself.

After she boarded and took her seat there was a two-hour delay before the plane even warmed up its engines. She tried to read the magazines and newspapers. But she couldn't concentrate. There weren't any other passengers sitting near enough to talk to. The plane looked almost empty. Finally things started to happen. Signs flashed; announcements were made. The seat shook as the engines were raced. She hadn't been in a plane in thirty-five years, never a jet.

It was such an unusual feeling when the plane started down the runway. She had wondered what her reaction would be. Were the doves dead? The orange-beaked bird? The plane started lifting off. It was so unlike when their wings began to flap inside, beating back and forth in flight. She was being transported, and there was no cooing yet. Was she leaving them behind this time? Maybe she could go horseback riding in Halifax, find a stable, rent a horse. Follow a beaten path and not get lost.

Agents of Grace

Go outside after one o'clock and you pay for it with three gallons of sweat. How could he have forgotten that? The only other movement on the block was the mailman in a blue pith helmet pushing his three-wheeled cart down the sidewalk, envelopes shimmering in the heat as he slid them into the mailboxes. The cement felt like it was beginning to soften under his shoes. He had been back a week now.

Heat was cumulative in the Valley, he decided. Four days over 110, then seven days, and it didn't cool off in the evening, and you heard the motors of the air conditioning units night and day. The millions of acres of cotton, vines, and fruit trees had to be absorbing some of the heat, because the gray dirt between the rows looked like it was smoldering into ash.

From the park he could see the stained glass windows of St. Candace. Father Al. You couldn't see one without thinking of the other. He had already visited the rectory twice since he'd been back, had dinner, talked over old times: how the Valley All-Star team won the state soccer championship. Father, who had been the assistant coach, liked to talk about that season game by game, the same way he reviewed all the nuns who had left the school and the hospital, one by one. Father was all alone now. Mrs. Oliver, the housekeeper, let him in.

"Frankie Iturbide, All-League forward, two years running," Father Al said, getting up from his chair. "Do I have a deal for you." He was imitating a TV commercial, exaggerating his usual singsong Okie tenor, which had always been puzzling because Mrs. Oliver had told him once that Father was born in Columbus, Ohio, and his mother was Norwegian. "It must be those years in the seminary with the Irish priests, Frankie," she'd added. "He went in when he was fourteen."

The rectory was cool but it wouldn't have made any difference: Father always wore his black suit and his collar—outside too, no matter how hot it was. He was thin, his gray hair was neatly parted, and he wore stainless steel–rimmed glasses. And he didn't look sixty-three; he didn't look anything. He made quick jumpy movements after he was on his feet, like his weight wasn't evenly distributed.

"Wait until you see what I've got, Frank." He unlocked the big cupboard behind his desk and brought out a violin case. "Take a look." Father Al's enthusiasms had always been so intense they were almost palpable: in soccer, his fists clenched, "It's up to you, Frankie; it's your turn; we need another goal to be safe," kicking his legs in turns as if to show him how.

He lifted a violin wrapped in chamois out of the case. Took his time sliding the chamois off, exposing the shining straight-grained pinewood top. "A woman brought this in yesterday. Her late husband's. She wanted the church to have this instrument. She suggested we might raffle it off and spend the proceeds on the church. But I thought of you. You need a good violin for when you start recording. You're a professional musician; the best is not good enough for you. Look at the handle: do you see what I see, Frankie?" He turned the instrument lengthwise to the scroll. On each side of it, a diamond the size of a thumbtack was set in the wood. The faceted stones caught the light and turned pink. Father Al tried to hand him the instrument.

"I don't play the violin anymore, remember? I switched to the viola to have a better chance at an orchestra." He stepped back.

"You're trying to Jew me down."

"No, there's too much competition with the violin. I don't need a violin; I have a good one. But maybe one of the kids in the youth symphony could use it."

"This is valuable."

"We could have it appraised."

"Oh sure, and the diamonds come up missing. That man owned the biggest dairy in the county. Well, Frankie, since you say you're not interested, I guess I'll have to raffle this off," Father Al said, wrapping the instrument again.

He walked back toward his mother's house. His shoes felt like they were sticking to the sidewalk. If he'd driven it would have been worse; his car didn't have air conditioning, and it was like getting into a oven. You didn't need air conditioning in Santa Monica: there was the ocean. On clear days you could see the flat blue expanse from the apartment balcony. Here all there was was cotton. He crossed the street to avoid having to pass Mrs. Stark's place on the corner. Her mother might see him; she stationed herself in the glassed-in sun porch, watching. He didn't know if she expected to see UFOs from there or not, but she believed in them, believed in the presence of interstellar extraterrestrials living among us, trying to save us from ourselves, as she explained once. He'd tried not to smirk, for his own mother's sake. Whenever there was a cancer breakthrough Mrs. Stark's mother would say, "We know who to thank for that. They work hard to keep us safe," and Mrs. Stark would listen noncommittally, waiting politely for her to finish.

He'd landed in Mrs. Stark's fourth-grade class when his father refused to pay the parochial school tuition after the divorce. Mrs. Stark believed in music and California history, she'd said once, when a girl asked which church she went to. Within a month she had him staying after school for the Washington Elementary orchestra. "I have an extra violin," she said, "but you have to promise to practice at least an hour a day." That was the easy part. He could go three or four hours and not know it, as if it were all physical and it was just a matter of his body getting used to the exercise. He was playing with the county symphony by the sixth grade and going off to music camps all over California.

Just before he was ready to graduate from high school he stopped going over to see Mrs. Stark on his own. Before, it was like he was constantly traversing a triangle: home, the church, and Mrs. Stark's, all within six blocks. He had never explained to himself why he stopped. Of course he'd gone to visit when he came home from the conservatory during school break; he couldn't refuse his mother when she'd tell him they were invited. He must have outgrown the need for a mentor. Like he hadn't lost his faith as much as stopped using it. He didn't go to church, either; it just wasn't necessary anymore.

He was past the corner now, but he heard the violins, two or three, beginners. What were they doing? He'd played that. What was it, Brahms? He had to stop to listen, sweat from his forehead running down into his eyes. He could remember Mrs. Stark in the knotty pine–paneled music room, standing in front of the old chrome stands watching you, it seemed, more than listening, as if by your effort she could tell how well you played the piece. Then the music stopped as if he'd been imagining it, and he was standing dripping in his own sweat. Didn't she ever rest?

He got home just a little before his mother. She went to work at six in the morning. She'd asked for the early shift to beat the heat. She did private nursing now; he supposed it wasn't so tiring as being supervisor at the hospital. No matter how hard he'd tried, he had never been able to dislike his mother. That was a strange thing to think. She was too good, and it was too easy an option: it made him think of his father. The third daughter of her family, the one who went to nursing school because some teacher in high school said she was so good in chemistry she had to go on. "Frank," she said, putting down a bag of groceries, "do you have to go back for practice with the kids tonight?"

"At seven-thirty. Maybe it'll be a little cooler when the sun goes down."

"We'll eat early," she said. "I'll fry the chicken." He could say, Not in this heat; it's too much work, but she would protest and do it anyway. Crispy fried chicken was one of his favorites. It had been his father's too. He hadn't looked him up this time yet. Not the last couple of times he was home, either. It was just too awkward; he didn't know what to say anymore; there were too many silences. The third wife trying to be kind, his father going on about real estate prices, calling him by his stepson's name. He'd got his blue eyes from him. He claimed he was pure Castillian Spanish on both sides of his family, which made his mother and her brother Jack roar. "He's dark as an Armenian," his uncle would say.

They sat in the crosscurrent between the fan and the air conditioner vent as they watched TV and ate their dinner. The weather came on and they both groaned when the temperature was predicted at 112 for tomorrow. "This place is going to dry up and blow away," his mother said. He still had two hours to practice his viola before he had to leave for the auditorium.

Some of the kids' parents had come, but a quarter of the students hadn't. The music room at the auditorium was too big to cool properly. He was already sweating. He got them all seated and settled down, on the right page. Then they played. It was awful. Why did they bother to come if they hadn't practiced? "Again," he yelled. Because their parents wanted them to. Because of him, a town legend. He had wanted to play the minute Mrs. Stark handed him the instrument. It was as if the notes constructed in quarters and halves covered him up, protected him. But at some point he stopped getting better, stopped getting the oohhs and ahhs. He was on the list as candidate violinist for the San Francisco Opera orchestra. A serious auditioner and a possible replacement for three West Coast symphonies. Practice had got him there, but not a hundred hours a day would get him a position with the L.A. Philharmonic. But his name might do that for him. Iturbide. He was tired of waiting for someone to die. That's one reason why he was switching to the viola at twenty-four; there were more openings for the viola.

Mrs. Stark came in and the kids sat up straight in their chairs and paid attention. He was always yelling, "Concentrate!" Mrs. Stark was moving behind the kids, changing their hands on the bow or violin, whispering to them. He raised his voice to say, "Again."

The summer he was twelve, after music camp—it had been two weeks in the cool Sierras—his uncle Jack had told him, "Work for me and I'll get your hands dirty." Uncle Jack was a labor contractor and had some forty acres in vines of his own. So he picked grapes. The traditional way in the Valley for kids to earn money for school clothes. Spiders, dust, and the awful heat, and filling the pans full of Thompson's seedless for jug wine. He wouldn't give up. Never in front of his cousins, who watched him, waiting, or the green card Oaxacan pickers who spoke more Zapotec than Spanish and reminded him of calves with big brown eyes, sitting in the crowded bus three to a seat, going from vineyard to vineyard. He picked after his cousins quit. He kept up with the Indians.

He owed a lot to his uncle Jack, who must have thought he was going to grow up a sissy, playing the violin, with no father. He practiced even harder after picking, transferring the energy he'd learned to store for that into playing. The same with soccer: it gave him more energy to use for his music. More strength. He picked those grapes with a vengeance every year until he was halfway through the conservatory, halfway to his master's in music, and found out that practice helps but so does having a good teacher. And so does being born with the ability to be a great musician. There were musicians there so far ahead of him he didn't belong in the same practice room. Jean had said, "It's all relative." And about his stage fright, she almost convinced him, "You just need some confidence. You can learn that." But she could say that because she'd given up the violin and didn't have to face an audience; she was trying to be a conductor now. What a hick he'd been.

He didn't understand why, but he was enjoying this summer with the kids more than he wanted to admit to himself. He had never been interested in conducting or composing, especially not teaching, but this was different. This was like teaching forty-one nursing puppies how to eat: you keep shoving their muzzles back into the dish of food until they can do it for themselves. Most of these kids wouldn't be playing in a few years. But a few would find out how delicious it could be. Parents drifted up to ask how their kids were doing. Maybe Mrs. Stark should put name tags on the kids; he wasn't sure who was who. Some parents were assured; some were diffident, like his mother had been. Did they think this was a way into the middle class, some world of higher culture? He had bet fifteen years of his life on that, on what, and where was he?

He'd only been home from practice a half hour when he got a call from Father Al. His mother was already in bed. He glanced through her bedroom door and saw her lying in the middle of the bed, the outline of her body like it was already in a casket, as the phone rang. "Frankie, I know your car doesn't have air conditioning, but I need a ride." Father Al hadn't driven since his heart by-pass years ago.

He drove over in his mother's car, the air conditioning blowing so cold his shoulders hurt. Father was waiting at the curb in front of the rectory. "It's another one of those things," he said, getting in. "You know how they are. Every little freak of nature turns into a miracle. Christ on a tortilla. Statues that cry real tears. I got a call from a woman who said she was the Virgin Mary. Could barely speak English. She was going down to get herself notarized, as if that would make a difference. Take a left here." A string of cars in front of them was slowly moving down the street. "This is supposed to be authentic," Father said. Groups of people were standing on the sidewalk in front of one of the houses: it was the only one with a porch light on. When it was his turn he stopped the car in front of the house. The outline of a cross, Christ on the cross, showed on the stucco wall, life-size, in silhouette. A woman on the sidewalk close to the car was making the sign of the cross. "Will you look at that. It's that sycamore that's casting the shadow; they need to trim the damn thing. Why do they need this kind of entertainment. Drive on, drive on." Father Al seemed irritated, but what difference could this make to him and St. Candace?

They went to Farm Boy's for coffee; sat in a back booth. This was like old times when he was in high school, driving Father someplace, stopping here. "They might as well have captured Elvis. What do they want me to do, call the Pope? Ignorant people. What can you expect. How's your mother?" He never waited for him to answer. Father had visited her at the hospital, took her communion. "It's a screwy world we live in," he went on. "One thing after another."

He got up early for the meeting. His mother was making coffee, putting the place mats on each end of the table, cloth napkins. Where had she learned all these middle-class things? When they'd put the swimming pool in, his mother hadn't known how to swim. He'd caught her holding onto the edge, going around the pool, and tried to convince her to let go. "Don't you dare," she yelled at him, frightened.

"You don't know how to swim? You didn't learn, not even in high school?"

"They didn't have a pool then. The only water I ever got into was in the irrigation ditches next to the fields. And on Saturday night in a wash tub, after my two older sisters took their turn. The same water."

"Why don't you go to the Y? They have adult classes."

"Because I don't want to learn, that's why."

She handed him a cup of coffee. He tried to keep his eyes away from the front of her uniform. She hadn't phoned him before the operation or even when the biopsy showed that the tumor was malignant. "I didn't want to worry you," she told him later. He'd found out when Mrs. Stark called him after the surgery. There were a lot of things he didn't understand about his mother. She still wore the old starched white RN cap and dress that most of the other nurses had stopped wearing years ago. "You're a contrary person, aren't you?" he said. The phone rang and she got up to answer, laughing. She started speaking in Spanish and he knew it had to be family, a sister, Uncle Jack. His parents had spoken fast in Spanish when they didn't want him to know what they were saying. He had taken it in high school, and Italian at the conservatory, but it was his uncle Jack who taught him how to think in the language. His cousins laughed at first, but that's all Jack would speak to him, picking. "Your grandfather, my father, wouldn't even speak English; he said it wasn't a Christian language," Jack had told him. He learned, just like he learned to forget that a black widow spider might bite him when he was reaching up to cut a cluster of grapes loose. He got so hot, so tired, that he didn't think about black widows or the fact that he was yelling in Spanish for his cousin to share his Coke.

He wore a white shirt and a tie, despite the heat, for his meeting with the executive board of the County Fine Arts League. He'd looked at these women for years, at first puzzled, later condescendingly. They always looked back charmed. Since his first solo with the symphony, when he'd had to stand on a special platform to be seen by the audience, they had always responded. Acclamation, of course, scholarships; they even raised money to send him to New York to study with a famous teacher. The Fine Arts League. Why would anyone bother?

"We need more violins," he said. The secretary was writing it all down. "Some of the musicians are having to take turns on a instrument, which means no practice time."

"Frank," Mrs. Stark said, "the supervisors cut our budget in half again this year. Both school districts have cut the orchestra from the curriculum."

"They never cut the marching bands because they play at the games," someone else said.

"We don't have any money," Mrs. Stark went on. "We're going to have to scrounge around for used ones."

"If we don't start these kids when they're young, there won't be any county symphony in another generation." They all knew that, but he had to say something to follow up Mrs. Stark. She cared so much about this. The concert mistress of the symphony, a violinist and a quality cellist in her own right. She had taught him for five years, until he was good enough to go on to a better teacher she'd recommended. He had paid her in yard work, along with the four or five other kids Mrs. Stark's mother supervised.

The league, these women, were why he was here. The executive board had applied for a state arts grant to organize the summer orchestra program. It was Mrs. Stark who wrote the letter to him asking if he'd be interested in the conductor's twelve-week position. The grant was paying him more than he made in six months in Santa Monica.

The meeting went on and on. He didn't make much effort to hide his boredom, or his yawns. Later that morning he spent fifteen minutes with each musician, mostly getting them to hold the violin correctly and sit straight before he stepped back and listened to them saw. Mrs. Stark worked with the cellos and another woman with the basses. They sounded worse, if possible, and some of these kids had been playing for three or four years.

"You know your problem is you don't practice," he snapped at one little girl with dark hair in pigtails, the first violin. The kid froze on the gray metal chair. "Who can play that?" he asked the whole group. No one moved. He grabbed her instrument, adjusted the pegs, and played the piece. And played it again, exaggerating the vibrato. Again. Then he handed the violin back, saying, "Practice, practice, practice."

"How's your mother?" Mrs. Stark asked after the kids filed out.

"Fine, she's fine." His mother was already after him to go over and visit Mrs. Stark. He wasn't ready yet. He waited.

"Would you like to come over for lunch? Nothing special, just what's in the refrigerator."

"I'm afraid I've already promised Father Al. But thanks, and tell your mother hello for me."

When Father Al treated, it was in the Sacred Heart Hospital cafeteria. "I talked to someone on the phone who's an expert," he said, polishing his fork with his napkin. "There's no ceiling on that violin. It could be worth a fortune. That's not including the stones. I wish there was some way to contact one of those collectors who have all the money in the world." Father Al started in on his spoon.

"Too bad I don't know any." In spite of himself, he thought of Jean. "And besides, you don't know that those diamonds are real. They could be glass." He enjoyed saying that. He didn't care if they were real or not.

"Maybe, but that violin is old. They bought it in Portugal on one of their visits. I phoned the woman. She doesn't know how much money her husband paid for it."

"Have it appraised. But you're going to have to actually show it to someone in L.A. or San Francisco." Because he was with Father Al, they had given him three times the usual portion of food. Tamale pie. He wasn't going to be able to eat it all.

"I'm going to. I don't think a raffle is the best way to go. I don't think we'd sell enough tickets around here. How many people in the Valley want a world-class violin? You're just playing with that food. Come with me; I have to make a call on the fifth floor. Another aberration. Stigmata, this time. What next?"

They took the elevator upstairs. There was a crowd out in the hallway. More people in the room, some saying the rosary out loud. There was a small man in the bed, asleep, his hands folded over his chest like a religious painting. "Speak to him, Frank. See what he's trying to pull." They were standing at the foot of the bed. He spoke softly in Spanish. The man opened his eyes but didn't respond. He picked up the chart at the foot of the bed. The name looked Laotian. He had been taken for Japanese or Chinese himself by other Asians in L.A. "I don't think he speaks Spanish," he whispered to Father Al.

A doctor came in. "What's the story?" Father asked, in a loud voice. Everyone seemed to jump at the sound.

"He was admitted this morning with severe dehydration and what looks like puncture wounds in both hands but just his left foot."

"What is that supposed to mean?" Father Al was getting angry; he was speaking in his purest Okie at his highest pitch.

"I don't know what it means; I'm not a theologian."

"I'm a director of this hospital; are you getting smart with me?" The doctor's face turned red, but before he could reply, Father Al asked, "Did he say how it happened?"

"I didn't admit him. He's on Medicare. On the form it said the punctures were there when he woke up Tuesday morning."

The man was smiling at them now. With English he must have learned from TV he said, Good afternoon, like an announcer. The doctor slipped the bandage up on his right hand. There was a hole in the palm that came out the top, but there wasn't any bleeding; it was just red meat. "Was that self-inflicted?" Father Al asked. The doctor shrugged his shoulders. The people in the room and the hallway pushed closer, jostling them. "What do you want?" Father shouted. They were trying to touch the patient, reaching for his feet or just the bed. "Get out of here, all of you. Vamoose. Vamoose."

He followed Father back to the elevator. "This is obscene. What do these people think they're doing? Superstition, that's what it is." It made him feel like old times, Father Al upset. It was like when they were impossibly behind in soccer, and Father stopped shouting and started to look sad, defeated. He was an expert at all the emotions. Back in his office, he went to the big cupboard behind his desk, unlocked it and got the violin out and unwrapped it like a relic. "We can put a new roof on this place if I'm right," he said, holding the instrument with both hands. "Buy a new altar; paint the whole building. This place should celebrate the Glory of God. It's becoming a hopeless task. We depend on Wednesday night bingo for the salary of two of our lay teachers. The feds won't pay Medicare unless we let the indigent and the illegal in, and the doctors are gouging us out of most of the money. School enrollment is down, collections are down, the nurses want to join the Teamsters' union. I don't have an assistant anymore because there are no priests." The phone rang and Father Al picked it up and started talking, holding the violin against his chest like a baby. Frank caught his eye and mouthed, I've got to go.

God, it was hot. He wasn't going to make it home. He'd lost his tolerance for the heat. He'd forgotten how the lawns died yellow every summer and the trees drooped to the ground in collapse. It made you doubt the very possibility of coolness or rain or the windshields of parked cars covered like milk with frost. He got the mail out of the box at the curb and wanted to break into a run to get up the front walk and into the house. He was awash. How did people stand it before air conditioning? Swamp coolers. He had to get back to the city.

He put some water on to boil for iced tea for his mother and automatically started doing the breakfast dishes. His mother hadn't wanted a dishwasher, though she'd let his father put in a garbage disposal. "Lucy, what kind of a person would turn down a dishwasher? Are you crazy?" his father had yelled. "You want to throw away the Whirlpool and go back to a washboard?"

"It's not the same thing. I get to think when I'm doing the dishes."

"You're always going to be a wetback," his father had said. They had argued like that for two years before he left.

When the phone rang he knew who it was before his mother spoke, from the way she broke into a big smile and then started to giggle when Mrs. Stark said something funny. They'd liked each other from the start, when he began fourth grade in her class. His mother had joined the Friends of the Symphony and took trips with them all over the state to attend musical events. Mrs. Stark had been in the recovery room waiting for his mother after her double mastectomy. "You can talk to him now, Leila. He's sitting in front of the TV pretending to read."

"Frank, I found four." Her voice was excited. "We went to Bakersfield. One at the Goodwill, that needs a bridge and strings, and three at the Next to New place that are in good shape, but one doesn't have a case."

He tried to sound enthusiastic. "Good, good, we can use them."

She went on, "We got them cheap, too; forty dollars apiece at the store and fifty at the Goodwill—they wouldn't come down."

He remembered when he was twelve and had gone with Mrs. Stark and a couple of her other students to Stockton. He was playing in the county symphony then; so were the two girls. Mrs. Stark had explained that he needed a better violin; that he'd gone as far as he could on the one he had. He hadn't understood. "The sound you make is too much for that instrument. You need a better one." They had gone into a pawnshop and he'd played one violin after another. He could do a good vibrato by then, and he made people passing the shop stop on the sidewalk to listen. The owner had applauded. Out of the five or six, they found a much better violin than his old one. He had his own money from working in the grapes, and Mrs. Stark talked the owner down to half the price marked on the tag.

By chance he and Jean had found a violin in a used furniture store while they were looking for a bureau for their apartment. He played it just long enough for Jean to squeeze him around the middle and whisper, "Get it, get it." The owner made him buy the chest of drawers where they'd found the instrument too—two hundred dollars for both, take it or leave it. Jean was actually squeaking by the time he got out his wallet, the tone was so good. He still used that violin.

"We've never had so much interest as this summer," Mrs. Stark was going on. "The kids, the parents coming to rehearsal; it's been wonderful. We're building an audience for the next generation. She stopped short of saying, It's you, Frank. It's your energy that's creating this excitement in the youth orchestra.

There had been a lot of write-ups in the paper about him over the years. How many times had he gotten a clipping in the mail from one of the Fine Arts League members? Last week there had been a caption under his photo: Frank Iturbide comes home to give something back to his town. Had he said that? It was Mrs. Stark. She liked to say things like that, putting it all on a higher plane. But art was like religion: it didn't always bring out the best in people. She should know that by now.

"Isn't she something," his mother said when he hung up.

"Who?"

"Leila Stark. Never gives up. Always trying. I don't know what I'd do without her."

"Whatever happened to her husband?" He'd never thought to ask before.

"He died. He came back from Southeast Asia and had problems. He was a navy flyer. He drew a bath and shot himself through the heart, but he didn't die right away. I was working ER at Sacred Heart when they brought him in. He lingered for a month. It was awful. I didn't know her then; you weren't in her class yet."

Father Al phoned. "Pick me up, Frankie. Let's go the Pump Room, watch the World Cup." He drove to the rectory in his own car. Even with all four windows down it was like sitting above a burner on his mother's gas stove. He should have taken her car. They went to the back room of the bar where the 36-inch TV sat on a big table in the cool dark. Father drank his free beer out of a coffee mug. When Al had brought him here for the first time—he must have been sixteen; he'd just got his license—he'd raised the coffee mug and winked. "Not to alarm the parishioners unnecessarily," he'd said. "Why hasn't pro soccer caught on here? It's a more clever sport than American football. It takes ten times more skill than both baseball and basketball put together." Father was musing, sipping out of his mug, watching the game, which was tied up, one to one.

"It has no tradition here, I guess. No history." He didn't really know why it hadn't caught on. The conservatory didn't have a team, of course, and he had missed the exercise. He was good enough to get on a club team in the city that played on Saturdays. He played forward; he could go to a practice field and kick goals all morning, when he had the time. It was like the violin in a way, where he could go into a practice room and play for five or six hours and not even know how much time he'd spent. It was wonderful, just him and the instrument. It was when he had to play before a audience that the music seemed diminished, as if he'd lost something. It didn't seem natural; it confused him. He found out anyone can practice, but playing in front of an audience is a different matter. You can destroy yourself with nerves and anxieties before the frog-eyed audience even hears you. Jean never really understood. She had seen him quaking before a student performance and said, "If you want something bad enough, forget everything else and just do it." Another time: "You look blissful when you practice, and you sound superb. Why should people listening change that?" And when she started giving up on him; "People's minds don't want them to be happy. It's the brain's job to make you miserable. It's your body, your hands, the intuitive part of you that makes you good. You either have it or you don't. You have it, Frank. You just won't allow yourself to disconnect that brain of yours."

Jean was born to play, was a prodigy. At five years old she was playing professionally. Burned out by the time she was fifteen. Married at seventeen. Stopped playing. At twenty she started at the conservatory, divorced by then, was going to be a conductor. She was always making suggestions to him but would never pick up an instrument herself. He had yelled at her once, "You gave up and you want me to take you seriously?" That was unfair. She didn't speak to him for weeks. Once, on a whim, he drove her down to the Valley for the day. She didn't disbelieve his stories, but she looked skeptical sometimes. Once they turned off 99 he realized he had no intention of taking her home. He wasn't embarrassed by his mother. But he couldn't make himself drive down his street, or even phone. He went to Mrs. Stark's.

Father Al came back to the table with a refill. "I forgot to mention I have a party in St. Louis that's interested in the violin with the diamonds. Wants me to send it along." Father Al was watching the game as he talked. "I'm reluctant. It's too risky: even with insurance, special handling, somebody could steal the thing. I don't know what to do." A player got a penalty kick and Father stopped talking.

It had been the Saturday after Thanksgiving. He hadn't come home for the holiday. He had to stop, show Jean he belonged somewhere. Mrs. Stark opened the door as if she were expecting him. They were in the middle of making fruitcakes, and Jean started helping, cutting up the candied fruit. When the first loaves came out of the oven, Mrs. Stark poured brandy over the tops. She tried to cut slices from one while it was still too hot and it broke into pieces. He didn't know if it was Leila or her mother who phoned his mother, but she came over. It felt so awkward, introducing his mother to Jean that way. He hadn't known where to look.

Mrs. Stark asked Jean to play; she remembered her, had seen her perform as a child. Jean picked up an old first-year-student violin and started playing while they sat around the kitchen table eating fruitcake. If the violin was supposed to be the instrument closest to the human voice, Jean could summon a whole choir when she played. She was born to play the violin; it was an extension of her body. She must have played for half an hour, and when she stopped it was as if something important had left you, like spirit or grace. Mrs. Stark was crying and trying to clap and hug Jean all at the same time. His mother had droplets of tears falling down her cheeks. He had never heard anyone better. He did what she said after that. All but the part about getting nervous. When he had to solo or play for an audition, he was a wreck.

He drove Father Al back to the rectory. "I forgot to tell you: the self-inflicted stigmata patient disappeared from the hospital. But I want you to know that the Virgin Mary is alive and well and here in the Valley, and ready to reveal herself at the right time. According to her brother. I can't get them to understand the church is not interested." Father got out of the car but leaned back in the window to say, "I should have gone into an order. Parish priests are like family doctors; everyone wants to dump them for a specialist. I can't keep up. It's the Jesuits who get everything. See you later, Frankie."

Mrs. Stark had arranged an ice cream social for the youth orchestra after practice Friday night, in the park next to the auditorium. League members scooped ice cream out of five-gallon containers into the kids' plastic dishes, and the kids got to choose from cans of topping. His mother was squirting whipped cream on the top. "Enough?" she was asking. "You want more?" Parents were coming up to ask how their kids were doing, to meet him, shake his hand. He kept trying to get away, but the kids were hovering around, eating their ice cream. He had one scoop of vanilla to be polite; he didn't particularly care for sweets. It was dark now and the street lights had come on. One of the kids was asking him about the pizzicato in the piece they'd practiced, plucking with ice-cream-sticky fingers on his beginner's violin. He had no intention of playing when he took it to demonstrate, but the instrument was up on his shoulder, tucked under his chin, and he heard Mozart. He didn't try to force the music for an audience; he let it come out of the instrument the way it was supposed to. When he stopped, everyone was clapping. Someone's grandmother came up and hugged him and said in Spanish, "You are a cabbage with a bow around it." Cheryl's father translated for everyone, and people laughed. He laughed. He couldn't believe how happy he felt. He hugged the old lady back.

❦

He wasn't practicing as much as he used to. Since he'd been home, the whole structure he had built up while he was away was falling apart. He wasn't sure why. He practiced, but he wasn't concentrating, wasn't listening. He went into the back bedroom so he wouldn't bother his mother watching TV. Took his viola out of the case. He was beginning to like the instrument, the lower range, the heavier feel, the thicker strings. But he didn't want to play an instrument that was mostly a foil for the violin. He thought of Jean, the last time they were together. They had started arguing. Over what? Him playing the viola? Her playing the violin? "You don't know what it was like. I never had a home; I lived in hotel rooms. I never had any childhood. No one baked me fruitcake. I played the violin. I was a monkey on a string, until I got too big, too tall, and they had to buy me a bra, no more braids and pinafores, and all of a sudden I wasn't so brilliant anymore. I was a freak. And you want to know why I don't play?" He waited her out until she was breathing easier and said the line that always made her giggle. "Sweetheart, I could play you like a fine violin." Her response was always, "You mean more like a double bass"—she had stopped smoking and gained some weight. But this time she jumped up and started dressing. He knew she would come back; she always did. But a couple of days later, when he got home from rehearsal, she was gone. He hadn't seen her since then. He'd heard she was in Chicago.

He was standing in front of the closet door mirror, and he realized he had stopped playing; he was just staring at himself. There was a knock at the door and his mother pushed it open. He watched her in the mirror, not turning. "I didn't know if you were still here. I just wanted to say good night."

"Do you still go to church?" he asked. "To listen to Father Al?" and he tried to smile.

"Every morning. I stop on the way to work."

"Why do you still do that, Mom?"

"You practice your violin every day. I practice trying to be good every day. And I go to Mass to remember why I'm practicing. It's like you practice to be ready for the performance, to be ready to participate in a violin concerto, whatever, something beautiful. Well, I practice so I can participate at Mass in something beautiful. Father Al doesn't have anything to do with it."

"Why"—and he hesitated, wanting to get it right—"Why does everything have to be so complicated?"

"There wouldn't be any reason to get up in the morning if it wasn't," she said.

❦

Father Al phoned. "I understand you have the Gutierrez girl in your orchestra. He's a doctor, an orthodontist."

"I'm not sure which one she is."

"I'll bring the instrument by Wednesday night. Just let the family take a look at it. They like fine things; they drive a Mercedes."

Mrs. Stark was going to play with the youth orchestra; it was her idea. A good one. They'd sound a whole lot better, of course, and she'd be there as an example for the kids to follow, too. All the parents had been invited to the rehearsal tonight to hear the kids play through the entire piece they'd been practicing for the last five weeks. There was a kind of excitement before any performance that always made him feel sick to his stomach. But this was not bad. He felt exposed as he raised his baton, but not terrified. No one was expecting anything of him. There were the kids, their eyes wide, watching him and the sheet music at the same time. He moved his arm and they started playing. Some lost their places and just pretended to play. Others were three or four bars behind everyone else. But most were doing better than he'd ever thought possible. When the music stopped the parents started clapping. Father Al was the first one to stand, clapping, the violin case tucked under his arm. Frank motioned to the orchestra to stand and bow back to the applause. They didn't get it; this all had to be practiced. He pointed at Mrs. Stark, who bowed alone. Father Al was beaming now, holding the violin case at the small end like a baseball bat and heading for the Gutierrezes.

He had been surprised at the sound, ragged at times, but they'd be ready to play with the regular symphony in the park on Labor Day evening. He strolled over to where Father Al was showing the violin to Cheryl's father. "This violin is exceptional, Doctor. There's not another one like it in the Valley."

"I don't want to play the violin," Cheryl was saying. "Mrs. Stark says I'm getting better on the cello."

He wandered off over to where his mother was pouring punch into paper cups. He took one and picked up a cookie. "You never eat sweets, Frank."

"I'm changing my ways. What did you think?"

"About what?"

"The music, Mom."

"It was fine. I enjoyed it." They both laughed. His mother.

Father Al caught up with him later. "Why didn't you back me up? There's a new roof for the church in here," he said, shaking the case. "He's going to think about it, Dr. Gutierrez." Somebody came up to talk to Father then, and he got away.

It didn't matter what you paid for an instrument. Jean had told him that in the practice room while he played and she read. "I had the best, an Amati. It had been repaired, pieces replaced, but it was authentic. What a tone, what resonance. I hoped my imagination, my ability would stretch to meet the instrument. It made a difference, but then again it didn't. Do you understand that?" He shook his head. "If you could wear a funny hat that would make your nerves go away, would you do it?" He shook his head again and started playing. He didn't like dwelling on his stage fright. Later he asked what had happened to the Amati. She knew what he was talking about. "Nothing, I still have it.

It's safe in a bank vault. I can't stand to play it, much less look at it. It's a curse."

They went to Mrs. Stark's for dinner. His mother talked him into going. "You can't just keep saying no. You're being rude." He went. He used to like going; it was like a special holiday. Linen tablecloth, candles, hors d'oeuvres, everyone expectant with each course. It had turned into a task, somehow. He wouldn't take his viola when his mother asked. "Have it your way," she said. He used to play duets with Mrs. Stark after dinner.

They walked over; his mother took his arm. He tried not to notice the sweat dripping down his back after half a block. He'd never even thought of the heat when he was a kid. "What did you do without air conditioning when you were a girl?" he asked.

"If we had a refrigerator, we'd fill the freezer with grapes, and when they'd get hard we'd put them in our mouths to cool off. Jack tied a hunk of ice to the top of his head once with a towel, I remember, to show off."

It went like it always did. The meal was excellent; the conversation continuous, Mrs. Stark's mother making them all laugh with her theory that the recent earthquakes were caused by microwave ovens, which generated waves that caused disharmonies along the faults. "Mama, you told me extraterrestrials invented microwaves."

"They did. They wanted to totally automate the kitchen for us, but they didn't realize the effect the waves would have on the Earth. They're not always right; they're like us, in that respect."

"What will they do now, then?" he asked. "To fix the problem, I mean."

"I'm not sure. They were sent here to help humans, so I suppose they will do something. I stopped using our microwave a long time ago. You have to help yourself in these situations."

After dinner they listened to Mrs. Stark's tape of the youth orchestra rehearsal. They didn't sound half bad. He listened for the cellos and thought about Cheryl Gutierrez; she'd been taking lessons from Mrs. Stark for two years.

"What's next for you after Labor Day, Frank?" Mrs. Stark asked.

"That's a good question," his mother added.

"Go back to the rat race. Keep auditioning until I find something."

"One of the elementary school districts needs a music teacher." He couldn't believe his ears. What was she saying? "The program has special funding for two years; it can't be cut." He couldn't take her seriously; he was better than that.

"But I'm not interested in teaching," he said. "I just want to play."

He couldn't wait to leave after that, trying to hurry his mother, who was offering to help with the dishes. He finally got her out of there. "Could you believe that?" he said, once they were outside. "Why would I want to be a music teacher in this hellhole?"

"Because you'd be good at it," she said, as if she'd been waiting for him to ask that. "And it would be a way of paying back all the help you got." He wanted to yell, I don't want to be a music teacher, not here or any other place, but he didn't. They walked home without saying another word.

"You better phone Father Al," his mother said when he came home from the auditorium. Now what? he thought, dialing.

"You won't believe what has been happening around here." Father Al sounded breathless. "You already know we definitely have the Virgin Mary living here in town. They won't leave me alone; they insist they want to see the bishop. They propose to come over tonight and convince me to take them up there. But that's not what I wanted to talk to you about. I spoke to the Gutierrez girl's mother; she wants what's best for her daughter. They're not Catholic, believe it or not; somewhere along the line they became Nazarenes. Mrs. G. wants you to decide; she'll buy the violin if you recommend that Cheryl switch back. Frank, are you there?"

"I'm here, Father. Tomorrow I'll mention it; they'll be at the practice. Have you had it appraised?"

"I have a priest from Modesto coming down to take a look at it tomorrow morning. He played in a band on TV when he was a civilian. I'm supposed to send the diamonds up to the bishop after the violin is appraised; he wants them for safekeeping, which is a good idea. There's no telling what could happen around here anymore."

He went into his room for something and ended up sitting down at his desk to write a letter to Jean. He had her sister's address in Decatur. He knew it was crazy but he started to feel better as he wrote, almost happy. He told her what he was doing for the summer and invited her to the Labor Day performance. He put in a P.S.: I don't know why, but I feel hopeful after writing the above. And I miss you. Did we love each other? Do we love each other? He had never said anything like that to her before. He almost ran to get to the Post Office before it closed to send it overnight delivery. He was dripping sweat, coming back the two blocks, but he could imagine Jean's face when she read the letter, holding it close in her nearsighted way, squinting without her glasses on.

After dinner he remembered to tell his mother the latest on the violin. They were sitting with just the TV lamp on, waiting for the weather. But she didn't laugh this time. She usually thought the things Father Al did were funny. "You're going to tell them to buy it?"

"Why not?" She didn't say anything. He waited.

"Because that's not the way it should be. And she wants to play the cello."

"Mother, she'll drop both by the time she's fifteen and the hormones start raging. Then they can sell it to someone else."

"That doesn't make any difference."

"It's a decent violin; I played it. I'm no expert, but she'll never outgrow it, and they have the money."

"That's not the point. You're not being honest."

"Honest?" He was yelling. "Who's ever honest around here? How sick are you? Are you in remission? Are you pretending to be okay? Honest? I'm an average professional player, honest, and I'll never make it. If it wasn't for being Hispanic I'd be out on my ear. That's honest. I threw up all over myself the last time I had to audition. Jean called me a practice room virtuoso. And Mrs. Stark dedicating her whole life, that's bullshit, because she doesn't have anything else except her goofy mother. And you, what do you have besides me? And that's not much. Those old people you like to take care of, they're vegetables. They all die." He was going to say something about his father and her, but she got up and was gone. He followed her, yelling through her closed bedroom door: "Father Al is a bigot and greedy and stupid and no one will ever tell him that. How do you like honesty now? You can't hide from the truth."

The hell with this, he thought and went out the front door. The heat hit like someone was throwing hot towels over his head. He was going to sit in the little park by the church, but when he got to the bench he saw the emergency blue and yellow flashing lights in front of the parish house. By the time he got there they were taking Father Al out on a gurney and loading him into the back of an ambulance. His nose was bleeding and he had his eyes closed as if he were asleep. There were police too, and they were putting people in the back of two cars, pressing down on the tops of their heads as if the door openings were too small and their bodies had to be forced inside.

He caught up with the housekeeper, Mrs. Oliver. "What happened?"

"Some crazy Mexicans. I came running when Father started yelling. When I got there he was on top of his desk and this demented woman was telling him, 'Just let me show you the proof.' He must have kicked her because that's when one of her brothers punched him in the nose. There was nothing I could do but yell, Stop that! Then I ran and phoned 911. When I came back it was all over: Father had got himself locked inside the cupboard and the woman had her clothes back on."

He thought about walking over to the hospital to see how Father was, but instead he went home to go to bed.

He had to get up early in the morning for rehearsal. The paper had a long column of print under the headline PRIEST ATTACKED. His mother wasn't talking to him, except to say good morning.

When he got to the auditorium the kids were already in their seats, some warming up, four of them playing patty cake patty cake baker's man. He watched; he hadn't seen anyone play that for years. He saw the Gutierrez girl come in. "Let me hear you play just one page," he asked her. Her face flushed and she sat down, opened her music, and started playing her cello. He reached over for another kid's instrument and sheet music and tried to hand her the violin. "Now let me hear you on this."

"I don't like the violin."

"Neither do I, but please try."

She took the instrument and started playing. Once she relaxed, she was good. "That was fine," he told her. He took the instrument back. He wanted to say something else, but Mrs. Stark came in.

By one o'clock he was so hungry his stomach was making loud noises and he hurried home. As soon as he opened the front door he heard the phone ringing. "Frank, those son-of-a-bitch fanatics, did you hear? Mrs. Oliver said you were over. I got a shiner and a broken nose too. But the worst of it was the damn violin. When I got away and jumped into the cupboard and slammed the door shut to get away from those looneys, I kneeled on the case in the dark. I didn't know until I got back this morning. I stayed overnight in the hospital because they thought I had a concussion. Those crazy Basques own a big sheep ranch in the foothills, biggest wool growers in the Valley. The top of the violin is cracked a little, and the handle where the diamonds go isn't straight anymore. I don't think it's damaged much; probably just needs a little glue. You might want to take a look at it."

"A little glue, Father?"

"We'll lower the price some. I have to go now; the diocesan attorney just drove up. I'll call you later, Frankie."

His mother came in and he listened to her moving around in the kitchen. He went and leaned against the doorway. "Did you read in the paper what happened to Father Al?"

She started giggling. "I'd liked to have seen that. People can be so funny," she said.

"The violin was damaged. Father crunched it during the visitation." His mother started laughing again. "Mother, the Gutierrez kid plays the violin better than she ever will the cello. She's good. She can develop into a competent player."

"What did Leila say?"

"I didn't ask her; I'm the director." With the same breath he added, "But I'll see what she thinks. I don't care if Mrs. Gutierrez buys the violin; that's not the point. It doesn't make any difference to me."

"It should," his mother said. He felt himself start to get angry. He wanted to yell, What do you want me to do? He tried to smile for his mother and repeated, "Let's see what Leila says."

When he walked into the music room the five cellists were dueling, faces right next their music on the stands, playing furiously, as if to see who could play it fastest. He stood by them listening until they finished. Clapped loudly for them. "Brava, brava, you know that passage now. I'm proud of you. See what practice does for you?" The five girls beamed. He looked at their name tags to be sure and made a comment to each of them. "Hold a little more on the quarter notes. Keep your back straight. You too, Aurelia. Tighten up your bow; you're going to shred all that horse hair. Cheryl, don't keep time with your foot; this isn't a bluegrass band." They laughed. Mrs. Stark was late.

He got the boys to sit down; they were always antsy. Somehow there were almost as many boys as girls in the orchestra. When he had been in the elementary school orchestra he'd been the only boy in the string section. He got them to settle down. Then he had to change a broken A string for one kid. Then four hands went up: they had to go to the lavatory. He tried to explain that you had to be prepared to play, once the conductor was ready.

He tapped his stand with the tip of the baton. A ripple ran through the group as everyone straightened up, some a little slower than the others, till they were all poised, alert, ready to start. It was like a cloud traversing the sky to block the sun, diminish the heat. He waited. Mrs. Stark came in then, right behind three little girls in white who couldn't be the minimum age of nine. Were they triplets? Were those their First Communion dresses? They must be the kids he'd heard that day, passing by her house. Leila was carrying three violins in one hand and with the other guiding the new kids to vacant chairs while he waited.

The Money Tree

A dog had got out. One of the run fences had sagged inward where a post had snapped off, probably from the wind last night, enough for the setter to escape. The other dogs all yapped as I approached: they knew I should feed them. But there was no time now. I made sure it was just the one dog missing and ran for the house. I didn't notice my body, I was in such a hurry. I pressed once on the doorbell and waited but no one came. Then I held my forefinger hard against the plastic button. I kept telling myself, Why should you care? They don't. On a Saturday they wouldn't notice anything until noon.

Margo opened the door. I must have been excited, because I was on my toes, I realized, and she said, looking me over, "You're jiggling, Carmen." I stopped, put my weight on my heels, dropped back my shoulders, and lifted my chin. "That's better," she said.

I realized the chimes were still sounding behind her and took my finger off the button. "The setter got out," I said.

She held the screen door open. "Come in; I'll get Simpson up." I followed her across the living room. She moved regally. Even in crumpled pajamas that were two sizes too big for her, her body moved like the languid swish of a fish across the dusty rug. She went into the bedroom and I turned into the kitchen. I did the coffee, rinsing the pot out, filling it with water, counting out the spoonfuls, and plugging in the cord. The dishes hadn't been done for a couple of days, not since I had helped her clean up on Wednesday after school.

Margo came into the kitchen, erect, as I was filling pots with water to soak off their inside rims of hard-stuck food. He came behind her, coughing, wearing his old woolen robe. You could count the bones in her face and neck. The skeleton of her thin hands seemed held together by large blue veins like twine that ended in the calves of her thumbs. "I should never have taken in that goddamned animal," he said.

I wouldn't look at him; it was too early in the morning to have to look at someone that stupid. "We should get going," I said. "If he goes for the highway. Before the traffic gets heavy."

"I took a taxi back last night," he said. "The car's at the club." And they both waited. I heard the pot beginning to perk, and the first faint whiffs of coffee came out of the spout in puffs of steam. "I'll go by the path," I said, working out the best way to handle the problem. "When you get the car, go the other way to the overpass. I'll meet you at the roadside rest."

Stately with poise, I walked around them and back across the living room. There was no time for coffee. I started running as fast as I could once I got outside, counted to fifty and stopped, walked for the same amount of time, catching my breath, then started running again.

He was right. Setters were one of the dumbest breeds ever developed, and it was probably run over by now. Which was the most likely possibility: The owner would take the Simpsons to small claims court? The owner would do nothing? The owner would curse the Simpsons? One woman had carried it further: while crying in outrage at their stupidity, she had scratched Simpson's face with her fingernails.

I had gone to small claims court the last time, when an owner sued because his collie had mysteriously died at their kennel. He wanted the maximum allowed, fifteen hundred dollars, to replace the dog. The Simpsons were to meet me at the county complex, but they never showed up, which meant that they would lose and forfeit the money, which they didn't have. When the judge asked who was there from the Good Life Kennel, I stood up, confident, my shoulders back. "I work for the kennel," I said. Everyone looked at me.

"The plaintiff has stated his dog was not cared for properly. It was left outside in the rain and caught cold," the judge read.

"The dog was nearly fifteen years old," I pointed out. "Also," I added, "it was a crossbreed and its market value would not have been more than seventy-five dollars as a puppy." But the judge remembered the other times the Simpsons had been there. The last one was when the

Pekinese escaped while Margo was grooming it on the kitchen table; Simpson had opened the front door and the dog ran for it. That had cost four hundred eight dollars. For the collie we paid a hundred and thirty-seven dollars plus court costs. They were thankful, too, when I found them sitting in the dark house and told them. Margo bought me a scarf.

It was a wonder that anyone ever brought their dogs to the Good Life Kennel. But it was the only one around, so far, and they advertised. And in their own way the Simpsons looked, at first glance, competent. But more important, they knew how to react to things, especially disasters or reversals. A telegram to an owner when a boarded dog fell ill. Or sending me around with photocopied flyers to put on telephone poles: REWARD, LOST DOG, with a photo and a good description. And both Mr. and Mrs. Simpson would join any owner who showed any emotion for his dead or missing animal, the tears bouncing down Margo's bony face like spray over stones in a stream, while manful Simpson sniffed beside her through his bulbous nose, his gray-blond hair slicked back with water. They had seen much better days.

I stopped at the top of the first hill, but it was impossible to see the highway yet. The dog was nowhere in sight. This was hopeless. I didn't want to go on with it. I looked back the way I'd come, over the mile of round hills covered with foot-high grass blown in opposite directions like green fur. To the kennel. To the old house where the Simpsons lived. Past that to the estates, where I lived. I could just pick out where our house must be. Two stories, on a half acre landscaped with seven-year-old redwoods. We'd moved in three years ago. Now the place looked like it had been there forever, as if we were the original inhabitants. But it was the chicken ranch that had been there first. Flies from the chicken ranch had hovered like smoke over the estates, and the county health department forced the ranch owners to shut down a year after we'd moved in. They had all the buildings torn down but the old house. Then the Simpsons came, their imaginations running rampant: who else would have thought of leasing what was left of that failed place to start a kennel? I watched from my bedroom window as the slipshod wire fence went up around the runs. Read the advertisement in the city papers: Your dog deserves to board in the country. Grooming. Training. By the day or the month. Special rates for multiple-dog owners. People trusted the Simpsons with their animals. They looked so self-assured. Well dressed. Well spoken. If the actual kennel didn't measure up to the owners' expectations, it was irrelevant to the Simpsons. They didn't make explanations—that they were remodeling, or they couldn't get help. And the business flourished, no matter what they did.

I went down the hill, making my own path in the new grass. I had to pay attention to the direction I was going and be on the lookout for the dog at the same time. I sighted in on the only tree left along this section of the highway to be sure I would strike the road above the roadside rest. The highway went straight up the state, like an open pit six lanes wide. I'd followed its whole length once from the window of an airplane. I had been here in time to attend the small ceremony at the rest stop when they officially opened the highway. It had taken months before the rabbits stopped running onto the smooth warm surface to get flattened and picked to pieces by the crows. But now the ground squirrels had adjusted enough to live on the shoulders, standing on the edge of the slow lane, watching, as if they were counting the cars that went by. I used to come to the highway nearly every day. For the walk. To see the changes. Count the out-of-state license plates at the rest stop. I'd seen every state but Delaware and Kentucky. And then walk on to the construction: motels, gas stations, restaurants. I always thought of the rest stop, the businesses, the weigh stations as trim to the highway, like flowerbeds to the sidewalk. There was always something new, different, coming up.

I trudged toward the tree. Dogs run. The more stupid the breed, the faster they run. That's an Irish setter. Skittish. Beagles will rest when they are suddenly free. Stop by a gopher hole for a quick dig. Take a roll in some fresh excrement or dry dirt. Stretch out in the sun for a snooze. I don't even have a dog.

The first time I met the Simpsons I was walking to the freeway. I took the shortcut from the estates through the old chicken ranch. The kennel runs were being built on one of the chicken house cement floors. There was a lot of noise: hammering, an electric saw. Both Margo and Simpson were standing near their Mercedes watching the workmen. Margo spoke to me as I passed. "Don't hunch your shoulders, dear." I wasn't sure she was talking to me, but I stopped. I watched as Simpson poured a drink from a silver cocktail shaker into her glass. She took a sip. I was not indignant, just surprised. "Poor posture can become a lifelong habit. Now is the time to make corrections, while your body is still malleable." She looked me up and down over the rim of her glass and then took the few steps between us, switching the glass to her left hand. She put her right hand under my chin and lifted it slightly. Her hand was cold, and I felt my whole upper body tilt back. "Now take a breath, inhale, pull in your tummy, lower your shoulders. Down. That's better."

I did what she said. I didn't feel exposed. This was astonishing, since my breasts were the size of two separate planets. Two perpetual motion machines. I didn't dare look down. I was amazed at myself.

She took several steps backward. "Now walk toward me." I took the four steps between us too fast.

"You're jiggling," she said. "Turn around. Now walk from the hips down. On the balls of your feet. Turn around. Tummy in." She took another sip from her glass. I would never do this for my mother, I thought.

"Much better," she said. "Call me Margo from now on," she added. "We're starting a new establishment here." She then went on to explain her past. I stood there straight, the way she'd left me, as she spoke.

One, she had studied piano from the age of two until she was thirteen. She was a child prodigy and gave concerts.

Two, she was also a child model, then an adult model, with an international reputation.

Three, she married Simpson, who was a male model, at twenty.

Four, she had three daughters.

Five A, opened a modeling agency of her own.

Five B, operated the business for twenty-five years, made piles of money, and spent it all.

Six, opened Simpson Export Business.

Seven, Simpson Travel Bureau.

Eight, Simpson Kennel.

It was a wonder to hear her. It was like the words of a book coming alive on the page. A parrot pecking at your fingers. A wind getting sand in your eyes. Wild thoughts racing up your nostrils into your head. Then the sounds of the harpsichord. A mouthful of fudge. You could taste her words.

I told my mother, who had just gotten home and was washing lettuce in the sink, for our supper. "Sounds like an interesting woman," she said.

"If it's true," I said. "She offered me a job. After the fences are up. They're going to live in the old house; they have a five-year lease." My mother hummed at me, listening in her fashion. We both had the same bodies, but she was never in hers. Her mind was either on my father, who traveled up and down the state as a seismologist, or on her own job teaching physics at the college. She bought my bras. I was too embarrassed. They were getting bigger and bigger. I don't think she ever noticed the size of her own chest as anything unusual. She had poor posture. Her back must have hurt like mine did. "What am I going to do?" I asked her once, pointing at my chest with my thumb. She thought I was talking about which sweater to wear. "The green one's better," she said. I felt all my growth was going into my upper body. I swear I didn't wish for them, ever in my life. I tried to console myself: there were worse things. I could have been born without arms and legs. I stole an envelope and a sheet of letterhead from our doctor, who I saw every month for my allergies. Signed his name to a letter to my high school excusing me from P.E., so I didn't have to take off my clothes.

In retrospect, my parents would have listened if I'd had the patience to explain. Would have probably allayed my apprehensions if they'd known. They were secretly amused by me, wondering out loud why I wasn't more contemplative, why I allowed my imagination such scope. To them I was a twenty-year experiment. A diversion. My father would say to me, "There is no reason to pout." When I would rage, my mother would say, "Contain yourself." I was an exceptional student in spite of myself. I could not let the other kids get ahead of me. But I kept up a studied indifference at school and did not mingle. At home my parents didn't care if I cleaned my room or not. So I did.

Once the kennel began operation, I forgot about my own problems and picked up theirs. Not a heavy burden. Mostly coping with their incompetence. And Margo had a kind of genius for spending money. She could send a whole department store section into a tizzy looking for the right blouse. My mother met Margo once when she gave me a ride home, and listened for an hour and fifty minutes to her stories, standing at the curb. Margo could captivate anyone. But the stories were not always true.

I had gone through her things: dressers, closets, trunks, boxes, purse. She kept everything. Brochures on her businesses, along with all the receipts. Newspaper clippings, along with boxes of photos. Tax returns. The evidence was all there, but it wasn't easy to line it all up with what she said. It took time to work out the sequence. I knew they had both been convicted of tax evasion when they had the modeling agency. Fined and put on probation. Accused, according to what I could piece together, of burning down their warehouse for the insurance money when they were in the export business. Those charges had been dropped for lack of evidence. And there were other things Margo would hint at that I could never pin down: "We warned them what would happen," she would say; or, "We have friends."

Within a couple of weeks I stopped thinking so much about my own two great burdens bouncing in front of me like two attached basketballs. My back didn't hurt anymore and neither did my shoulders from the harness. It could have been from my new posture or from the way I walked now. But the most important thing was I did not see them looming in front of me anymore.

I heard the first sounds. If you weren't aware that the highway was there you'd never guess that noise was made by hot tires against the blacktop. Flying insects, maybe, or fire in dry grass. The sound in a conch shell. Your feet had to be almost on the black macadam before you realized there was a highway slicing through these hills.

The tree was in a small ravine that ran between the foot of the last hill and the highway embankment. I had to go down the hill on the sides of my shoes not to slip. There was still no sign of the dog. He was either dead, mangled beyond help on the road, or foraging in the garbage cans at the rest stop. I slid down the last ten feet to the base of the tree on my rear. I didn't notice anything unusual at first. The tree was a eucalyptus, so it constantly shed its leaves, and they were scattered underneath in different colors of decay. One of the large limbs had broken; it hung down, the leaves and branches resting on the ground. The new wood at the break was almost red and made me think of flesh, and the limb itself was the size of someone's leg. I had to concentrate to understand what I was seeing next, under the far side of the tree. Like cloth spread out over the leaves were sheaves of hundred-dollar bills. Some of the paper bands had broken and the money was spread out like decks of playing cards. I picked one up to be sure it was real. It felt crisp and smelled new, fresh. I searched for the source. Under the fallen branch was a case the color of the leaves. There was a metal hook screwed into the limb where the handle must have rested. It was all a very practical arrangement. Except the wind had broken the weighted branch and I had found the money.

I speculated on my options as I picked up the cash, which took some time. It was as if it had multiplied from its proximity to the green grass. I searched carefully even after I was sure there was none left. I had read too many newspaper articles not to know what the money represented. Or who it belonged to. For myself, I couldn't think of a use for the money. Turn it in? Be rewarded? Go on a spree? What did I need? What did we need, my parents and me? Uninteresting. Just keep the money? Too mundane, if not boring. Under my shoe boxes in my closet? I kept imagining Margo's face as I opened the case in front of her. It was an unusual chain of events that had brought me to the tree. It would be hilarious to show the money to the Simpsons, to see their reactions.

The case was heavy and awkward. I half dragged it up the ravine, making sure to leave enough signs in the soft dirt under the grass. When I got close to the rest stop I hid the case in a drainage pipe and hurried up the bank. There were the usual overnight cars and trucks in the lot, parked diagonally to the low brick rest rooms surrounded by lawns, picnic benches, trash barrels, telephones, and trees that never seemed to grow.

The Mercedes was already there. Simpson was pacing. In his handmade leather shoes, right in the middle of the drips and splashes of crankcase oil left by the thousands of cars that pulled in. He must have been almost perfect as a male model thirty years ago: above-average height, good profile, cleft chin. Trim then. But now it was as if someone had stuck a needle in his jowls and pumped him up with air. From a distance he seemed presentable: the well-cut, expensive clothes; the thick head of hair. But on closer inspection the clothes were stained. The hair sat on his empty head like dead grass. For a person who did nearly nothing, he was very impatient. He was smoking his pipe to demonstrate his displeasure with me for taking so much time.

He didn't notice me right off. Looking in the car, I saw the setter spread out on the backseat like a blanket, asleep. I got in and slammed the door closed, but Simpson didn't hear. I beeped the horn and made him jump and he came around. Before he could start, I gave the orders.

"Wipe your feet on the grass; you've been walking in the grease." He did. He got in. "When you get on the road," I told him, "get in the fast lane and make a U-turn across the center strip. Than make another so you're headed back toward the rest area. I'll tell you when to stop."

He started the car. "It was me that found the dog," he said. I moved my head in agreement, thinking of what must be done. There wasn't much traffic and Simpson managed the car well, considering that he'd probably spent half the night at the country club. They had a membership but never played golf, just ate and drank, when they had the money. When they didn't have the money, Simpson went alone and cadged drinks, Margo mentioned once.

When he stopped on the shoulder of the road above the drainage pipe, I went down and got the case and brought it back up. There wasn't room in the front, so I slid it in the back on the floor. No one saw me, I was sure. Simpson didn't even seem to see the case. It wasn't in his nature to question. We headed back to the kennel.

Margo must have been upset; when she worried, she cleaned. Not the obvious, like doing the dishes or vacuuming. Instead, she'd take the light fixtures apart and remove the dead gnats. When I opened the door she was polishing the claw legs of their oak dining room table with oil. "Simpson found the dog," I said. She got off her knees, back straight, and stood up.

"Well, happy days," she said. She meant it. They couldn't afford a lost dog. They couldn't afford to pay their rent either. Among other things. I'd seen the notices. The envelopes bore threatening messages: NOTICE; LAST WARNING; URGENT; IMMEDIATE REPLY REQUESTED.

I got the money case up on the cluttered table as Simpson came in behind me. Neither of them was curious about what was inside. I could leave the thing closed and they'd never go near it. They never used the table, so they'd never consider moving the case. Simpson sat down and put on his glasses and read an old newspaper. Margo went into their bedroom. I opened the case and then sat in a straight-backed chair to watch, legs crossed, poised, with a certain amount of presence and with perfect posture, thinking about the time I'd met the Simpsons' oldest daughter, Doris, an airline stewardess. The first thing she asked me when I was showing her around the kennel was, "Do they pay you?" I shrugged, something I since have stopped doing. "Mostly," I said. "Make them," she replied. They did, in their own way. Margo would buy me things. T-shirts. Makeup. Or take me to her hairdresser and pay. They invited me out to dinner and we had lobster and steak. Once. When an owner picked up her three dogs after fourteen months of boarding. They spent the money that afternoon and night. It was a joy to watch them. Rarely, Margo would make a great show of writing me a check and tearing it out with a twist and fling of her wrist. "Here you go," she'd say.

They must have smelt the money. Simpson suddenly put down his paper. Then Margo appeared at his side. Both came directly to the table after only about four minutes. I sat in my chair watching them. No one asked where the money had come from. They didn't want to know about the tree.

Simpson immediately got out his calculator and started counting, restacking the money on the cleared space on the table as it was tabulated. I never saw him move so fast. He must have worked in a bank at one time, the way he fanned the white borders of the bills back with his thumb, then let them go, counting each one. "We must keep this quiet," Margo said in her best teacher manner. "It could be dangerous." Then she lowered her voice: "We must tell no one."

"I won't," I said.

The eucalyptus leaves—I had unwittingly put some in the case—Simpson put aside in their own pile. The money looked less, diminished, stacked on the table beside the open case. After Simpson calculated the last stack, he ripped off the long strip of paper and showed Margo. She looked it over, holding it close to her face. She was so vain she wouldn't wear her glasses if anyone might see her. "We must each sign the receipt, and I'll put the date and time." And she carefully did that, using the yellow no. 2 pencil she kept in her hair.

"A pact," I said, enjoying the situation beyond measure. Simpson signed the receipt and handed it to me. I didn't look at the total; I just signed. I felt a rush of well-being like I'd never known before. I wanted to leap up and hug Margo. And Simpson too. But it would have broken the spell.

Simpson started putting the money back into the case. We watched. When it was all in, Margo put in the paper with our signatures on top and then closed the case. For good measure, she sealed it with a six-inch piece of Scotch tape.

If they had any conscious plan, they didn't elaborate. We agreed that the money was to stay in the suitcase under their protection until further notice. Was that until another meeting of the signatories, I wondered. Or were we going to keep the money until the rightful owners came forward? Or until the bills themselves became collectors' items?

Margo dug up an old wig on a dirty white styrofoam head and started brushing it. Simpson went back to his newspaper. I got up to go out to the kennel to start hosing down the runs and feed the dogs. "Well, I better get to work," I said. Neither answered, so engrossed in their own projects. If Margo's thoughts could appear across her forehead, chipped there with a chisel and hammer, the words *greed* or *avarice* would not appear. *Fur coat* would. *Ruby ring* most definitely. And *face-lift*, a really good one this time. Simpson's would appear in pictographs of his senses. Smell of that good brandy he always talked about. Smoke of the best pipe tobacco made. The feel of a new, unstained, no-burn-holed camel's hair overcoat.

Nothing happened. I watched the tree every day after school for an hour or two. Until Thursday. I was lying in the grass on my back, looking up, with the breath of the beagle I'd brought along for a walk on my cheek. It had been there as long as the place had been open. The Simpsons received a check for him every month. Why have a dog you pay someone else to keep? Margo had trained him as a pup, after I'd gotten several books from the library and photocopied the right sections. They didn't know any more about the business than I did. She told me once it was either the kennel or suicide, but she always talked like that. She turned out to be a good trainer. She had loads of patience and never tired of repeating herself. The beagle and I were both her successes. I'd actually learned to contain myself. To limit the amounts of anxiety that I dwelt on. To disregard what I thought others thought. Absolutely. My body was the instrument and I the song. It was amazing that it took almost fifteen and three quarter years for someone as intelligent as I am to understand that.

The beagle started licking my cheek, so I rolled away onto my stomach. It didn't register at first that what I was seeing was what I had envisioned since I'd found the money. The men by the tree, three of them. Spreading out, following my trail toward the rest stop. Stopping at the drainage pipe for a look, than going up the bank and walking along the shoulder. They acted like they'd done this before. There was a car beyond the tree with a man sitting in back looking out the open window. I got down lower in the grass, although I knew they couldn't see me.

I tried to think what they thought. Money: it wasn't at the tree. Did someone find it and simply drive away? Or did someone who lived near the rest stop find the money and take it home? How do people answer questions like that? There had been an ad in both the lost and found section and the personal section of the two city papers:

Lost, Highway 5
First North roadside rest after Road 111 exit
Green suitcase
Notify Atty Lester Tribb
408/733-2220

I didn't tell the Simpsons about the ads, but that's why I was watching the tree.

After awhile they left. I woke up the beagle and we started back. It was over three miles from the kennel to the tree. They couldn't know the place was there. It depended on how clever they were.

I got to the last hill and looked down at the kennel. The beagle ran for home and I watched as his tail, straight up like a rudder, guided him toward the new Mercedes parked in front of the house. He raised his leg against the right front tire. I remembered Margo saying, elaborating, on a theme she'd been developing all week: "We won't touch the money until the proper time. We mustn't." It irritated me sometimes, but I never pointed out, ever, that it was I who found the money. It was mine if it was anyone's, legally. "No," she said, "we will wait. There's no rush."

She bought me a bracelet, gold, heavy, ostentatious. Presented it to me in a red velvet box. "Here's something for you, Carmen." March was almost over and it was eleven days since I'd found the money under the tree. There was a sports coupe, red, foreign, parked next to the new white Mercedes now. They had bought bundles of clothes. So many there was no possibility of hanging them all up in the closet space they had—if they had bothered to unwrap most of them. There was absolutely no attempt on their part to deceive me about spending the money. Each purchase must have caught them by complete surprise too. Once bought, it was dismissed promptly, forgotten.

Feckless Simpson was the most changed. It wasn't just because of the really good clothes he wore now. It was his whole demeanor. The money finally proved to him he was a cut above most people. And the more he spent, the higher he rose in his own estimation. He was actually condescending to me several times, Simpson, which I tried to enjoy in all its ridiculousness, but it was hard.

Margo kept herself intact; she adorned herself too but didn't allow the money to really alter her. She could still be snippy at times, easily irritated: "Carmen, sit still. Don't you have anything to do out in the kennel?" But essentially she was the same, with a secret source of instant gratification. Neither could ever become sated, I was sure.

I watched. They made no excuses, gave no explanations. What was there to say, on my part? I didn't care about the money. Even they couldn't spend the whole three million dollars. They didn't have the imagination necessary for the endeavor. They were talking of tours, collecting brochures on cruises. They had canceled their ad in the local paper, and the dogs stopped coming in. There were fewer than a dozen left out in the runs.

They began to resurrect and elaborate their pasts. Margo had the photos of herself playing the piano as a girl blown up and framed to hang on the wall. Then her triumphs as a model were framed. She was pretty. Straight as an icicle. She bought an expensive portable keyboard to get her timing back. And ordered the baby grand over the phone as she showed me her first concert program, just matted and framed. "I might as well," she said.

Simpson had an old animal skin I'd never noticed before cleaned and patched and then hung, spread out, on one wall in the living room. I looked at it a few times before asking him what animal it was. There was a lot of hair missing; the tail had got stiff like a whip. "Zebra," he said, getting up out of his chair. "I bagged him on safari during an assignment in central Africa."

I'd thought the faded stripes looked somehow familiar, but I couldn't image anyone shooting a zebra. "You shot a horse?" I said.

"A zebra, running, at a hundred yards." I stopped myself from saying anything else. He got out his rifle to show me. An elephant gun, he called it. The bullets were as thick as his nose. He'd had the barrel reblued and the stock refinished. "Here," he said, "hold this." It was heavy and I almost dropped it on the floor. He grabbed it back and brought it to his shoulder, pointing it at the opposite wall. "There are some things a man has to do," he told me.

After about a month I thought I should do something, not to stop them, but at least to slow them down a little. They were becoming a spectacle. My mother, who wouldn't notice such things, had seen the Simpsons buy dinner for everyone sitting near them at a restaurant, on a whim, because someone had had a birthday and they'd joined in the song. They paraded around with a retinue of new friends. They rented the country club for a banquet. Their pictures were in the paper: Mr. and Mrs. H. Barstow Simpson celebrate their thirty-fifth wedding anniversary with gala. And then, former musical prodigy Margo Simpson has convinced the noted soprano Marcia Smith-Milham to come out of retirement for one last farewell concert performance at the civic auditorium.

But before I could think of anything I got the call. It was Margo, crying. I could barely understand her. I hadn't been over there for a couple of weeks. It was too hectic for me now. There were too many people. I should correct that: I *had* gone when I knew no one was there. Had used my key. The suitcase was in the corner of their bedroom, empty. The money was hidden in two pillow cases tied to clothes hangers among the press of their clothes. I counted out my share, my third, and took it away. There had been only two dogs left in the kennel when I came for my money, the beagle and a Pekinese. I'd given each of them a long scratch through the fence.

I knocked on the kitchen door. No one answered. It was locked from the inside, so I kept knocking. It would be impossible for them ever to notice that my third of the money was gone. "Carmen?" I heard Margo yell out.

"It's me," I yelled back, "open up." It took some time. She was shaking so badly when she finally pushed open the screen door that I had to grab her. She had cracked, shattered. She looked the same, the haughtiness, the posture, but there was a gap, a space between what she could see and what was there. She was terrified. She took hold of my arm and wouldn't let go. Simpson came out of the hallway carrying an old toilet plunger held to his side like a club.

I came down on my heels and kept my shoulders back. "What's wrong? What's happened?"

"Go out to the kennel and see," Margo said. Because she wouldn't let go of my arm, she came along with me. Simpson followed us. I didn't know what to expect.

Someone had put a wire noose around each dog's neck and then thrown them over the horizontal bar that supported the fence. The dogs had strangled, scratching and biting each other in their frenzy for air. Under the beagle's collar was a lined page from a pocket address book. Without having to touch the dog or the paper I could read what was written there: a dollar sign with three question marks in red ink.

I found a pair of pliers in the shed. Margo, who still had a firm grip on my arm, came with me. The worst was when I cut the wire and took the paper from the beagle's collar. I wanted to squeeze his paw as if he were still alive. Margo looked like she would cry if she could manage but was too terrified to try.

They had certain options left. I rather liked these kinds of problems. Simpson was standing like he might stay there forever. "Go get the shovel; we'll bury the dogs." He did what he was told. With Margo still attached to my arm, I went back toward the house. "Take the collars off," I called back to him. "I'll send them to the owners with an explanation."

Margo had been scouring the copper bottom of her frying pan with steel wool, salt, and lemon juice when I came, so I set her back to work at the sink and put on some water for afternoon tea. There was such poor light in the kitchen: only one of the five bulbs in the fixture worked. Why had they stayed here anyhow, after the money? I knew they had spent some nights in hotels in the city. Inertia? They had the dogs to care for?

Margo wouldn't join me for a cup of tea. Neither would Simpson, when he came in and put the two collars on the kitchen table, next to my elbow. I was going to miss the beagle. "You could go to the police," I announced. "Turn in the money. Report the killing of the dogs. Show the note."

"We've spent some of the money," Simpson said, as if it were probably a great surprise to me. Margo kept scouring away. "She bought you a bracelet," he added.

"The police won't know if there's any missing. It was found money. Do you think the real owners will go and claim it at the police station?"

Mulling it over as he spoke, Simpson said, "We could put it back in the tree."

"I hadn't thought of that," I said to humor him. "You could leave," I suggested. "Just get into your cars and drive away."

"They'd find us," Simpson said. "Hunt us down." His answers were making this more interesting.

Saying it a little louder for effect I repeated, "Take what's left of the money and go."

Margo surprised me by speaking up. "I think his idea is a good one," she said, rubbing the frayed lemon half across the bottom of the frying pan. They had some resources left. Things had taken a turn here; I couldn't tell the direction.

"If you want to try it," I said.

"The money," Margo said. Simpson moved fast. He came back with the suitcase and opened it up on the sideboard by the sink, then got the pillowcases and emptied them inside. The money in disarray filled the case to overflowing again. "This will work," Margo said with her old enthusiasm.

I didn't want to see them hurt if it could be helped. They weren't bad people. What were they? Irresponsible.

"Would you take it back to the tree?" Margo asked, coming over and putting her tapered fingers lightly on my perfect shoulders.

It was almost dark. "What if some else finds the money?" I asked. "Then you wouldn't have anything to give the owners. And why would they be checking the tree?"

"We should take the chance," Margo said.

"Take my flashlight," Simpson said. If they were ready to risk the money, I could always go pick it up in the morning. I finished my tea. Margo embraced me when I stood up. "You've been such a help," she said. Simpson handed me the two-battery flashlight and then the suitcase.

I went, but I didn't need the flashlight yet. The big persimmon-colored sun was bouncing just above the horizon, flashing orange all over the sky. I followed the shortest path to the highway, but it took time. That suitcase was still heavy. The grass had dried up and was as stiff as wire. And the conical bumps of hills I'd walked in the daytime were steep and made me breathe hard now. I had the feeling I could get lost if I weren't careful. I was almost to the gully where the tree was when I first thought someone was following me. I couldn't be sure, of course. But who else would be out here? And for what reason, walking parallel as if he knew where I was going? I slowed down. He slowed down too, across the field maybe two hundred yards away, not making any attempt to conceal himself.

It was them, then. They must have been watching the house. I'll just hand over the money, I reasoned. They would be glad to get this much back. I'd even throw in what I took if it came to that. "We've tied up all the loose ends," Margo had said as I left the kitchen. The phrase kept whipping around my head until it began to hurt. Was I a loose end too? I dropped down in the grass and opened the case. There was enough light to see that most of the bills had no zeros. They were dollar bills.

I took a breath that I couldn't exhale. To think. To think. Then I ran. I left the case and ran back the way I'd come. I was down a gully and out of sight in a minute. I knew these hills better than anyone. He couldn't follow me. I cut back toward the rest stop, but way to the left, to miss the tree.

It wasn't my own cleverness that trapped me, it was theirs. I always underestimate people. That's what comes of thinking you're smart. Did they hang the dogs themselves? Had they been contacted by the owners? What was the sequence of events? Poor Margo.

I waited in an erosion cut until there was no more sun. Then I started walking past the rest stop toward the first cluster of businesses on the highway. I stayed up on the bank, well away from the headlights of the cars. I could see the neon in the distance, the blue-white and the faded greens and pinks. It seemed unnatural in the dark of the hills, more so than the yellow headlights and red taillights of the cars. It was startling, sliding down the bank on my heels onto the flat surface of a parking lot. People moving about. The steady light. Inconspicuous, but with presence, I found the phone near the reservation desk of the restaurant. I dialed their number. Margo answered in her usual voice.

"You're going to die," I croaked.

She didn't respond at first. Then, "Wait, she has the money at the tree. Like we promised. The girl. You said we'd be even. She's smart. She's hidden it somewhere. Get it out of her. She knows where it is. It was her idea."

I started laughing. I couldn't help it. "I'm still alive," I managed to say.

"Carmen? Is that you, Carmen?"

I wasn't laughing at Margo but at myself. I had to hang up, I was so overcome. It took me a while to regain my composure. Clever is not smart and neither is a dead dog dead. I liked riddles.

I phoned their number again. "Margo," I said, "my advice is you'd better run for it."

"This is your fault," Simpson's voice came in on the extension. "You did this. We never wanted that money."

I could hear her breathing. "Margo, why didn't you give them back all the cash you had left instead of putting those dollars in the case? Did you think they'd be fooled? That I could spend three million dollars?"

How far would she go? Would she actually have me murdered? In a pleasant voice Margo intruded upon these thoughts. "Where are you?" she asked. All at once I felt something worse than fear or apprehension: it was as if the receiver had suddenly become the blunt head of some serpent, bared fangs next to my cheek. I dropped the phone and got out of the booth. Hearing her voice was like she was there with me. It frightened me.

I had been so silly. I understood it, finally. But now I knew what to do. If Margo and Simpson had been contacted by the owners and had made up this version, it was up to me to provide the owners with a more accurate account. I knew the number by heart. It was the kind of phone call I could make with perfect assurance. I stepped back into the booth and picked up the receiver.

Stepsister

It had been a day and a half. An ex-priest, a now-married priest, someone from before she was chancellor, was saying very early mass at one of the churches the diocese had closed. Old St. Thomas. With the encouragement of his former parishioners. They'd gotten a key somehow. "Times have changed. We have different needs," the spokesman for the delegation had said that very morning. "Not in this church," she'd said back. She had new locks put on the doors and bars on the windows. Added the place to the security patrol list. Who did they think they were? She spent more time with the diocesan attorney than anyone else. She had heard it all. But teaching sixth grade had been worse. She had to keep remembering that. And she had wanted this position too. Running the diocese. Chancellor. A niche heretofore filled only by priests. She was the first nun in the whole state of California to be a chancellor.

She was tired when she got home at seven. Home was a room at Mercy Hospital, where the nursing nuns used to stay, when there were any. It was just another hospital room, but it was her home. Why was she always having these long drawn-out conversations with herself over a word like *home*? She had tried an apartment once, back when they started modernizing the order. She'd felt like an impostor at first. The apartment had been too noisy. The sound of the refrigerator could keep her up all night, not to mention her inconsiderate neighbors. So she had gone back to the convent. Dormitory atmosphere. Someone to gab with in the TV room, if you so chose. But she had hidden sometimes too, just to be by herself. The building had been sold when the order dwindled. She'd heard it had become a bed and breakfast.

Slipping on her comfortable shoes, she looked over her mail, which had been put on the gray metal bedside table. She wasn't hungry, but she had to eat; she went back out and down the stairs to the hospital cafeteria. She'd never had a weight problem, she thought, as she pushed her tray down the runners. One-oh-five since she was fifteen. Petite, Eleanor had called her. Petite like a railroad spike, she'd kidded back. "The beef stew is good," the server said. It looked disgusting, in fact, but she nodded. "I'll take some," she said. She carried her tray over to a table—she was the only one in the place—and sat down. She said her prayers and added, "Please don't let me die of ptomaine poisoning, oh Lord," and giggled to herself. The food was worse than it looked, the meat the size, shape, and hardness of small rocks. Institutional food. She worked for an institution. She lived in an institution. She was institutionalized. She chuckled out loud. Thankfully, the server had gone back into the kitchen.

Back in her room, she read her mail. A fashion catalog with women almost naked to the waist in the ads for underwear. Once, as a teacher, she'd allowed her students to ask any questions that came to mind about nuns. To clear the air. A whole drove of them had suddenly left the order—it was early in the seventies—to get married or join a commune or become jet pilots. It was the first time lay teachers had outnumbered nuns, and it was the beginning of the end of Catholic education. She'd never felt she had a student with a vocation, after that. The first question she had heard before: she removed her coif and veil. Her head wasn't shaved. They were fascinated. But she wasn't ready for the next one. A ten-year-old stood up and asked, "Is it true that nuns have their tits cut off when they take their vows? My uncle said that." No one even giggled; no one was even shocked. Except her, of course, yelling, "Outside, outside, go to the office." Eleanor was principal then. Never mentioned the incident, specifically. Took her into the teachers' room after school for coffee. Told her some anecdote about some old nun that she'd stopped listening to after the first couple of sentences.

Five pleas for contributions. They were getting better at disguising the envelopes to look like real letters. How had she ever gotten on these mailing lists? The last letter was from a lawyer. Just what she needed. Three of them together, she noticed from the letterhead. Reynolds, MacIntosh, and Reynolds. They liked to cluster like vampire bats. She skimmed the letter. They were kidding her. She'd been named executrix in her cousin's will. She didn't have time for that. She'd phone in the morning, beg off. San Francisco was too far; she didn't have anyone left there.

When she finished her correspondence, it was almost nine. She was getting home later now: up at five thirty, at work an hour later, back after seven. But there was still time to go up to the terminal wing. She felt comfortable up there with them, at her ease. The people there were so glad to see anyone who came in. Soothe them; listen to their cares.

She had her hand on the phone to call the San Francisco lawyers. It was after ten; the gentlemen were rarely in before that time, though. She had been at her desk for over three hours. Was she getting sanctimonious too, besides everything else? Father O'Reilly came in like an iguana. The auxilliary bishop, her boss, the person she reported to. He never knocked. An old-timer. Never comfortable with the fact that a nun was doing this job now. A token to the times, surely; she could only speculate on that, and a reward for faithful service, but still he never accepted the fact. One of the few Irish alcoholic priests who should never have stopped drinking. Should she go on with another almost-related thought? The non-Irish bishop before this one had been critical of the Irish, so the story went. For a century, almost since the Gold Rush, in fact, it has been traditional for the diocese to be sent Irish nationals for priests: grown, she sometimes pictured, for export. It suddenly stopped cold, for seventeen years. If only she had been chancellor then. Because the then-bishop had retorted at dinner one evening, "The Irish need to be taught table manners first and to speak the English language second before they're fit for one of my parishes." To the Irish consul, no less. It had been she who'd kept prodding Father O'Reilly to enter the clinic. Forty years in this country and his brogue was as thick as peat and he savored it as much as he used to the first sip of a good scotch whiskey.

"Top of the morning to you, Sister."

"Good morning, Father." She didn't use her imitation Irish brogue with him. Sometimes on the phone she did. The foreignness of it was an advantage. And if the caller was of a certain age and remembered the movies, all to the good. Eleanor had insisted she watch them, *Going My Way* and all the rest, whenever they came on TV. "Put that book down; you can learn something." She had, after awhile. At first she'd complained that the banter between the priests and nuns could give some credence to the lies about the babies buried under the nunneries. "No one believes that foolishness anymore," Eleanor had said. "These roles give us a resonance, a kind of credibility that Protestants can never have. Because their sacrifice is so much less." The thing she ended up learning was that she was a perfect mimic. She could sound more Irish than any colleen that ever danced on the village green.

Father O'Reilly hoped to be charming but didn't know how to go about it. "You're looking well, Sister. It must be the change in the weather. Fall can't be far," he said, looking out the window.

"No, it can't," she said, "since it's almost November." She watched him grow more and more uncomfortable.

"The bishop is feeling much better now."

"I've been praying," she said. "For his full recovery." The man had a heart condition because he was too fat. Obese, to be tolerant about it.

Another long pause from the auxilliary bishop. Father O'Reilly, when he jutted his neck and chin out of his collar, looked like a shore bird that had swallowed a plate. It was said that when he was young he'd looked like a romantic lead. He still cultivated the image; thirty-five-dollar haircuts, tailored suits, all free, of course, from Catholic businessmen. She noticed for the first time how his nose was pinched at the bridge, forcing the flesh down into a purplish horn the size of a small pear. He offered her the file folder he'd been holding behind his back. "Here are the papers on the diocese versus the latest plaintiff. We decided to settle out of court on this one. People must think we're made of money. Slip on a bit of popcorn at Tuesday bingo and the church will take care of you for life."

"It's the times," she said. The case should have been fought. It shouldn't have been paid off with one penny of church money. But it wasn't her decision. It was his. Protestants fight to the bitter end, no matter what they're caught at. We stand on our moral dignity. Our righteousness. We maneuver like Irish sumo wrestlers to get the sympathy.

"We must be more careful, Sister." Was he blaming her for the popcorn on the floor? He had tried to get rid of her at first. Accused her of being too inexperienced. Unyielding. No knack for the position. She'd heard that. She had thought of going to him for confession, telling him off, in veiled terms, of course. But that wouldn't have been charitable. Instead she had become so efficient she was perfect. Or nearly perfect. He could find no fault.

Eleanor had met Father O'Reilly just once, but that was enough. He could see a rich parishioner who was waiting to write her will standing in the doorway a mile off, she'd said of him, but he couldn't recognize a moral issue if it was taped to his forehead.

"Father, I have to make a personal call, if you don't mind." He could stand looking out the window for twenty minutes.

"Excuse me, excuse me; I'll see you later. Top of the morning to you."

❦

The diocese didn't have a spare car for her to drive. The extras had been sold in an economy move, Father O'Reilly reminded her. A two-hour trip by car turned into a five-hour trip by bus. It had been her idea to sell the cars.

Seething. I am not seething, she told herself. I am not. She recalled that in the old days wearing a habit had been a certain protection from the attentions of the ordinary. She hadn't worn a habit in fifteen years. When the first changes came, she'd welcomed them. She was firm in wanting to be the bride of Christ, but she didn't need to wear the wedding gown every day as a reminder. It was made of gabardine and was hot in the summer and itched all the time. She'd thought that for Sister Eleanor, her mentor, it would have been more difficult to shuck off the habit, but she did it with ease. "I don't feel any different," she said. "I'm still the same person that took my vows." Eleanor was always counseling her about their vows. Patience: "Patience is a subtle part of the vow of obedience." But it turned out both she and Eleanor had been impatient. The other vows she'd never been taken to task for. Poverty had been easy: she was born poor; her father was a park gardener for the city, and he used to bring her mother home little bouquets of wild violets for her birthday. And the vow of chastity, it was the easiest; it was a release to be just the devoted bride of Christ. But after all these years she was still impatient. "Hey lady, do you have the time?" her seat companion kept asking. I pray for these people, she reminded herself.

Travel had deteriorated. These days, if you were too poor to fly, you were abject. Five hours to think about mothers stuffing soiled Pampers under their seats, winos passing paper bags shaped around quart bottles back and forth for a sip. Juveniles and their radios. Has the whole world stopped bathing? she wondered.

She had made a mistake, telling Father O'Reilly about the San Francisco lawyers who wanted to see her. She should have just passed it off as personal and taken the day off. "Go," he'd said. "We'll get along."

"Oh, I can't; there's so much to do."

"I insist," he'd said.

Eleanor would have said you can tell how important your position is by who they replace you with when you're sick. They replaced her with a twenty-three-year-old secretary who couldn't spell. One of our good Catholic girls, as Father O'Reilly referred to her, paying her the minimum wage. The Irish scut.

The city had grown taller, but Market Street looked almost abandoned on a Sunday. Where had the big department stores gone: the White House, the Emporium? She remembered coming downtown to shop for her school clothes. Parochial school uniforms, which she had been perfectly willing to wear. Brown plaid skirt, white blouse, green sweater. You could wear any kind of shoes as long as they had laces.

Her parents had been so proud of her for joining the order. Sending treats. Visiting. But she noticed each time there was less and less to talk about. Less and less in common. By the time she was teaching, their get-togethers had tapered off considerably. It wasn't she who stopped writing after her father died. She always remembered Christmas, Easter, and her mother's birthday. And she had been busy. It was a neighbor who'd phoned the convent to say that her mother was in the hospital. She just couldn't get away at the time. You just can't walk out and leave a whole grammar school to run itself. Her mother died the next morning.

The hotel was near the attorneys' office, an easy walk tomorrow morning. The room was a better shade of green than her hospital room. Fewer pictures, but a double bed that almost filled the place. It was only for one night. She had asked the hospital cafeteria to make her a lunch, which they did grudgingly. A cheese sandwich, a half pint of milk, a bag of potato chips, and an apple. She ate that now in her nightgown, sitting on the edge of the bed. It was almost like home.

It was Eleanor who always brought it up: "You've never wondered about having a normal, regular life? Wife, mother, children, home? What kind of person you would have been?"

"Never."

Eleanor was good at pursuing anything disquieting. Another time: "You've never questioned anything? You've always been obedient?" It was her first year of teaching. She was having a hard time of it. She had slapped a girl across the face for talking back in class that day. She knew what Eleanor was doing, trying to make her see that she had been like her students once. Feeling their oats. Like frisky little animals. "Didn't you ever do anything really silly?" she asked. "Or something that mortified you later, down to the roots of your hair?"

She wanted to please Eleanor, but most of all she wanted to get out of this situation, of teacher-called-in-by-the-principal. She would learn to do better. So she told the most horrifying, shameful, embarrassing thing that had happened to her in her twenty-two years of life on the planet. At St. Catherine's there were dances on the first Saturday of every month. Boys from Catholic high schools were invited. The odd thing was that most of the kids who went were the ones who thought they might have a vocation. The dances were well chaperoned by both the nuns and parents, and most of the lights were on as the dancers circled the wooden auditorium floor to the music from records approved by the principal. There had been a young Irish priest who taught religion at St. Catherine's who'd hold impromptu sessions where he'd challenge the students to ask him anything. One Monday after a Saturday dance her whole class of over a hundred girls had been invited to the auditorium, and at the end of the session she, Marynora Sorensen, stood up straight and spoke up for the first time to the priest standing alone on the stage with her question about the dances. "Why do so many of the boys carry flashlights in their pockets when they dance?" she'd asked. Another girl stood up and said she'd wondered about the flashlights too. But most of the class was cracking up, laughing so hard that some were crying. The priest excused himself. The sisters began calling out, "Back to your homerooms, girls, back to your homerooms." The worse was, she hadn't understood what everyone thought was so funny. Eleanor had roared. She'd tried to join in too, but it was still too difficult.

Walking up Market Street to the attorneys' office, she felt lighthearted, as if she might start skipping down the sidewalk. Maybe she'd have time to go out to the park. It was one of the two things she missed about the city, going out to Golden Gate Park to look at the sections where her father had worked. He used to take her, once she got old enough, whenever he had to go in on a Saturday. She'd help pick up paper with a stick with a nail in the end. Dive bombing, he called it. She found a five-dollar bill one time. "It's yours," he told her. "Do what you like with it." She'd put it in the collection basket on Sunday. The other thing she missed was going out to the zoo. When she was teaching, she always arranged a class trip to the zoo. After her first year she knew the classroom wasn't the place for her. Eleanor knew too and sent her to night school to work toward an administrative certificate. Even when she became principal she went on the zoo trips. Zoo Day, the kids called it. She was there with them once when a male lion started roaring like a mad thing, the sound carrying everywhere, drawing a crowd. By the time she got there he was just showing off his big teeth. If she were an animal, she'd be a fox.

She thanked the woman who ushed her into the office. She chose the chair in front of the big polished desk. William T. Reynolds III, the name plate said. He took his time, and when he did come into the room, it was from the same door she had. As he passed behind her he asked, "What would you like to be called? Miss Sorensen okay? I'm not Catholic." She didn't turn her head. Because lawyers had a specialized knowledge, albeit a critical one, they thought they were above the common crowd; just like priests, they were the direct link, the ones who negotiated the questions and then interpreted the answers for the rest of us. And when they became bishops or judges, mercy mercy. "Marynora will do," she said. It had come out too Irish and in a stage whisper. She wanted him to understand her.

"I'm glad you've come, Marynora," he said, stopping to smile down at her. She recognized the Rolex watch he wore on his right wrist: someone had given one to Father O'Reilly; certainly over thirty-five hundred dollars. Four thousand, possibly. William Reynolds, the son of the owner of the firm. Fresh-faced. Unformed.

"This is going to be the easiest job you've ever had," he said. "All you have to do is sign these papers." The folder was already laid open on the desk. He turned it around for her and handed her a pen. "Where the red Xs are," he said. She took the pen. "You're a cousin, I believe?" he asked. She didn't pay attention, was already reading the second page. "That's not necessary," he said. "Mr. Sorensen was a client of ours for years." He was speaking faster now, as if he were trying to wedge words between the sentences she was reading.

"How much did the company gross last quarter?" she asked, taking off her glasses.

He looked puzzled. "Something like 14.2 million for the whole year. It was a very good year, mostly because they sold off some excess property. The year before, they'd lost 2.8 million dollars." He sat back in his chair and looked at her. He was going to wait her out.

"If the probate process takes six months, why do you want me to abrogate my position as executrix now?"

He spoke carefully, slowly, as if he were talking to a child or an idiot. "The heirs want to sell the business. They have taken our advice on this matter. It's a good time; it netted a small profit last year. We handle things like this as a law firm. Financial planning. We might have a buyer now, if we make certain concessions before the business goes on the market. An executrix is, in this situation, mostly an honorary . . ."

"I'd like to see the plant or factory, whatever it is," she cut in. She should have let him go on and on; if necessary, until he ran out of words. He would feel better for it. Impatience was so hard to control. It wasn't something that could be easily mentioned in confession, and though she watched for it every minute, it still tripped her up. When she was teaching, she couldn't stand the thought that some of the children were not keeping up. Two pages of math a day; the spelling workbook. Eleanor the sage had said teaching is a task that should be as imperceptible and cumulative as the movement of a glacier: a glacier that can cut valleys through mountains was how she put it.

⚘

They left the freeway, crossed railroad tracks, and drove into an industrial park. Stopped in front of a solid-looking, cement-gray, windowless building the size of a football field, with an office complex adjoining. Lawns, a border of flowers, a sign: TRADE WINDS: HERBS AND SPICES. Why am I doing this? she thought. Not because William here doesn't want me to. I'm past that, I hope. Not, most certainly, for a new challenge. The diocese provides that for me. I don't know why yet. I'll admit there is no reason. Beyond, I want to. Mr. Bill hadn't said one word, not one, the whole drive. But his thoughts were as loud and clear as if he were yelling them: Frustrated old maid. Nun. Anachronism. Bitch.

She had heard them all. *Anachronism* had been yelled by a former nun picketing the cathedral. Of course, that was not going to stop her from hearing mass. She had prayed thanksgiving for the grace that had made her join the order. Adversity and conflict had their own reward. She often thought that. She thanked heaven for Father O'Reilly sometimes. He was almost as good as being tested by a leper. For the Lord, of course.

William, overtly rude now, led her into another office and then left, without a word. Poor man. An office with a view of the insides of the plant. Several men in coveralls and paper hats were operating large gray machines the size of city buses. The overalls were the same color as the machines. The floor was filthy. A forklift and driver came into her field of vision. It was all a vignette, an asterick on the company's gross income the year before. William came back, followed by the superintendent, almost out of breath. Had he hurried to see the nun running amuck? What had William told him? She would have to guess. Did she have any idea yet, any thought what she was doing here? The Lord would provide. She tried not to let them see her smile.

"I'm pleased to meet you," the superintendent said, avoiding using her name. Bob, his name tag said. A big, blond, red-cheeked man with a bemused look, responsible to the plant manager for daily operations. He was going to fat over the responsibility, like a priest who'd found a good housekeeper who could cook but whose parishioners gave him no time to exercise properly. Why did priests have housekeepers and not nuns? She'd ask the bishop the next time he announced his open door policy.

She started questioning Bob while William glowered. Bob gave full replies, as if he were an auditor. "One hundred seventy-one full-time in two shifts; that includes twenty-three in the office but does not include work we contract out. Janitorial is always out. All security is outside. External maintenance of the buildings . . ."

William couldn't stand it anymore and interrupted Bob in the middle of a sentence: "I don't see what purpose you can possibly have for this information."

If impatience was her major fault, she decided, knowing why she did things must be her major virtue. Why had she become a nun? To become independent at eighteen. To get the education her family couldn't afford; she could always decide to leave the order afterward. To get away from her parents, who loved her too much. Because she had a vocation. Because she believed so fervently that it was her only choice. All of the above, or choose one. She was a hypocrite. "I intend to fulfill my duties as executrix during the probate period, which means I'll be managing the business, among other things, of course. I think my cousin had more reason for wanting me as executrix than you know, William," she added, to round out her thoughts.

Her father's cousin Albert used to send them spice racks at Christmastime. Little jars filled with juniper berries, tumeric, vanilla beans, exotic things they never used, that faded and shriveled after a few years. She didn't remember him much as a girl, but he must have been around. He knew her. He bought football uniforms for the team when she was principal of the junior high. The things Catholic schools had to do to compete with the public school systems. You'd think they'd be more appreciative, taking some of the burden of educating children away. Later he used to phone her sometimes, just to talk. Never about the business or his children, who got their names in the paper, messy divorces, drunk driving, but about baseball or her father. He'd been the major contributor to the new gym the first year she was chancellor. She had it named Sorensen Gymnasium. He had done so much.

William didn't speak, driving her back to her hotel. She thought of what Father O'Reilly would say about her absence. He would be relieved. Happy. Ecstatic. How would he feel in six months, when he realized what she actually did for the diocese? She could always go back to teaching; she'd be better now. She wasn't bored being chancellor though.

When William stopped in front of the hotel he didn't come around to open the door, as he had that morning. She didn't like irritating people; that was never her intention. "I'll see you tomorrow," she said, "at six-thirty. I'd like to get to the plant before the first shift goes on . . ."

"I have better things to do than be your chauffeur," he said. The car lurched forward, then stopped. He yelled back, his head out the window, "Take the bus," and was gone.

She had brought tea bags, and she brewed a cup using hot water from the tap. She had to phone the diocese, of course. While she was thinking of the best way to break the news, she sat down on the bed. She caught herself at once: early convent training; never, never sit on the bed during the day. The bed is for sleeping. She didn't know the reason for the rule. She had obeyed it for twenty-five years. She sat back down. It would be truly sacrilegious to put her feet up too. She tried the left foot first as she dialed the number.

She couldn't sleep that night, and it wasn't because of the conversation she'd had with Father O'Reilly. It was about taking the bus to the plant: there were three transfers, according to the schedule she'd picked up when she went out to dinner. That apprehension made her think of the first time she wore the habit outside the convent. She was a city girl, so she'd been asked to lead a group of visiting sisters to the cathedral. She kept counting them on the bus, looking back from her seat to be sure that no one had gotten lost. Turning once, she realized they *did* look like penguins in their old-fashioned habits. She had to concentrate before she could recognize their faces again.

She had to stand, jammed in, only able to maneuver a little to a new position in the moment when the door opened and a bunch left before the new commuters got on, but it was better than nothing. She made the connections easily and finally got out at the stop in front of the industrial park and started down the sidewalk. She suddenly felt buoyant, like she had as a girl on the first day back to school after summer vacation, as if just getting there was enough, took priority over what she would learn. Learning had not been so difficult. She'd had to study. Hard, sometimes. She had tried to please her teachers and her parents too, of course, rather than herself. She was the best-behaved student any of the nuns had ever had. They'd all commented on that, under *Deportment.* But not now. Now she did what she wanted.

"Call me Bob," the superintendent reminded her, standing up when she came into the office. Before she could speak, he said, "Mr. Reynolds phoned; said I was to do anything you asked." He seemed amused.

"Can you get another desk in here?"

"There's a vacant office the last manager used—they didn't replace him when he retired last spring—over in the business complex."

"I'd like to be here where I can see . . . ," she couldn't think of the right word and paused a second before adding, ". . . things." He got on the phone without another question and ordered a desk brought in. He'd make a good priest.

"Bob, do you think you'd have time to show me around the plant?"

"All the time in the world," he said.

"And my name in Marynora," she said.

He was still smiling as he handed her a blue hard hat. "Blue is the top honcho color," he said, and then added, "Mary." His hat was red. When he opened the door into the plant the noise hit against them like the force of a strong wind. She followed him, the noise pounding against her head and neck, getting louder and louder as they went. Her nose was burning from something pungent in the air.

Bob stopped at the entrance to a room the size of a school auditorium. She looked past him. Fifty or sixty women in aprons and plastic shower hats were standing in front of bottling machinery as little jars marched along a track in fits and starts. The place was filled with a white smoke, thicker than incense. "We're running garlic power today," Bob said. She'd known the odor but hadn't been able to name it.

The next stop was a processing room, the air thick with dust, where a dozen men were operating refining machines. Three others emptied hundred-pound sacks, one after another, into a blender. They wore masks and paper hats. Bob waved and they waved back. Forklifts passed, carrying finished boxes of the product out to the loading docks. They followed the forklifts and watched as the big semis were loaded.

Coming back, Bob stopped at a door and looked at his watch, then turned the knob. Five men were sitting on sacks, reading magazines. "Hey, Bob," one said. The others kept reading. She knew what kind of magazines they were; the centerfolds were hanging out. "Get going, you guys; it's time," Bob said, and walked away.

She waited until they got back to the office to ask. Her desk was already there. "What were those men doing?"

"Goofing off. Waiting for a batch to get done in the cooker. Then they go back to work."

"Couldn't they be doing something?"

He thought for a minute. "I suppose. They could get some more materials for tomorrow. Go help on the line. Good guys; they do their share."

"Tell them I don't want them to goof off anymore. Explain to them that the company needs everyone to do his best if it's to keep going. Tell them to keep busy." Bob wasn't smiling anymore. "No more reading magazines on company time," she said. She sat down in her chair and Bob went out.

The rest of the day was uneventful. She left early to catch the bus. She was tired now; no hope for a seat at the rush hour, though. To her surprise, people didn't crowd her or step on her shoes. She even ended up sitting for the last part of the ride. Then, when she lifted her hand to look at her watch, she got a whiff and understood: she reeked of garlic. No wonder, she thought.

ꕤ

After a long shower she stretched out on the bed. She'd already washed out her clothes. She had brought two complete changes. That's all she needed. At first, at the convent, that was all they were allowed. She had learned so much about herself there. "Vanity deposed," Eleanor the mandarin like to say. It was like a course in survival training, preparing you to be dropped on Mars. After the old-timer nuns stopped being wary and decided she was going to stay, it got so they treated her like one of them. About forty percent had disappeared from her novice group. A dying vocation, Eleanor had said fifteen years later, when she mentioned that she was the only one left of her novitiate.

She had gotten to like the gab sessions when she was a teacher, late at night in the convent recreation room. But she knew she wasn't as good a teacher as some of them. Her enthusiasm didn't go as deep as theirs for bright students, the lesson plans, correcting the endless papers. By the time she'd gotten her administrative certificate they were running out of nuns. During her first year as principal she'd had to hire lay teachers. The nun teaching first grade was eighty-one years old. The first lay teacher she interviewed was Mrs. Jensen. The salary was a third of what the public school districts were paying, but Mrs. Jensen needed the job, having just moved to California from Texas. "And when do the kids go home?" Mrs. Jensen asked.

"Three thirty."

"And the teachers?"

"I usually stay until five thirty, then eat dinner, come back at six thirty, stay until nine or so." She hadn't realized Mrs. Jensen thought she would have to do that too. She never phoned back.

Nuns were leaping the wall that year as soon as they figured out which direction it was in. They had to combine the second and third grades, and she taught both, besides coaching basketball after school.

Eleanor used to hold forth with eloquence on staying, half joking, half serious: "We've got to hold out. As long as we can. The Irish monks kept the Greek and Roman tradition alive all through the Dark Ages. That's our job now, to hang on as long as possible, during this age of shadows when there are no rules and the blue eye of the television set provides our morals." Eleanor the apostle was full of such wisdom. Dominated the order and the diocesan school system. When Eleanor became principal of the high school, Marynora became principal of the grammar school. But the number of nuns kept diminishing despite her eloquence. The year before she accepted the position as chancellor, she and Eleanor were the only two nuns left in the diocese.

A month and a half and she'd finally gotten used to the noise. They were running allspice today; she was going to smell like a bag of cookies on the bus. She walked around the plant by herself now. It was fascinating. The employees accepted her as manager with a "Good morning, Mary"; they didn't know she was a nun. She was the boss. The heirs were already asking William about trying to talk her into staying on. She couldn't, of course; she had responsibilities, obligations. Her vows. Production had picked up almost twenty-three percent, and they were staying in the black. There wasn't the tension here in the plant that there was in the diocese. The structure was much looser; the traditions less strict, less inhibiting. This was indeed a vacation for her.

She got some wonderful ideas, just strolling around. Staggering one shift for about a third of the employees, having them come in two hours later, when the line was set up and ready to go: it saved something like four hundred manhours a week. Contracting out most of the inside plant maintenance: why have a plumber stand around waiting for something to happen? Call one when the cooling system broke down. She had cut down on the overtime by twenty percent by reevaluating all the job descriptions and combining some of the jobs. There were a lot of similarities between manufacturing and school systems, she thought. In the bottling room especially she couldn't help thinking of the little glass bottles as students filled with over twelve years of product. The foremen wore white hats and waved as she passed.

She didn't plan on it, but she opened that same door that Bob had the first time he'd taken her around. The exact same five men were in there, reading the newspaper this time. "How you doing?" one said. His name tag said *Stan*.

"I'm fine," she said. "And you?" Apparently he wasn't being smart with her.

"We're all fine too," Stan said, turning the page. The others were still behind their papers.

"Didn't the superintendent ask you not to read?"

"He mentioned it, but there's nothing to do right now."

Three of them were smoking, she noted. The bales of cinnamon bark they were sitting on would pick up the smell of the tobacco smoke. She remembered from the time cards she went over every night that these men got at least fifteen hours of overtime a week. She was becoming irritated.

"Would the five of you please find something to do while you're waiting for the next batch? Something that might lessen the amount of overtime we have to pay you." Everyone was attentive now.

"Now listen," Stan said, pointing his finger at her.

She felt the same way she had when a student challenged her. But she didn't lose control like she used to. She was rational and spoke with an offhand ease that would have made Eleanor proud of her. "I'm going to give you one minute to get up and get out on the floor and start to work." She paused. "Or you're terminated. Do you all understand that?" She stepped back out of the doorway and looked down at the second hand on her wrist watch. Started walking when the point hopped on the six as if she were propelled by a rocket toward the office. She had the men's names; she knew who they were. She told Bob, who sat down abruptly, his eyes blinking as if she'd struck him. "Fire them," she said. "Give them what we owe them and get them out of the plant."

He swung his chair around to the loudspeaker microphone and asked the shift foreman to come to the office. They waited in silence until she remembered something. "They were smoking in the restricted area, too." He didn't answer.

She had met Tiny before. He must have weighed three hundred pounds. Due for a heart attack, at his age, she thought. Hoped it wouldn't be in the plant. Could she start a diet program for the workers: bring health food into the lunch room snack dispensers, yogurt and granola instead of candy bars and potato chips? Her father had taken breaks too, hiding behind trees, smoking, reading the sports page, but never challenged the city over his right to do so.

Tiny leaned over the desk, talking low to Bob. She didn't try to hear. Tiny went back out, putting his white hat on at the door. She went to work, checking the time cards against the department production records. She didn't notice at first when the door opened. Then she saw a woman her age standing in front of the desk: she was wearing safety glasses and a paper mask, a plastic cap full of dust at the creases, a stained apron and long, faded yellow rubber gloves. She watched in fascination as the woman pulled down the mask, stretching the elastic until the paper cup–like filter rested under her chin. "Bob," she said, "rescind the firings or we walk."

Bob stood up. He was embarrassed. "Mary, this is the union's chief shop steward, Mrs. Russell." Neither acknowledged the other. Bob went on talking. "Mary here is the manager; she's responsible for some of the innovations that we've been trying. To save the place. What she says goes. She has the complete backing of the family."

She stood up too. She had the feeling something dramatic was going to happen. She was ready for anything.

"This is not a game we're playing here; it's not basketball. No one wins on points. It's a job. This place is where we work." Mrs. Russell didn't sound excited or angry or even upset. It was as if she were merely mentioning something in passing, reading someone else's point of view on the subject. "We've gone along with some of the crap, but it was a mistake. The goddamn family has been running this place like a three-ring circus for years, and *now* they want to save it?"

Marynora felt she was a flexible person, but this was too much. "The company is ready to file a Section Eleven, go bankrupt." She pointed down at her desk, covered with papers. "It's inevitable, unless we can cut costs and raise production. Those men weren't doing their jobs."

"Those men do a day's work for a day's pay, just like the rest of us. A batch takes an hour to make and ten minutes to mix in the mixer. For the next three hours they take the batch out and bag it in a hundred-and-five-degree heat. So while the batch mixes they take a break. All of them have their ten-year pins. I've been here twenty-one years and that's the way it's always been done."

"Then we have to change that, Mrs. Russell. Those men are terminated. You agree, Bob?" He didn't answer. Mrs. Russell turned around and walked out of the office.

She noticed it immediately. The sound stopped. There was no background hum. No gentle vibration of pencils on her desktop. Bob went out. She picked up her hard hat and followed. The place was empty. They walked the length of the plant to the loading dock. In the parking lot the employees were standing around or sitting in their cars.

"Hire more hands," she said. "And get them out of our parking lot."

The department foremen pitched in and the bottling room started up by noon. Some of the office staff who were nonunion helped. She boxed bottles, then stacked twenty-four cartons to a pallet for Bob to take away with the forklift. They got all the next day's orders out. Her back ached by four, but she had never felt so good in her life.

She got on the bus and realized that she hadn't thought of the diocese all day. She had been eating at a cafeteria, and she went straight there instead of to her hotel room. Filled already with senior citizens. She fit right in; they were all past caring what they ate. Macaroni and cheese: it looked like mounds of tiny ninety-degree plastic pipe fittings. But it tasted good. She had an appetite.

She spent the rest of the evening going over the company contract with the union. They had to come to their senses about this, she decided. Production was cut eighty-five percent when they walked out. She was not being hypocritical when she prayed for the factory workers and their families.

By nine o'clock the next morning a meeting had been set up for that afternoon between William, herself, the union business agent, a Mr. Kliess, and the union attorneys. They hired more employees, filling all the jobs by two o'clock. They were running paprika; she wore a mask, but her nose still twitched as she worked. The city police finally made the former employees move out of the parking lot. They carried signs now as they walked up and down the sidewalk. UNFAIR. LOCK-OUT. It struck her as a contradiction in terms. Who was being unfair to whom?

They met in the spacious, unused manager's office in the business building. She didn't sit in the manager's chair behind the desk. No one did. It was almost like being in front of an altar. The glass-topped desk reflected the sunstream coming through the high windows. William opened the meeting. The three union lawyers resembled him a little: they were alert, knew the importance of dress, had their attaché cases of answers at the ready. Attentive. Like seals at feeding time.

"We have a slight problem," William started out. Everyone laughed but her. She didn't think it was funny. The business agent was an old man, older than the bishop. The liver spots on the back of his hands were the size of the rings on a leopard's fur. His head was perfectly round, rimmed by a fringe of almost white hair.

William went on with how the company and the union had always gotten along. "Then let's put the men back to work," Mr. Kliess interrupted. "We have a contract, good for another eighteen months. We'll straighten all this out then."

She spoke up. "The contract was voided when the employees walked out. If they'd honored the contract, we wouldn't be here."

"The people who work here are individuals; they walked out for due cause. And they won't come back until you start treating them fair and like human beings." His face was getting redder as he spoke. As if his empty head was heating up, she thought.

"We don't want them back," she answered in a reasonable, even tone. "We have new employees now. In fact, we have petitioned for a vote to find if these new people even want a union, much less the one you represent."

The business agent jumped up. "Come on," he told the union lawyers. At the door he turned back toward her. "You'll get yours, lady," he said.

It was easy, she thought, stopping on the way to her office to pick up a sandwich at the vending machine. She hadn't had time for lunch before the meeting. She sat at her desk to eat. "The Teamsters won't cross the picket lines," Bob said. He didn't come all the way into the office, just held the door open with his foot, as if he might be contaminated. She finished chewing the food in her mouth before replying.

"Get the list of nonunion truckers that William gave me. I left it in the receiving office. Start phoning. There must be some people who want to work."

Back on the line she noticed the work was going faster now. It wasn't a complicated task, this. There wasn't much thinking involved. It was like fractions; anyone could do them, given a little encouragement. It wasn't skilled; it wasn't like teaching.

She was no Joan of Arc. Why did they burn her at the stake, anyway? She used to know that. Her shoulders hurt worse tonight than they had the first night. She ran the hotel shower's hot water for ten minutes against her back. A luxury. She took three-minute showers usually, no more, no less. Life had to have a structure, a form that a person could adhere to. She was not a martinet. She was flexible. And she felt a surge of giggles, thinking, As long as people agree with me.

William phoned first. "Are you really comfortable in that hotel room?" he asked. "We could arrange for an apartment, or you could stay with us: we have a guest house," he started out kindly.

"I'm fine here," she said. "Don't worry about anything; it will all work out for the best." She said that for him. He was cooperating during the crisis.

"But I *am* worried. It doesn't look good. They filed suit today accusing us of breaking the contract, among other things, by firing the employees."

"But they went out of their own free will."

"This is a labor-leaning city. And there are a lot of ways to interpret the situation."

"I see, I see." She didn't see: this was a smoke screen on William's part and the union's. Or maybe they were going to try to smoke her out.

"I tried to get in touch with some of the family this afternoon. They were all out. As of now they haven't returned my phone calls," William said.

"Production is up to about forty percent today. And these newer workers come in considerably lower on the pay scale."

"Do you think all this is necessary?" he asked. William was trying to be reasonable now. "Those people worked here a long time. They're going to be bitter, no matter how this turns out."

"That can't be helped," she said. "People must be responsible for their actions."

"What bothers me . . . ," he started out.

"William, we're in the right. That's what matters," she interrupted.

"But I've never gone through this kind of thing before."

"You'll get used to it," she said. "It's nothing."

Father O'Reilly phoned a couple of minutes later, using his unctuous voice this time instead of his Irish brogue. "Have you seen the *Chronicle*? There's a story on you: NUN IN CHARGE. A photo of you walking past plackards with slogans that are not very flattering." She didn't remember getting photographed. Wouldn't Eleanor have been pleased at her notoriety. They were sly. She knew what they were trying here.

"Don't be concerned, Father," she said.

"The bishop has been made aware of the situation, Sister. He asked me to phone." It was as if cluster after cluster of grape-shaped bells went off in her chest. She swung her feet off the bed and onto the floor to steady herself. To recharge her nerve. What would Eleanor do? Say?

"Apparently," Father O'Reilly went on, "the bishop has received calls from our people down there. And the archbishop of San Francisco is also supposed to be inquiring into the situation. They are all very, very upset."

She was shaking. Literally. Her arms and shoulders were quivering. "I can't help that," she said.

"It is my guess the bishop wants the problem resolved as quickly as possible."

"Tell the bishop . . . ," she began. An exact answer was needed. It was so important to be precise. She had made a choice before, when

Eleanor left without her. She was responsible for her actions always. "Father," she said, "I'll have to call you back. A messenger is at the door. Perhaps with a counteroffer."

She hung up the phone and put her feet up again. What did all this have to do with Eleanor? She thought back to that time. She was leaving with Eleanor; it was all decided. The decision was a long time coming for both of them. On her part, the religious life had become meaningless, ridiculous, mindless. They were the last nuns in the order now on the West Coast. Who were they holding out for? Everyone did what they wanted. What did they represent? And who cared anyway? Even as a school administrator she'd had to put up with guff from everyone. A parent told her once, after the tuition had gone up again, "Go out and get a job and see what it's like to pay out this much money." She'd had enough.

Eleanor's dissatisfaction was more general. She had become almost obsessed with the new pope. *Dislike* was not strong enough a word. She saw in him the erasing of forty-one years of her efforts on the church's behalf. "All for nothing," she'd say. "Why live a life that sucks the possibility of hope out of the very people that we serve?"

"He won't be there forever," she'd point out. "Remember"—with some pleasure—"the Irish monks had to wait five hundred years."

"When the others see that it's possible to return to the past, the next one will be worse," Eleanor insisted.

They had been promised positions; Eleanor had made contacts outside. It sounded so exciting, like they were escaping from a dungeon. She actually looked forward to teaching again. She was ready for a classroom in a private school, where the kids wanted to be there and the parents backed up the teachers. But then Eleanor went into insulin shock. She'd had diabetes for years but never took care of herself, didn't follow the diet or the regular hours. It was she who had to remind her to take her shots. Eleanor was hospitalized. The doctors cut off her right leg just below the knee when complications set in. It didn't slow her down. She was getting too loud. "I'll leave if I have to crawl," she'd say from her wheelchair. They couldn't fit her yet with a prosthesis. She had to be taken everywhere.

Marynora was having second thoughts—first thoughts, really. Not for herself. The doctors were talking about the difficulty of regulating the diabetes. "Are you ready?" Eleanor asked. It was late July; they had to make a decision, if they were going to teach that fall.

"You know I am, but why not wait until you're better. They'll take care of you here."

Eleanor stayed; she talked her into it. How likely would that private school have been to take a sixty-one-year-old ex-nun with one leg? Eleanor started doing exercises to strengthen her good leg. Followed a diet. Stopped talking about leaving. She got better. But she kept talking about the pope. She could be right at times: "Our pontiff chooses his nationality first, his gender second, his holy position third, and the church fourth. Believers come last."

Then the pope came to California. Eleanor confided her design. She was going to confront the man over abortion. She had bided her time until this occasion, stayed on to do this one last thing for California Catholics. She had made elaborate arrangements to get close enough to challenge him to debate the issue. She had been one of three hundred nuns invited to hear him speak. Marynora knew she'd let it go too far. With great patience and tact she tried to talk Eleanor out of it. And when she became so excited over the event that she forgot to take her insulin, it was with Father O'Reilly's help that she got Eleanor admitted to the intensive care unit at Holy Name Hospital until the pope left.

When Eleanor recovered enough she was really ready to go, leave the order, and she wanted to go out with a bang. A press conference, no less. By then Marynora was convinced she was mad. "The pope, the pope," Eleanor raved; she frightened her. It was up to her to defuse the situation again. It was for Eleanor's own good. The diocese helped again; they could be subtle when they had to be. Strings were pulled. Eleanor's last dance was almost alone. One reporter from a weekly showed up, but there were no TV crews in attendance.

Somehow Eleanor knew; she knew. She didn't seem surprised when Marynora said she'd changed her mind, explained she'd never really liked teaching all that much. Eleanor left. Went to a residential care complex. Marynora became chancellor.

She went to visit, taking Eleanor flowers from the bishop's garden.

Eleanor sat, blouse rucked up under her arms, in a deep soft chair, like some disheveled dove. She was glad to see her. She still wasn't taking care of herself: trouble with her leg; coffee stain on her blouse. She caught a slight body odor when she bent over to kiss her. Eleanor seemed happy. Was going to ball games; teaching illiterate adults twice a week. Had published two articles in a radical Catholic magazine on her ideas for restructuring the church. Went to mass every morning at five A.M. at a very progressive church. Eleanor didn't need her. "I can go to the zoo every day now," she said. That had been their sort of humorous goal, when they were going to leave together.

"I envy you," Marynora told her.

"When you're ready," Eleanor answered, "there's plenty of room here."

She didn't laugh; it wasn't funny. But Eleanor did, down to her toes.

It was too late to phone back that night. She rehearsed the call going to work on the bus the next morning. Waited till nine; she knew he'd be alone in his office then, and the bishop wouldn't be available till ten. She dialed the number with perfect calm.

"Father, you might mention to the bishop that I intend to stay here until the six months are up. Do you understand that?" She had to take control. "I'm on a leave of absence that you, as auxilliary bishop, authorized, if you'll recall." She'd have given anything to see his face when she said that. There was a long silence.

"Do you think that course is wise?" Father O'Reilly asked. He didn't sound indignant, as she'd hoped. He sounded concerned.

"Trust me, Father. I've written a letter to the bishop with a much longer explanation than I can give you on the phone. But I will say that this situation will work out to everyone's advantage. What's most important to remember, and I'm sure my cousin chose me for this reason, is that the diocese will benefit." She was truly divinely inspired. "You remember how the bishop always talks about his wish list? I can make it a reality. A new emergency wing at the hospital: how long has that been under consideration? Or your own pet project, the area behind the high school football field made into a playground for preschool kids."

"Sister, the bishop was most explicit; he wanted you to desist . . ."

"Have I ever failed to think of the diocese first? Have I?"

"No, in fact you haven't."

"Father, there could be a trust fund with revenue, two or three million dollars annually." It sounded like the phone went dead. "Did you hear me?"

"I'm here, Sister."

"It's up to you to prepare him for my letter. It's up to you."

"I'll try, Sister."

"Good," she said. She knew she sounded positive.

She had things to do. Some thinking. The letter had to be just right. She was capable of a perfect letter. Father O'Reilly would see to that end. And she had to keep the plant going, the negotiations progressing, the heirs happy, and William willing. She could even fit in seeing Eleanor. Would *she* be surprised. She'd never gone back. Eleanor had phoned several times, but she'd always been out. Or busy. But a day didn't go by that she didn't think of her. Not one. She'd learned so much from her. She'd visit, make the time. Maybe take her some bottles of herbs and spice. Today was cinnamon.

Double Smart

He gave up early—there was no business—with every intention of going home, but he found himself parking in front of the bar. It was on the way. Didn't see anyone he knew inside. The bartender was someone new. Drank his drink. Had been coming here for years. Before he'd opened the restaurant. Two meatpackers came in off the swing shift. He thought he recognized one, but it was darker in here than outside. He looked closer: it wasn't who he thought it was. He missed the ribbing he usually got. "Al, how many of your meatballs does it take to make a hamburger? About a hundred?" Never mind, he'd always answer. He gave a fair value when it came to food. Spaghetti Al, they sometimes called him.

There was a running argument going on between a shuffleboard player and three or four customers sitting at the bar. You'd never know it was 1949, to hear them. Veterans, going over the war again. Younger than he was by five or ten years. They didn't take into consideration the ten years before the war, the Depression. What it was like then, a dollar a day, not a dollar an hour. On the East Coast people were starving. He'd come west. The further west he got, the better it was, and the best was in California. There was no Depression, not until he lost his job in a tuna cannery in San Diego. But it was never like it had been in New Jersey, where he was from, two thousand men laid off in one whack.

The Depression caused the war. The first war caused the Depression. Cause and effect. Ross was right about that. You look for the reasons. You already know the effect; you just have to line up the causes. And it usually equals out. He picked up his change after one drink and headed out the door, home to bed. There hadn't been a woman in the place.

❦

Al had to concentrate, making the sauce. How much celery had he already diced? How many heads of garlic? His investments kept popping into his head like toast. *Investments.* What a nice-sounding word. They were for Linda; she would get everything. Maybe he'd leave something to his sister, Vera. But his daughter got the investments. He laughed aloud at himself and turned his head to check on Jack, who was doing the plates, standing on a wooden Golden Glow beer box to reach the sink. He didn't grow, that boy. Hair in his eyes and his face red with the steam from the hot water. Jack was the best dishwasher he'd ever had in the place. But he never told him that. It had taken too much work and patience on his part to enjoy giving Jack any praise.

A dump truck passed. It didn't take anything big to make the old building shake. A Hudson could make the water glasses closest to the edge of the shelf clink against each other. A good wind could make the old plywood construction shack billow like a tent. When the rains came the roof leaked big drips, enough to fill a bucket overnight. Two women walked by on the edge of the road, and he could hear their voices as clearly as if they were inside the building.

Had he cut everything? Onion. Garlic. Celery. He didn't stint on the ingredients. Herbs. He took out the cans of oregano and bay leaf. Salt, pepper, and paprika. He had to have everything lined up. It was like getting ready for surgery. Things had to be just right or he forgot. He made enough to last a week, only adding a little water toward Friday to make up for the simmer. "Jackson, go get me three number ten cans of tomato sauce." He watched the boy get down from his box and head for the storeroom. His apron was hiked up, folded in the middle, but it still dragged on the floor. White paper hat resting on his ears; the sleeves of his white T-shirt rolled up.

He'd seen Jack's father, uncles around, in the bars. Not often enough to say hello. They were always up to something; he'd read about them in the paper once or twice every couple of years. He hadn't recognized Jack that time he'd caught him; the kid wouldn't be washing plates now if he had.

He'd walked into the storeroom that time, then forgot what he'd come for. He was standing there trying to remember, eyeing the shelves of restaurant-sized canned goods, the cases of beer and soda stacked on the floor along one wall. All at once a long-necked bottle of Regal Pale beer lifted out of its case and slowly rose toward the ceiling. He followed it with his eyes until it disappeared. All he could think was that the Okies, when they wanted that brand, ordered a tall blonde. Another bottle started going up. This time he moved underneath it and looked up: there was a hole in the roof; he could see sky. An old vent. He watched as a line came down with a loop on the end and landed on the neck of another bottle. The noose tightened and up it went.

He tiptoed outside, found where the ladder was, and went up on the roof. It was amazing that it held his weight. There was the kid, working the line, with four bottles beside him. Al wasn't pissed off; in fact, he was amazed that someone would have thought this up. A kid that size, stealing beer. He crept over closer, and just as he was going to yell, the kid turned his head and saw him. There was nowhere for him to go. His eyes closed down. "What in the hell do you think you're doing?" He didn't sound indignant enough, so he yelled, "You're stealing my beer, that's what you're doing. Where do you live?" Then he made the mistake of reaching down to grab him. The kid rolled away and went across the roof like a crab and hesitated only a second before going over the edge.

Al looked down at the body on the sidewalk maybe twenty feet below. He'd come down on a hedge with a fence running through it, bounced off that, and was laid out like he was dead. He got down from the roof in a hurry and went around to where the kid was.

There was no blood that he could see. He didn't want to touch him, though. The kid was breathing, gasping, in fact. "You did it to yourself," he said. The kid rolled over, holding his stomach. He reminded Al of an animal, hurt, but he was going to try to get away again. "Don't run," he said. "Catch your breath. It's a good thing you came down on the hedge." He stepped back and hunkered down. "How old are you?" he asked. "And what's your name?" The kid didn't answer. Al went on anyway. "You're too young to drink beer. What were you going to do with it anyway?"

"Sell it," the kid said, opening his eyes.

"As soon as you can, you go back up there and get those bottles.

Bring them inside." He never thought the kid would do it. He didn't hear him go across the roof, but the front door opened and he walked in and set the bottles on the counter.

He heard himself ask the kid, "You want a job? Do the plates, come in after school two or three hours, and maybe half a day on Saturday and Sunday?" He knew he was asking for trouble, especially when it came to him where he'd seen the kid before: at Noonan's, with his father a couple of times, probably sent down to get him to come home. He was going to say, Everyone has to work for what they want. But the kid would know that too. "Start tomorrow," he said. It was the old cause and effect, he thought.

Jack came back the next day. It didn't surprise Al. He showed him how, had to set him on a box first. He was okay. The tines of the forks were always clean, and he remembered to change the water so there was no grease on the plates. You couldn't ask for more. Personally, he'd rather do anything than wash dishes. Regular dishwashers didn't last too long. They had other plans—opening their own restaurants, or becoming executives for Standard Oil. He still ended up doing dishes sometimes, but the kid was good. Came in on time and had to be told to go home. Al made sure he ate, heaped a plate and floated the meatballs in sauce. Made him drink a glass of milk. Paid him fair. And let him practice on the shuffleboard for free, as long as a customer didn't want to play.

Linda didn't like Jack. "You know who that is?" she asked, whispering too loud, when she first saw him. "He's the one that was caught setting that shed on fire near the tracks. His sister is a senior this year." She rolled her eyes. "He tried to derail a streetcar once. I saw that, dragged ties across the rails. He steals bikes too."

"I'll watch him," he said. "Don't worry; I'll keep an eye on him."

At first he did, too, but now he knew exactly what Jack was up to by the sounds. He'd gotten the key from the hook and opened the storeroom door. He took his time getting the right cans. Once he'd brought in a can of beets instead of sauce. It was all he could do to carry the three cans; he had to put them down to relock the door. Then he opened the other door and slipped inside the other room, the one he wasn't supposed to go into, and quickly checked the pay chutes on the rows of slot machines to see if anyone had left any money. Shut that door quietly and went over to the shuffleboard table. He started lagging the weights down to the far end. The table was freshly waxed so there was almost no sound—until a car door opened out in the lot. There was only one person in the entire county that could make the leaf springs on a Ford make that noise when he got out. "Jackson," he called out, "quit that and get in here." The kid came running with the cans. "Stay here, too," he said, wiping his hands on his apron. He went out, filled a white mug with coffee, set it in front of a stool, and stood behind the counter.

The sergeant wasn't just fat; he had gone beyond that. He always reminded Al of the snowmen they used to build, snowball head too small for the rest of the body. The grips on his thirty-eight were ivory, and he always had a pair of black leather gloves stuck in his belt. The sergeant never sat down or drank the coffee, but he always took out the gloves and set them on the counter.

"Here he is," Al said, trying to put some humor into a situation that made him sick to his stomach. "How's the sheriff?"

"Getting ready for the election."

"It's that time again, isn't it?" Al said. "Well, he has my support, I can guarantee you that. What kind of chance would we have here, out of the city limits? If it weren't for him," he added. "No one cares about the unincorporated area except the sheriff. The city cops, you can forget them."

"All you have to do is call," the sergeant said. "We'll have someone out here."

"I'll remember that. There's not much trouble here, but it's nice to know." As he talked, he was rolling up twenty-dollar bills and putting one in each finger of the sergeant's gloves, holding the gloves below the counter as he worked. When he was done the sergeant picked up his gloves and tried unsuccessfully to suck in his gut enough to put them back under his belt as he walked to the door.

"Piece of shit," Al said several times, opening the cans of tomato sauce. The slots weren't worth the aggravation. He had to pay out half the profits to the owner, and then the sheriff got his. He was everyone's bank. Who was he kidding?

❦

It was slow until the first construction worker came in. Laced work boots, khaki shirt and trousers, a Caterpillar tractor watch fob dangling from his pocket, sunburned face. This one had left his hat in his pickup. "Al, give me an order of that red stuff you call food and ten dollars worth of quarters." He put the roll of coins on the counter and went back into the kitchen. Jackson was watching in the two-way mirror over the sink, but he still said, "Keep an eye out." The rhythm of the place would start to pick up now: after-work customers, nickels in the jukebox, "Brokenhearted Dreams," "Quit Driving Nails in My Coffin." It was something you could see and feel as people came through the door. The noise of the slots, the arms yanked down, the payoff coins ricocheting out, even the pop pop of the sauce bubbling on low heat, Jackson clinking the plates, Linda pressing down on the keys of the cash register, and the ding as the cash drawer sprang out. The sounds of making money. Sometimes he liked to think it was the sound of happiness.

He threw a fistful of spaghetti into the pot that was already on the boil. He brushed the special butter on the garlic bread and heated it, taking his time. A roll of quarters took about six or seven minutes. He couldn't rush; that's when things went wrong. He understood that now about himself when he cooked. It wasn't the food he made his money on, he reminded himself. Two more customers came in, and then another one before he could get out in front. It was always like this; everyone came in at once. But it was almost five-thirty; Linda would be here soon.

Cooking didn't come naturally to him, he once decided. He'd fallen into it like he'd become a cement finisher and a shoe salesman and a wiper in the merchant marine. But the difference was, here he was in charge; the restaurant was his. He was a bona fide businessman.

Marta had taught him how to make the sauce, to cook the pasta just right. She was half Italian, his second wife. The only experience he'd had was a couple of years on the breakfast shift as a fry cook. He had trouble with eggs. Yolks would not stay whole for him. If he didn't outright pop the yolk, the yellow frying like a stain, then the yolk broke underneath and leaked all over the hash browns. People didn't like it. That's why his own place was only open for lunch and dinner, eleven to three A.M.

Linda opened the door at ten after six. His daughter, in spite of the way she looked. It seemed like she was trying to look ugly. Peroxide hair. Makeup too thick. So much lipstick it got on her teeth. "Hi, how's business?" she asked.

"How's school?" he asked her back. He noticed now how she avoided saying "Dad." She was ashamed of him, he supposed. He was ashamed of her too, the way she looked. Fifteen years old. She didn't have to work here, but it was one way he could keep an eye on her. He left it up to her. Keep the money in the family. The tips she made. Got along with the customers. The Okies idolized her. Tried holding her hand when she counted out their change, teased her, undid the strings on her apron, gently tugged her long hair as she passed.

Linda went right to work. He'd seen whose car she got out of. He would handle that later. Without letting her catch him looking, he watched her hurrying back and forth, taking the dirty dishes off the counter, back into the kitchen. Probably taking time to drip water down Jack's neck and duck the gob of soapsuds he threw back. Clearing out the sink behind the counter so she could fill it with hot water to wash. Letting the glasses soak while she emptied the ashtrays and wiped the countertop. Things he should do, try to do anyway, before he opened. But the cooking took time too.

Ross came in. It was always good to see him, no matter what condition. All cooks drank. He did himself on occasion. He controlled it because of Linda. Because of the business. Ross, as young as he was, drank like a fish. He opened a beer and put it on the counter in front of the stool at the end where Ross could rest his back against the wall. He'd fallen off a stool once when he was in better shape than he was now.

"Al," he said, putting out his hand to shake, "give me an order of that Armenian spaghetti." He sat down like an old man, using the edge of the counter to lower himself.

They had worked together before. Ross was a good cook, could always get a job. And he was the kind of person who always took the time to show someone else how to do something too. A good all-around cook. Had offers to manage places, big ones, two hundred–seat restaurants.

Armenian or not. That was an old joke between them. As far as he knew, he wasn't one. Not his father or his mother. Because he was close with his money, or because he was hairy? He used to have dark wavy hair and needed to shave twice a day. His hair was thinning now and turning a little gray. Had he ever met an Armenian? What did they look like? He had a pot belly. A face, that's all, with a big nose and a good set of false teeth. Blue eyes.

It was because he was tight. He had four nickels from the first quarter he ever made. He wanted to know what percent of fat was in the hamburger he bought. When it said a hundred pounds on a sack of potatoes, how much did it really weigh? He was cheap. He was making money for Linda. There was nothing wrong with being an Armenian. Someone told him once it took five Jews to take an Armenian to the cleaners. If that was true, it took a hundred Armenians to take one Okie sheriff.

Ross was at the stage where he wouldn't talk. He got him a plate of spaghetti, putting on two full ladles of sauce and twice the meatballs he usually gave. Jack saw. He looked surprised. That kid had eyes in the back of his head. "You're supposed to be looking through the mirror," he said.

Ross cut up the plateful of pasta with his fork and knife like it was a thick pancake. Took swigs of beer between mouthfuls of food. He read newspapers, magazines by the dozens. There were paperback books in the glove compartment of his old car. He had been around: in the navy, oil fields in Venezuela, construction in Arabia. Knew the answers to things. Al had met people like Ross before; the year and a half he was in the merchant marine, there was always at least one on every ship. Had a book open when they had watch. Knew how to spell a word when you were writing a letter. Could read charts and knew where they were all the time. Ross didn't show off about it, like some did, and make bad feelings all around. He had a way of explaining things that almost made you think you'd thought of it too. Always using cause and effect. The cheaper the whiskey, the bigger the headache.

Al went into the kitchen and took a look through the two-way mirror over Jack's shoulder. He smelled of old piss. There were six people in there playing. One woman. They weren't as dedicated as men were; men could lose their whole paycheck before they would stop. Women stopped with the loose change they found at the bottom of their purse. No one ever seemed to be curious about the mirror at eye level on the wall. Nine by eighteen inches. They glanced at it, patted their hair, but that was it.

He remembered the new punchboards he hadn't put out yet. The amusement company always delivered them in an unmarked cardboard box. Hanging them up behind the counter always made him think how foolish people really were. He didn't make as much money on them as the slots, but it was almost pure profit without the aggravation. They looked like a child's game, a puzzle, the size of *Life* magazine and as thick as a book, the front stamped with hundreds of cellophane-covered holes. For twenty-five cents, a dime, or a nickel you got to punch a pellet of paper out through the back, then unwind the narrow slip to see what prize you'd won. No one could stop at one. The prizes were mostly candy, sometimes cash. A ten-pound box of chocolates was the top prize. There were a lot of one-pound boxes. He paid the company twenty-five dollars for the board and another twenty-five for the candy. And he always insisted that the boxes of candy be fresh. A couple of times when the boxes were opened the chocolate had turned white and the bottoms were pushed in as if someone had pressed their thumb against each one. On the big boards he took in five hundred; on the small boards, three hundred. After subtracting the overhead, the rest was pure profit.

He'd never gambled in his life. Maybe that's why he was so fascinated with watching other people do it. When there was nothing to do in the kitchen he could watch for hours through the two-way mirror, or happily hold the winning slips when four or five construction workers passed a punchboard back and forth, betting with each other over who would win what next.

If this kept up he'd be rich in about ten years. Retire in '58 or '59. Marta had walked out on him two years ago. If she knew what was happening now, she'd be kicking herself. She had been against opening a restaurant in the first place. Wanted no part of that dump. She still sent Linda little presents, perfume, a purse for her eighth-grade graduation. For a stepmother, that was nice. Linda's real mother he never heard from. She'd left when Linda was four. He could do without women from now on. His sister kept an eye on Linda, only lived a block over.

He always knew he wasn't going to work for wages like his father had his whole life. Go into business for yourself. You never get ahead working for someone else. Never. He could send Linda to college, take a vacation, go back to New Jersey to see his mother. Hadn't been back in six years. Not since he joined the merchant marine in '43.

❦

The sheriff himself called. Al had just finished tallying the proceeds from everything for the last month, sitting in a booth, the papers spread out, his old Underwood adding machine at the ready. It was unbelievable, the total. He could retire a lot sooner than he thought. The phone rang a half dozen times before he got up to answer it. He was thinking about buying a motel somewhere up in the mountains, renting cabins and fishing all day. It took him a minute to realize it was the sheriff himself.

The sheriff needed another two hundred dollars a month to help his campaign. He was being challenged by a man who wanted to clean up the county. Just until the election was over. Al would understand.

Al did understand. He was being taken, but there wasn't anything he could do about it if he wanted to stay in business. There was no money in spaghetti. Refuse and he was out on the street.

He made a call to the Acme Amusement Company, the people who owned the slots and sold him the punchboards. They listened. We'll get back to you, the manager said. What did that mean? He was in no position to ask. But he didn't say thank you.

There was nothing he could do about Delbert, either, who had more oil in his hair than there was in the crankcase of a Chevrolet. He'd gotten a good look at him when he'd stopped for a traffic light in front of the Mobil gas station where Delbert worked. Linda hadn't seen him. She was sitting on the fender of the boy's car, fawning on him, lighting his cigarette as Delbert waited, leaning against the hood of his DeSoto. All he could do was watch. His sister had explained: the more forbidden the fruit, the sweeter it seems. "You'll only make it worse if you say anything."

"It can't get any worse," he'd answered.

❦

When he got home he was so tired he couldn't sleep. He couldn't eat, although he'd brought home a meatball sandwich on a bun. He never had time to eat at the restaurant. But now he couldn't make the effort to open the brown paper bag to get the sandwich out. He sat in his chair trying to read the paper, but he couldn't concentrate. He decided to take a bath. Running the hot water, he took off his whites.

He lowered himself, one leg at a time, watching his skin turn pink. Laying back, he felt his body let go. Relax. He could almost hear ping ping, as if his body were made of tiny springs that were uncoiling now that the weight had been taken off them. He floated, listening to the pings.

When the water turned tepid he woke up and dug the drain plug out with his big toe. After a minute he turned on the hot water with the other foot. He opened his eyes briefly and saw that the steam had clouded the mirror. Then he went back to sleep.

His dreams were always funny, cartoonlike, in color. This time it was Uncle Scrooge diving into his hoard of coins. His nephews Curly, Moe, and Larry were trying to slip some into their pockets. But it was him, Al, who grabbed Curly by the ear. But that wasn't right either; it was someone else.

Bang. Bang. Bang. Someone was kicking the door. "You're always doing this. I have to use the bathroom. I have to go to school," Linda yelled. Bang. Bang. Bang.

"I'm taking a bath."

"You've been in there all night." He couldn't move; the water was like ice. She stopped kicking and he went back to sleep.

It was after ten by the time he was dressed in a clean set of whites and ready to go down to the restaurant. Vera phoned then and made him late. “Why don’t you go to bed?” she started in on him. “Linda needs the bathroom too. She had to come over here to put on her lipstick and pee. Are you turning into a seal or something?”

Vera could be funny. She never forgot it was him that talked her into coming to the coast. Got her out of their uncle’s dry cleaning business at nineteen. Got a job in the shipyards and married a sailor who stayed in after the war. Left her by herself with three kids to raise. She was working in a cleaners again, ironing. They laughed about that sometimes too. “Vera, I fell asleep is all.”

“You said that Thursday too.”

“I get tired, Vera. I work hard.” Then it was her turn. He listened. They went back and forth until he saw the time and got away. His Lincoln started up without any trouble for a change: with a twelve-cylinder engine, three or four ought to work regularly. From his rear-view mirror he watched the house disappear by pieces, the roof hidden by a tree, the weed-filled yard by a hedge, the unpainted upper story by a neighbor’s Plymouth. He’d bought it on a whim, after a week-long drunk. He couldn’t remember the occasion. Marta had kept the place up. The lawns. Inside was always clean. Now the lawns had died and the place needed paint. It looked like no one lived there. Neither he nor Linda were good housekeepers. Vera came over sometimes to clean. But the house was only a couple of miles from the restaurant. Once he turned the corner he could see it, down on the highway: it looked like two side-by-side boxcars with two lean-tos attached, the kitchen and the room for the slots. A worn-out apron of asphalt with potholes and wrinkles went all the way to the corner for a parking lot. Eucalyptus trees across the highway, taller and straighter than telephone poles. Texaco station on the other corner. He couldn’t see the place without feeling as if he’d just recognized someone that he’d been trying to remember for a long time. It had been his idea alone to open a restaurant there. The owner hadn’t been able to rent the place for a couple of years: it had been a real estate office before. He had the place painted on the outside and a sign put up the length of the roof: AL’S SPAGHETTI SHACK.

It had been a big step. It had taken some nerve to ask Ross, who took a lot of pride in being a cook, to help him. But he hadn’t blinked an eye when he'd told him his idea. "Why not? Every baker wants to open a doughnut shop, every bartender a bar. I've never known a cook who started up his own place, but why not?"

Ross knew where the restaurant supply places were, warehouses filled with used equipment, piled to the ceilings. Steam tables, stools, tables, booths, glassware, stacks of old plastic menu holders. That was the only time Al had second thoughts, when he realized that this stuff all came from failed businesses. He started buying: a counter, sinks, refrigerators. He found the shuffleboard table buried under boxes of old fluorescent lighting fixtures. It was a good buy: the legs were steady, no warp in the maple the whole twenty-foot length, and all the weights were there. Ross helped him install everything, even did some of the wiring. The owner wouldn't put a dime into the place.

He did all right at first. He couldn't expect to fill the place every night, but it was awfully sparse sometimes. He and Ross would sit for hours before someone else came through the door. Saturdays got good when he started putting on shuffleboard tournaments. Giving prizes. But the place turned into a gold mine after the sheriff called him. First the manager of the amusement company had come in, had a plate of spaghetti. Al hadn't known who he was. "This is some place," the manager had said, nodding his head in approval. "I'll tell my friends about it."

"Word of mouth is the best advertisement," Al said.

The manager left his card. Within an hour the county sheriff called. "You've been recommended to me," the sheriff started out. "Your food is good, and you have an ideal location to expand your business. Would you consider putting in some games of chance? Slot machines. It will stop a lot of crime," he pointed out. "The bookies are getting out of hand."

He'd been so naïve he'd asked, "Isn't that illegal?"

"The laws about slots are not spelled out very well. The state pretty much leaves it up to local departments. The way I see it, people around your location need some recreation too; that's something we all should consider. It's an unincorporated area. And we'll keep an eye on the place for you. Have a patrolman stop in every hour, if necessary."

"If you think you should."

"It's a good idea; there are people who come through here who think they can do whatever they want in the county. As soon as we catch one, two more show up with a new idea."

He was so dumb he didn't know that he was going to have to pay for the patrol. Ross explained it all.

They were big friends now, Linda and Jack. She'd take him glasses of iced tea with a slice of lemon while he stacked the oval plates. He'd hang around after work, sit on a stool by the cash register, and they'd talk. Al would have to remind him, "Jack, it's getting dark outside." Jack'd go to the window and look for the sun, see how much time he had left. Afraid of the dark. He was more like an animal than anything else. One time he came in wearing a girl's blouse. Didn't know. White, wrinkled, but clean. Al could tell by the puckered sleeves and the rounded collar. There were more kids in the house he lived at than rats. "Jackson, you taken to wearing female clothes?" he asked, laughing, thinking the kid must have worn it all day in school. Jack looked down at the blouse. "You make a nice-looking girl, I'd say." Jack undid his apron and started walking and then ran out of the place. Didn't come back for two days. "Why don't you leave him alone?" Linda had said. After that, he let up.

When it was slow, he'd give them chances at cause and effect. "If the sun comes up every morning when a rooster crows, what is it?"

"Coincidence," Linda said. They were all sitting in the booth where Al was going over the week's receipts. "The rooster had nothing to do with bringing up the sun."

"What do you say, Jackson?"

"If the sunlight wakes up the rooster every morning and he crows, that's cause and effect."

He was proud of them: he'd spent a lot of time explaining things using cause and effect, and they'd caught on. It had paid off. If we don't clean the hood over the grill, it'll cause the health inspector to dock us points. Our grade is low enough now. The hood was always clean now, without him having to say anything. Both Linda and Jack would give it a wipe when they had the time.

"What if the rooster dies?" Linda said. "What happens to the sun then? It has to be consistent."

"No one says it has to go on forever," Al put in.

"Then anything can be a cause and effect," Linda said.

"There must be a rooster somewhere that's crowing when the sun comes up," Jackson said. "You have to take the cause on faith."

"Faith," he said. "Don't give me that crap. Let's not get into religion now." The men from the Texaco station came in and they all got up and went back to work.

They played shuffleboard, enough to wear the wood down. Linda would stop to wait on a customer, serve his food, refill his coffee cup, Jack waiting. Then she'd go back over and lag a disk. He watched them sometimes when there was nothing else to do. Both were good, but Jack was better. He'd have to stand on his toes to slide the weights down the table, but he was a natural. No matter where she placed her weights, he'd knock them off the board, not with the speed throw or smashes most players used, but with little taps of his disk that sent hers off the edge into the gutter. Or better yet, he'd slide one past hers, outlag everything on the board. The game was to fifteen, and sometimes he'd get that in one or two turns, lagging fours, which meant the weights had to hang over the end of the twenty-foot board without being knocked off. The game was more complicated than pool. More direct, just hand and eye, no stick.

It was easy to lose track of time, watching them. "We're supposed to be working around here some of the time," he said. "There's plenty of dishes in the kitchen, Jack. And Linda, you haven't cleared that booth yet." Jack went back to the kitchen, but Linda stayed at the board. Sometimes she was more trouble than she was worth. It had been her idea to work, which was a relief: if dishwashers were a pain in the ass, waitresses could give you fits. Never on time, acting like they were doing you a favor to show up at all. He paid her the same as anyone else. She made good tips too. And she got the spillage when the amusement company sent men out to empty the slots. They used a hand-crank coin wrapper; dumped all the coins into the hopper, and while one man cranked, the other folded the ends of the paper coin wrappers as they came out of the machine. When there weren't enough coins for a full roll they gave the spillage to Linda. She never missed a Saturday morning. He got in on it too: the place was making the company plenty of money. He'd go through the coin boxes before they were emptied into the machine, looking for old ones. He had two-gallon mayonnaise jars full of coins: V nickels, liberty quarters, and halfs. Morgan silver dollars. Foreign coins. He kept the jars under his bed.

He was always running out of change. The amusement company traded him the coins from the slots for bills, but it was never enough. The slots were getting a lot of play. The times were good; people wanted to spend their money. Fridays were his best night. So he left after Linda came in and went to get more change. He'd already phoned Noonan, who was running slots too, three times as many as he had. The bar was like a bus station; so many people were coming and going. The bartender had five canvas sacks of coins ready when he came in for them. Ross saw him and called out, "Come on, you Armenian cheapskate, spring for a drink."

He couldn't refuse Ross. Had one himself too. They got talking. Noonan bought him a drink next, which was unusual, because he was tighter than the bark on a tree. And then Ross bought him one back. Ross was funny. He was going out with a six-and-a-half-foot Texas woman; he could tell a good story. Cause and effect. He had the whole bar laughing.

After a while Al didn't know what time it was or what the woman was saying that he was dancing with. He did know the name of the song because the record had been playing over and over: "I'm just here to get my baby out of jail." He kept seeing someone he ought to know as he shuffled around the dance floor. He finally recognized Jackson standing near the door in the semidarkness. Just watching him. Was he that good a dancer? Then he recalled the restaurant. But he couldn't get things in order enough in his mind to start his body moving in a different direction. It was effect and cause. He had to let the woman go and stop dancing first, then get the coins. Go out and drive back to the restaurant. He couldn't let go of her waist. When she went back to where she had been sitting on her own, he stood there on the dance floor.

Jackson came over carrying the sacks of coins, took him by the end of his apron, and led him out. Into a cab. Helped him out at the restaurant, which was dark. Linda was still there. She moved a chair from the door when she saw who it was. He had the keys; she couldn't lock up.

❦

"It was just a toot, Vera . . ."

"Leaving Linda there by herself." It had been almost a week ago, but that didn't stop his sister any. "I told her when she phoned me, Leave, walk out of the place. Let it get robbed. It'll teach him a lesson."

He wanted to hang up on her, but it would make matters worse. If he listened, she'd wear down. "Customer just came in, Vera. Got to go."

"Don't give me that; you're not open yet," she said. "You better get wise to yourself, Al, before it's too late," and she hung up.

Linda came in, eyes red, the high school class ring gone from around her neck. Delbert temporarily out of the picture? Sniffing as she wiped the counters. Women were their own worst enemies, he thought: they didn't know how to cut their losses.

Then Jackson came in to work and didn't speak. He was pissed because Al had docked his pay for breaking five of the big plates last week. He had to put his foot down somewhere. And it was the kid's own fault; Jack hadn't been concentrating. He wasn't made out of money.

The place was full, but no one was eating. He just watched. He wished he were Jewish, so he could make fun of everyone like they did. When he was a kid in New Jersey. It was only fair; everyone made fun of them. What would they make of these Okies? Ross said an Okie was anyone who came to California from somewhere else between 1925 and the end of the war that hadn't been to New York City. They weren't just from the Southwest; they could be from Nebraska, Montana, Colorado, Louisiana. Worked backbreaking jobs, had a lot of kids, spent all their money, and had nothing to show for it. Construction, steel mills, factories, meat packing, the new electronics plant. That last was a different type. More talkative, not so ready to bet how many toothpicks were in the cup by the cash register. Was that cause and effect: was there less push on the production line in electronics?

"Al, give me two rolls of nickels."

"Anything you say, Bud." He called them all that when he remembered to. He couldn't always remember their names. Some were old and some were young; some had big bellies but a lot were slim, with tight Levis that showed their balls, and they all had an angle, some hope that they were going to make a lot of money without breaking their backs all their lives. Gambling. Finding someone to finance a special machine they invented at work. The ponies. Knowing where treasure was buried during the war. Gambling. Drafting. Buy a journeyman's card, become a chiropractor or an optometrist in six months, be a white-collar worker.

Delbert came in around ten-thirty. He was a younger version, still in school, not ready to work full-time. His father was a heavy equipment operator, he'd found out; his mother worked in a box factory. Kept his head down, stood by the door. Linda didn't notice him at first. When she glanced up and did, she gave a smile that could have lit up the whole world. She was pretty then. Smiles can make you beautiful, he thought. But the idea started to depress him and he went back into the kitchen to work on the sauce.

&

Saturday night: no one worked tomorrow. No one needed to get up and punch in. They could all sleep. And go somewhere else for their ham and eggs in the morning, because he was going to be in bed too. Once he stopped frying eggs it had developed into not wanting to fry anything. The very thought of frying a hamburger or a steak made him grit his teeth as he slapped them on the grill. French fries were fine in the deep fryer. That didn't bother him. So was chicken; he'd drop that in with the potatoes. He decided he didn't like cooking. Except for making the sauce; that took some talent, and he thought he did it well. His sauce was exceptional. Ross told him once it was the best he ever tasted. Marta said it was better than her mother's. Linda, using the ladle, ate it out of the pot like soup when she thought he wasn't looking.

He noticed Jack was up on his toes, his nose pressed against the two-way mirror into the slot room. He should send them both home now. It was slow for a Saturday night, after nine already; the dinner crowd had gone. He could handle things by himself. It would be mostly the slots now, and the coffee royals, after the bars closed. He needed to order another case of half pints. He kept them hidden in one of the refrigerators under the lettuce. He charged a dollar for a shot of bourbon in a cup of coffee; he could get away with it because no one else sold whiskey after two A.M., the legal time.

"Jackson, what's so interesting? Jackpot?" The kid didn't answer. He went over and looked. At first he had to adjust his eyes to the sixty-watt bulb that hung down in the middle of the room. Then it was hard to take in exactly what he was seeing.

He'd had the machines lined up on a shelf that ran along three walls of the room. Their fronts were nickel plated, with little windows jammed with coins that promised jackpots, and a single lever stuck up out of the side like a gearshift that could take you to heaven. An Okie was playing a quarter slot machine. A woman was sitting up on the shelf, the machine pushed back behind her and to the right. The Okie was feeding the machine, reaching behind her; at the same time, her dress hiked up and her arms and legs wrapped around his waist, he had gained entrance and was keeping up a rhythm of pulling down the lever and driving home. She in turn, eyes closed, mouth open, was apparently singing into his left ear. The thrusts seemed to be timed to the three cylinders falling into place, one after another. Trying for the three bars? Would his luck be better for the attempt; would this cause a different probability? Just as he thought that the goddamn machine paid off, hit the jackpot. Coins came popping out, bouncing off the woman, falling to the floor. He noticed Jack was still looking. "You're not supposed to be watching things like that," he said. Jack just stared at him as if he were dumb. Then talked back. "You told me to."

Twenty-five dollars; that's what he paid extra for three bars. It gave him the edge on the other places that had slots. He went out front to get the cash. It was the fourth time tonight. Too many. He'd talk to the amusement company.

❦

Ross came in, early for him, three P.M., still sober. If you were going to describe him, it would have to be *clean*. High-polished shoes. Fresh dress shirt, always. Pressed slacks. Recent haircut. Close shave. Pale face, as if there were no blood coloring his skin. You wouldn't know he was out of work. You'd think he was on his day off from an insurance office. A young dentist. Anything but a cook.

Ross hadn't started yet, so he put a cup of coffee down in front of him, then decided to have one himself. He didn't normally drink coffee without something in it. He was a sipper; anything liquid had to have a bracer, from his orange juice to his milk. Always had been. Unless he was on the wagon. Ross was a funnel. He got a notion and he was off on a splurge. Drink anything and everything until there wasn't any more or he was good-night.

"You try the Cow Palace? I heard they were hiring fry cooks."

"I haven't tried there yet; I thought I'd give it a rest." He'd told him year before last he'd sent in thirteen W-2 forms with his income tax return. And he was the best cook Al had ever seen. Anything—he could do it. Chef, supervise twenty other cooks—he had a job like that once in one of the big hotels. All cooks drank. Or did just drinkers become cooks? It took a certain kind of person to stand in a kitchen for eight hours. They were like trapeze artists or deep sea divers. A lot of tension.

"I need a loan, four hundred bucks," Ross said.

He didn't blanch. He didn't loan money to anyone, not even his sister, but he went over and snapped open the cash register and took out twenty twenties and placed the bills in front of Ross.

"Do you want to know what it's for?"

"No, you don't have to tell me," he said. A customer came out of the game room then and said the machine he was playing was broken. Al went in for a look and knew right away what had happened. The customer had tried to put a wire up the payoff chute to control the spin of the wheels. People would cheat you in a minute if they could.

"It owes me a dollar seventy-five," the Okie said.

The gall. "You shithead. If I ever see you in here again . . ."

The bastard never gave him a chance to finish, turned right around, looking indignant, yelled over his shoulder, "If that's the way you feel about it," and left. When Al got back to the counter Ross was gone.

He got another call from the manager of the amusement company warning him to be on the lookout for a gang that was raiding slots. Using a drill, they made small holes in the sides to insert probes to manipulate the wheels. They could win thousands of dollars that way before anyone caught on. Not only did he have to worry about thieves that hadn't robbed him yet, he was getting taken daily. Players had been complaining for weeks that they weren't getting all their winnings. If a slot hit, paid off for three bells, eighteen halfs were supposed to come out. Maybe fourteen or fifteen would be there. It went on and on. He always told the customers, after examining the machine, that they couldn't count, or if they got tough, to go take a jump. Finally, after more complaints, he tried several slots himself. One gave him two quarters instead of five when he got three cherries. Did it again. He was going to phone the amusement company, but things got busy out front.

Just before closing he went back into the game room and looked the machine over again. Was ready to tape on an OUT OF ORDER sign when he noticed, tipping the slot up, that there was something white in the chute where the winnings came out. He reached under with his finger; then he tried a pair of needle-nosed pliers. He was able to work out two paper napkins that were partially blocking the chute and holding back seventeen dollars in quarters. The other machines were all right.

He kept looking at the coins and back at the napkins in his hand. Who would do this? He didn't have to think about it long. He put the coins and napkin in a jar and hid them in a cupboard. It was almost three. A last customer came in and ordered a coffee royal. He half filled a mug and carried it back to the kitchen, got a half pint from his stash in the refrigerator. He had a beer and wine license but no hard liquor license. Poured a fair shot into the coffee. If people needed a drink, they were going to get one.

The next morning he had to rush around before going to the restaurant: to the bank, to deposit; to a realtor he didn't trust, who was supposed to be lining up a twelve-unit apartment house for him cheap; to his bookkeeper, where they had long conversations which he usually began with, "What if we don't count the money from the punchboards?" Or slots. Or liquor. "No use paying federal and state taxes on something that isn't legal," he always said. "That would compound the problem, is the way I look at it." While the bookkeeper started tallying up figures on his adding machine, Al sat back in a soft chair, stretched out his legs. Wearing his whites; he had dozens of starched pairs, shirts too. He wore them all the time now, he realized. Sometimes he remembered to take off the apron. "Let's count the punchboards this year. They're the most legal," the bookkeeper said. "You have too much money not to." Al nodded. This was all for Linda; he hoped she would appreciate it someday. With all the running around, he almost forgot the napkins in the machine.

He got to the place just before opening time. Even did some of the glasses out front for Linda after turning on the grill and lighting the steam table. Got the venetian blinds up, the OPEN sign turned over. Sometimes he forgot the sign. But it didn't make any difference; his customers always tried the door. They were loyal if nothing else. Even if they tried to steal from him. He was waiting to watch at the two-way mirror: there was a mechanic at the gas station across the way he didn't trust. One of the napkins had a dark smudge on a corner. Oil? He played the slots. But he didn't come in that morning or afternoon.

Linda was on time for a change; he saw who dropped her off too. Jack came in, started right in on the piles of dirty plates from last night. Al felt a little guilty; he hadn't even scraped them off. There were stacks of them, utensils sticking out, balled-up dirty napkins jammed between, strings of clotted spaghetti, stiff now, red, the color of gladiolus his mother used to grow. Jack. Never said a word. Went to work trying to unstick the plates, sorting things out. Dried sauce hardened like a good glue.

There were no customers, a lull that sometimes occurred before dinnertime. Everything was caught up. He went out to his car and got the case of half pints; put them away. He was selling more liquor than beer. Linda and Jack were playing shuffleboard when he passed. He started chopping the white onions. He wasn't bothered if he rinsed the knife off occasionally. He went over to the sink and happened to glance through the mirror. Jack was reaching with his long thin fingers up the pay slot of the quarter machine by the door. He wanted to wait to see what kind of expression came over his face when he didn't find the napkin. But he couldn't.

He hurried around behind the counter and slammed the game room door open against the wall. Linda squealed. Jack looked up unsurprised, as if he'd been checking the empty coin wrappings for left change. But there were no paper wrappings. He left his hand on the base of the quarter machine.

"I trusted you," Al yelled, "and look what you do." He made a grab for him. Was surprised when he didn't resist; let him pick him up by his shirt front. His tennis shoes dangled off the floor. It infuriated him that the kid didn't change expression. His face was turning red but he kept looking unconcerned at everything that was happening to him. "Look what you do," he yelled again. He shook the kid hard back and forth and then bounced his feet against the cement floor and lifted him up to eye level. It was surprising how light he was.

"Let him go. Let him go," Linda yelled. He wasn't going to; he was going to teach him a lesson. Jack's face was turning redder. He didn't kick or yell. Just hung there like the rabbits he'd held as a kid by the ears, before his father clubbed them for dinner.

"It was my idea," Linda said, not loud now, almost in her normal voice. "I told him to do it." He looked back over his shoulder. Couldn't tell if she were telling the truth or not. He dropped Jack to the floor. The part of his shirt he'd held him up by kept the shape of his grip.

"We'll see," he said, and went back to the kitchen to finish up. Jack left; he didn't have to throw him out. He closed at eight thirty and took Linda home. He was tired. Seven days a week was too much. He fell asleep reading yesterday's newspaper.

He ignored Linda, which wasn't hard, not only because he didn't see that much of her until she came to work at five, but because she'd changed. It wasn't just her trying to steal from him, either. She was calculating. Seemed to take a certain pleasure in irritating the customers over little things. First cup of coffee was a dime; after that you could sip all day if you wanted to and it was free. She wouldn't hear when customers asked for a refill. When she had to, she'd slop a quarter of a cup in and splash some on the counter. It made for bad feelings. She made a big deal of him not trusting her in front of everyone, counting up her tips after her shift, lining up all the coins on the countertop. "Will you change these for bills, please?" As if she didn't open the cash register a hundred times a day, making change. Using bread again that people didn't eat. Taking half pats of butter left on the plates and putting them back in the crock for him to use for cooking. It wasn't his idea. He told her to stop it. He never stinted customers on food. Never. Full value. And worst of all, she was rude. If someone dropped food on the counter she'd wipe it up commenting, "You can't help it if you're a slob"; or, "You need a bib, Buster." No more hi's and good-byes. He told her to knock it off. She'd stop when she thought he was listening and then he'd catch her at it again. He started to hate to see certain customers come in that she picked on.

She asked him for a raise. It didn't surprise him. All in all she was a good waitress. He gave her twenty-five cents more an hour; that was ten cents more than he'd ever paid anyone else. And he pointed that out to her too. And some of her recent failings. She just looked at him as if she were trying to decide who he was. He wondered sometimes what she was going to come up with next.

He was still in bed, happened to open his eyes, and Linda was standing in the doorway. Ready for school. Even now, when he was coming home every night, he made it a point not to get up until after she left. He put his reading glasses on. She had an irritating habit of snapping her gum, her jaw askew, as she talked. The sound always reminded him of the pop of something frying. "Jack wants to come back," she said. "It wasn't his fault."

"No, goddamn it."

She didn't answer for a minute. Then she said, "I'm quitting. You can get someone else for me too. I save you a lot of money," she added.

He ignored that. It had been almost three months since he'd caught them. And he'd had two different dishwashers since then. Another was supposed to come in today. And probably wouldn't. If cooks were temperamental and erratic, dishwashers were crazy. "You tell him to come in tonight, but if I ever catch him stealing again I'm going to chop off his fingers with the cleaver. You tell him that." She turned around to go. "And stop snapping your goddamn gum," he called after her.

It almost made him laugh aloud the way Jack did his work after that. In a hurry. He wasn't always staring into the two-way mirror. He was doing the dishes—fast. Or sweeping or cleaning out the grease traps in the stove. Always asking what else? Any more jobs? He never took a break unless Al insisted. And never played the shuffleboard when he did finally go out front. He sat on the end stool, drank a quick Coke, and whispered to Linda. He overheard one of their conversations once. Jack must be in the sixth grade, worrying already: "Don't you miss grammar school?"

"You won't even remember you went there, once you get to high school," Linda answered.

It was Jack who noticed. He was peeling potatoes, sitting on his box, his back against the sink. The lights in the kitchen dimmed. Al was weighing out bulk hamburger for the meatballs. A few customers were eating at the counter. Linda was filling the napkin dispensers. The fan over the grill was making a lot of noise. It happened again, like someone had passed a hand over his eyes.

He kept on making meatballs. Jack got up and looked into the mirror. "Al," he said, "look." He went over to the mirror, a mound of hamburger in his hands. There were three men in the slot room. They had plugged a speed drill into the light socket, and one of the men was using it on the half-dollar machine. When he turned the drill on, the lights in the kitchen dimmed. Another was emptying the coin boxes in the machines they'd already opened into a laundry sack. And the third was standing by the door with a short piece of pipe wrapped in electrical tape in his hand.

At first he was so mad he thought of grabbing his cleaver and going in. But the odds were against him. He quietly phoned the sheriff's department; they said they'd radio the nearest patrol car. He got Linda to come into the kitchen to wait, and he told the customers something had come up, so he had to close. He kept hoping the deputies would be smart enough not to come up to the place with their sirens on. He should have reminded them not to, he kept thinking.

It was the fat sergeant who came through the front door suddenly, as if he'd dropped from the ceiling. Al pointed to the door of the game room and raised three fingers. He made a move to join the sergeant, but the deputy stayed him with a raised hand. As they watched, he crossed to the door and took hold of the doorknob. Just stood there for a while, like he was going to stay in that position forever. Then he opened the door, flew inside, and the door slammed shut after him.

Al ran to look through the mirror; he had to butt Linda's head aside to see between her and Jack. He got there too late to see the sergeant's move, but he saw the man with the drill join the one with the pipe already on the floor. The one with the sack of coins swung it like a club, missing the sergeant but hitting one of the posts supporting the roof. The bag split and streams of coins spread through the air. The sergeant hadn't bothered to move to avoid the sack but watched the spray of coins with a certain interest. Apparently as an afterthought, he took out a black leather sap and started hitting the man on the right shoulder. The thief holding the drill tried to crawl toward the door, but the cord was still plugged into the light socket. He pulled and the whole thing tore out of the ceiling and the room went dark.

It wasn't until the next day that Al noticed the blue denim shirtsleeve behind the slots. He didn't want to touch it, as if there might still be an arm inside. He finally got a yardstick and picked it up with that. The robbers hadn't been from around there. After they'd been taken to see someone from the amusement company, they'd been driven to the county line by the sergeant. "They won't come back," the sergeant told him on the phone. "I can guarantee you that." Al felt a little queasy when he heard that, as if he'd found a dead sparrow in the grill of his new Pontiac.

Ross didn't pay him back. He saw him a few times. Once at Noonan's, and he went out the back way. Another time he caught a glimpse of him in his car. He left word with Noonan to let him know when Ross came in. It had been over five months, when he promised two weeks. Four hundred bucks was a lot of money. Whoever made the rule never loan to family or friends was right. So when Noonan phoned, he told Linda she could handle things till he got back. He never considered what he was going to say. Just drove downtown, found a parking place, close, for a Saturday. Remembered to take off his apron after getting out of the car.

The bar was full of shot-and-a-beer drinkers, the working man's pleasure. The place was a gold mine. When he got enough cash, he'd like a business like this. He and Ross had discussed the idea seriously once. Ross was there, sitting alone. The way he held his head, Al could tell even in the semidarkness that he'd been drinking a while. Change and crushed bills were in front of him, along with his Chesterfields and lighter. Empty shot glass and half empty bottle of beer. Okies always drank out of the bottle, they'd decided once. He motioned to the bartender to give Ross a drink, and the same for himself. Ross had to notice him. He was only a couple of stools away. When the bartender put the fresh beer and whiskey down, Ross looked up and saw him. Nodded thanks for the drink.

Al was going to blurt it out, Where's my four hundred bucks? But Ross spoke first. "You should have asked me what I needed the money for. It's your own fault."

"What did you need the money for?"

"One thousand crates of frozen chickens. Surplus. At a fraction of their cost. The navy was getting rid of them. I heard about it and thought I could make a killing. You would have bought some, Al, a gross at ten cents a chicken."

He nodded, thinking it over. "I would have."

"I paid your money, my money, and my mother's money. Three thousand one hundred dollars. Greed. I meant when I started out to just use the eleven hundred I had. Anyway, I paid the navy for one thousand crates of frozen chickens. I had most of them sold. Went around and talked to everyone. A sure thing. No one wanted to pass up an opportunity like that. I wore a silk tie down there, Al, to show the government folks I was a responsible citizen and would spend the money as quickly as possible to help the economy."

"They wrote me out a receipt and when I was about to phone for the truck to come for my frozen chickens, two inspectors came over and started opening the crates and stamping the top row of chickens NOT TO BE USED FOR HUMAN CONSUMPTION. I politely asked them, 'Sirs, what are you doing to my chickens?' The chief inspector replied, 'You can't eat them; they're too old.' 'They were frozen during the war,' I pointed out. I had checked the whole business out. I knew about the time requirement. The man was a gentleman, Al, pure and simple. A patient fellow. He showed me papers. The chickens were frozen for the war, but the 1918 war." Ross picked up his shot glass and knocked it back, grimaced like it tasted bad, and took a swig of beer. Asked, "What do you think, Al?"

Al started laughing; he couldn't help it. "I think you're the dumbest Okie I ever met."

"But the very best part was I had to pay someone who just happened to be there at the time with his truck to haul my frozen chickens to his mink farm. Do you think that was a coincidence? Don't answer. Three hundred dollars, or the government would charge me fifteen dollars a day for storing my chickens in their refrigerator."

Al ordered them both another round.

"I was too shamed to come around and tell you about your four hundred."

"Forget it," Al said. "You'll run into another good deal and pay me back. But I *am* surprised that you didn't apply the old cause and effect to the one thousand crates of frozen chickens." Ross gave him a serious look and then made his eyes go cross-eyed, wiggled his ears, and touched his nose with his tongue. They both roared.

He wasn't drunk, he was past that, but he couldn't move. Somehow he'd gotten home and was laying on the couch in the front room. He wished he could move his face; the dust in the material was going to make him sneeze. He couldn't recall how he got home after the bars closed. Linda must have shut up the restaurant. She knew where the key was now. Ross must have gotten him home.

He was going to quit. He had promised before. A lot of times. His head didn't just hurt, it felt like someone was using a blowtorch against his forehead. He wasn't religious, hadn't gone to church since he was fourteen and had refused to go with his mother and sister one Sunday. So he didn't know why after all that time he couldn't help calling out now, "Lord take me, take me, I'm ready. Take me now."

He must have slept. There was a sound. Something was happening. He waited for the pain to stop. His brain was whistling, heating up enough to turn liquid and float out his ears. It was the phone. He had to roll off the couch and crawl over to the stand.

"Where have you been?" Vera asked. "I've been phoning you all night and half the morning."

"Vera, I'm sick."

"You got raided by the state. They took Linda down to the city jail. When I heard I went down to get her out. Three-thirty in the morning. I went by the place after, and they had sealed the door, put a padlock on it. The police said the state was bringing charges that you sold liquor without a license. And to minors too."

"That's a lie," he said, forgetting his head. Was he dreaming this? Didn't Vera know what this was going to cost him?

"Where's Linda now?" He knew she wasn't home; she always answered the phone. There was a silence. "Vera, where's Linda?"

"It was Delbert who phoned me about the raid. She went with Delbert when I got her out of the station. She went off in his car.

About eight this morning she phoned me from Reno," she said. "They were waiting their turn to get married in a chapel up there."

Why? He knew the causes. The causes were always there, waiting to jump out. But the effect: how long do you have to wait for that? Can the effect ever bring on a cause? Reverse the whole process? It was too late.

"And by the way, they took in your dishwasher too. Linda wouldn't come without him at first, but they wouldn't let her stay once I posted her bond. I didn't have enough for him. I told him you'd come down as soon as I could get hold of you. They're going to take him to juvenile hall at ten-thirty. None of his family showed up."

"I'll take care of it," he said. "I'll go down." He dropped the phone. His head started up again. Bad, so bad he thought he was going to be sick. He had to rest a minute after he stood up, but he made it into his bedroom and fell across the bed. He had to get downtown somehow. But he couldn't unless he could get his head to stop hurting so much. The pain was in his eyes now; he couldn't focus his eyes to see.

His cheek was against the cool plaster of the wall. It wasn't soothing, but it made him think. He had to bring about an effect. Between him and this very wall. He tapped the side of his head against the plaster, his eyes still shut. Another time, harder. Again. Harder. He could hear the pieces of plaster falling on the inside of the wall from between the laths. He opened his eyes; he could see. He hit the wall again, harder. The pain was going away. Harder. Effect. Effect. It was working. Once again, harder. Cause. Cause.

Talus

He walked up to where the gravel road turned off the blacktop and stood still for a minute, looking up the hill. Then he started. His feet got hot and he began to sweat in the California sun. Took off his jacket, then his sweater. As he went up he could see more of the valley. A lot of last winter's snow was still on the higher mountains. Nothing looked familiar. He wished he hadn't talked the bus driver into letting him off back on the highway.

He was leaning against his backpack in the shade of a pine when he heard a truck coming up the grade. He didn't get up. Not because he was shy, he told himself, though he hadn't hitched in twenty years. It was the thought of his own cars topping the grade: the first one, the VW bug he'd owned in high school; the second one, the Alfa Romeo Spider he'd sold last month.

The flatbed stopped. "You want a lift? I'm going all the way." The voice was a woman's, but when he opened the door it looked like a man sitting there: overalls and denim jacket, brown wad of Copenhagen showing against her lower lip when she smiled at him. She was big. Not fat, just big. The hands gripping the wheel had broken, dirty nails and scratches across the back. He got into the cab.

She never said a word until he asked, "Is there a place to stay in town?" When she didn't answer he added, "A hotel?" There hadn't been any when he was a kid, but that had been over twenty-five years ago.

"No," she said, picking her words carefully. "The Hilton is still in the planning stage." He nodded; what difference did it make anyway? He kept his mouth shut until she stopped the truck in front of the old grocery store, but he couldn't keep his eyes from sliding her way. She was wearing a baseball cap with white jagged sweat stains. The skin on her face was weathered; that was the only word he could think of to describe it. Like old bark left on the ground through the winter. Unplucked eyebrows and no makeup, but she had braces on her upper teeth. Maybe in her early thirties.

She went up the grocery porch stairs two at a time. With her long legs it was nothing. When she passed the two old men sitting there she murmured something—he heard the word Hilton—and they both cackled. She went on through the screen door and into the store. He stood by the truck. The gravel road ended in front of the store; a dirt road ran east and west. He wasn't sure which way to go. It was still a couple of miles to his uncle's place. He knew that. He tried to orient himself by the cliffs that went straight up like man-made cement walls behind the store, but he couldn't remember.

Was it a mistake to come back here? He was glad he had. He heard himself ask, "Either of you gentlemen know the direction of the old Watson place?"

Neither got a chance to answer. "I own that now," the woman said. He hadn't noticed her standing behind the screen door. She was eating apple turnovers out of a plastic-wrapped package. She had two or three in her left hand and was downing another in two bites.

"I thought I'd take a walk out that way," he said. "Warren Watson was my uncle, my great-uncle. I lived out there for eight or nine months when I was a kid."

She seemed to be thinking that over when one of the old men said, "I used to be in lodge with your uncle. My name is Chet Schultz." He got up off the bench and reached down over the rail to have his hand shook. "Just bear left; it's only two and a quarter miles."

"I haven't been out there in years," the other man said. "Rhonda, the house still got its roof on?"

"It did yesterday," she said, still eating her turnovers.

He thanked Chet, whom he didn't remember at all, swung his pack on his back, and started out. The dirt road curved around so he was out of sight of the store when he passed the Oddfellows Hall, old brick building where he'd gone with his uncle once for a Christmas party for the local kids. Most of the houses were kept up; a lot had the same yellow climbing roses swarming with bees. There were no new houses. He thought a section of the cliff looked familiar. There had been a dark stain on the face, in the shape of a fox's head. He wasn't sure now if that was it, there to the left. How could he come back to a place that he couldn't even remember?

He heard the truck again but didn't look back. She drove up alongside him and they both stopped. "It's not posted," she said, "but this is all private property." She was so sure of herself. He started to walk again. "Your name is Butch," she said.

He turned back around; it startled him to hear his old nickname, the name his uncle had used, and he said, louder than he meant to, "I've got nowhere else to go."

"Get in," she said. "It's all uphill from here."

He recognized the house. The stairs had fallen in and the hop vine had wrapped itself around the whole screened-in porch and buried itself in the roof shingles. She jumped up over the broken stairs and landed on the porch. He swung up, using one of the posts, and watched her fish out a skeleton key and unlock the front door. Except for the dust and cobwebs it was exactly the way he remembered it. Blue linoleum on the floor bordered with red and green flowers. Wooden table and ladderback chairs, wood-burning cook stove, pantry full of old cans. "It's like he left it," Rhonda said, "when he went into the hospital. I always meant to clear the place out but I never did." Wrought iron double bed in his uncle's room; another in the room where he had slept. The wallpaper was different. Several mice had gotten into the tub and died. Rhonda spit into the toilet and then tried to flush it. The sound startled him. Water rushed into the yellowed bowl and the old pipes groaned under the house. "It's working," she said.

He was going to say something but instead he just nodded, all at once relaxing. Feeling better than he had in a long time. "You're okay, Rhonda," he said. She beamed.

They went back outside and around the house. "You were three or four grades ahead of me," she said as she followed him. "I didn't recognize you. Not until you mentioned your uncle. You don't recall me but you must remember my brother Monte. He was in your grade."

He did. "Big," he said. She nodded. Monte had towered over everyone, but he left the other kids alone. Spent recess lifting stones or playing ball.

He looked around the pasture again. The grass was cropped, but no sign of any cows. The milking parlor was boarded up. "What happened to the dairy?"

"No money in it anymore. The valley is too small to run enough cows to compete these days. It's a thousand-cow dairy or forget it. We run some sheep now. And most of us own our own land, so we do all right. Don't ever borrow from a bank."

"My uncle used to say the same exact thing."

"They got you by the short hairs if you do." He laughed. Her tanned face reddened. She changed the subject. "I named a stone after your uncle. It's up there in the north pasture." They started walking back toward her truck. "I go up and lift it sometimes. He treated me awfully good when it came to buying the place."

"I'd like to see it sometime," he said.

"Well, how long are you going to be around?" She belched and her face reddened again. "Excuse me," she said. "I've got bad manners, my sister-in-law tells me."

ꕥ

That night he lay down on his old bed. He could smell the dust through his sleeping bag, even though he and Rhonda had dragged the mattress out to the porch rail and beaten it with brooms. She was funny. She knew it too. It was she who'd suggested he stay. "Might as well," she said. "Place is going to fall down without some nails to hold it together." It was better than camping out. They'd heaped her flatbed with trash from the house for her to take to the dump. After a couple of hours of going through things, hauling them out, she was punching him on the arm to make a point, making him laugh by trying on his uncle's old double-breasted pinstripe. She was a character.

He was up early. He wanted to keep busy. He'd found the tools yesterday, so he was ready to start in on the stairs. They were completely rotten, but he took them apart carefully to copy for the new ones. There was plenty of old lumber around. It took him forever with hand tools. He'd learned woodworking from one of his stepfathers. After that, he trimmed the vines and cut the grass in front with a scythe. Then he started on the inside, cleaning the ashes out of the stove. That had been his first job when he got here, his uncle sitting at the table smoking his pipe, making suggestions.

He must have been a sullen kid then, but his uncle never raised his voice, never whacked him. He was used to being left, though: grandparents, aunt, various in-laws, neighbors, now an uncle. Even then he'd realized this was the last place there was. His mother must have driven up there as a last resort; his uncle hadn't even known she was coming. She returned the same way ten months later, late at night, car still running outside, wanted him back, had remarried.

He'd written his uncle at first. Warren always wrote back. Mentioned his cows, old Mildred, who was still doing six gallons a day. He'd send ten dollars on his birthday and at Christmas. His new stepfather was an airline pilot and they went everywhere. Flew to Athens once for a weekend. He stopped writing a couple of years after that. But not his uncle. The last few years before he died—he must have been in the seminary then—he'd hold the letter up to the light to see if there was a check inside. If there wasn't, he'd put it away to open later. Never even went to the funeral. If there had been any money left after the hospital bills, he would have gotten it. His uncle had left him his gold watch and an ivory-handled razor.

Just before noon he heard her footsteps moving across the porch and then she kicked the bottom panel of the screen door. She was carrying a wooden lug box full of last fall's apples and several cartons of eggs were on top of that. She set the box on the table and opened an egg carton. "Look what I brought you; I've got extra." The eggs were huge and brown, with specks of droppings still on them. He'd forgotten about brown eggs.

"Well, here I am," she said awkwardly, her face reddening, "Miss Congeniality." He tried to pay attention. He was never sure what she was going to come up with. "Really," she said. "I was in the county beauty contest."

"That's nice," he managed to say.

"You don't believe me, do you."

He tried to sound sincere. "I believe you." He hadn't been following closely enough, he decided. He wasn't used to listening to conversations that veered like this.

"Let's go for a walk," she said. "I want to show you around." She was out the door and going down the new steps, it seemed to him, as if she were trying to cave them in.

He didn't try to keep up with her; just let her go on ahead, then stop and turn and wait for him. The pasture was covered with stones. Whether they popped up with the freezes or came down from the cliffs he couldn't tell. The stones had been cleared away when he was here, used for the base of a small reservoir his uncle had built. Everyone in the valley had shown up to help.

"Monte doesn't want you here," she said when he caught up. "He says it's not a good idea."

"Rhonda, I'll go. I don't need to stay here. You're not doing me any favors." He was shouting before he knew it. He stopped. She was watching him with interest from under her shaggy eyebrows. Was that a smear of lipstick across her lips? For him? She was wearing a new store-creased flannel shirt under her washed-out jacket. "You couldn't have been Miss Congeniality," he said.

"I was. I looked like a heifer in a silk sack parading around the stage in the high school auditorium." They both laughed. She slapped him on the back. "I was nineteen, a hundred and fifty-two pounds at six feet even. I don't know what got into me. I knew it was nothing but a ruse. Sell so many tickets and this might happen. But I had to try. They make you Miss Congeniality if you have absolutely no chance to win and you realize it and smile a lot and encourage the other girls. To make it worse, in the talent part I tap-danced while twirling a baton and singing 'On Top of Old Smoky.' In a blue sequined swimsuit. When I think about it sometimes I lay down and put a pillow over my head."

"I would have voted for you," he said.

"Go on," she said. "I've got my good points, but the starlet business isn't one of them. That's why I tried; they gave the winner a screen test. I wanted to get out of here in the worst way then."

"What about now?"

"No, I'm used to it now. I bought Monte out, when he wanted to buy a gas station down below. But he came back fast enough. I own this end of the valley now. It's mine," and she held out her arms. He looked around too. There was more than he had remembered. It was green from springs and from the creeks that came down from the high mountains. Lupine still in bloom. Pines scattered around, protruding from the cliffs as if they were falling down the rock faces as you watched. This was paradise, he thought. As close as he was ever going to get to it. She was watching him. It was like feeling eyes on you coming from some flowering bush.

"There's plenty of stones," she was saying. "I was always going to do it myself, but I never did. You can see where I've got the corners laid out. The sheep get past here and head right into the boulders where they break their dumb legs. If you worked on the wall it'd get Monte off my back. He's got a suspicious mind. You could use your uncle's tractor and flatbed. Now that man could build a stone wall."

She started walking up the path toward the face. There was more stone than green grass, big chunks of granite. All he had to do was look up to hear the sound of the stones coming down, hear his uncle's voice explaining how it happened. At night in the winter the water coming down the face would freeze, prying the rock apart as it expanded in the cracks, until the slabs split as if they'd been struck by lightning, and then the stones came down, shaped by their fall down the face, rolling once they hit the hill to end in the pasture. The next morning they'd go up to see. "Look at them," his uncle would say. "There's one we can use." He'd feel for a handhold, bend his knees slightly and bring the stone off the ground. "It's a good one," he'd say. "I'll be able to use that one all right." Then he'd go on to the next.

She stopped to wait for him again. "This is where I spread his ashes. It was where he told me to," she said. He looked around as if they were still there. "Here's the one I named for him." She put her foot up on a nice-looking oblong stone. It was set off by a circle of smaller ones a couple of inches apart. She moved her boot off when he came near. He got his grip and lifted. He didn't feel the weight until he tried to straighten up, holding the stone tight against his stomach, at the same time trying to keep his balance. He made it; his back was straight. When he finally put it down it was as if his whole body was lighter. He'd never felt such relief. She picked it up easier than he did. He noticed her eyes were closed and she swayed slightly with the weight. She seemed to hold it there forever as if she'd fallen asleep, and he closed his eyes too. He couldn't watch anymore. Then he heard it hit the ground.

He could see someone sitting on the porch steps as they got close to the house. He noticed the truck then, parked around on the side. Monte wasn't as big as she was, he thought, until they got up to him. "You remember Butch, Warren's nephew," Rhonda said.

"Can't say I do." He didn't get up or offer his hand.

"Butch is going to stick around for awhile and build a wall across the north pasture."

"Is that right." Nobody said anything else for a minute.

"Maybe we could get some of the folks out to help. Like it used to be," Rhonda said.

"Those days are gone," Monte said. "People don't do anything for nothing anymore. By the way, Butch, what line of work you in?"

"That's none of your business," Rhonda said. "You don't have to answer if you don't want to," she said, facing him. "Monte was resident deputy here before they cut back. He's nosy, too."

"I was a priest."

"You're kidding me." Rhonda was looking at him amazed.

"Like the pope? The Rome pope?" Monte asked.

"Not quite that high, but the same church."

No one said anything until Monte slapped his thigh and got up off the stairs. "I better get back to work if I'm going to finish before supper. Nice seeing you again," he said as he went through the gate.

She waited until the sound of the truck was gone before she asked, "Why did you leave?"

He'd been asked that before. He always made something up: I lost my faith. Misplaced my faith. Wrong vocation. I didn't like all the new changes. I disliked the old church. Celibacy issue. Money issue. Abortion issue. My own issue. I was allergic to animal hair and the monsignor wouldn't get rid of his cat. He'd like to tell her the truth, or as close to it as he could. "I had to," he finally said.

She nodded. Anxious to go, he thought.

The wall took all his attention. It took a while to get the knack, bigger stones on the bottom, the rows above locked together by their weight, rather than with mortar, like bricks. The damned tractor could never be depended on to start when he needed it, and the flatbed had two used-up car tires that always needed air. But he was enjoying himself. As much as he ever had. He still had to qualify everything. That was from being a priest for nineteen years. But he didn't think about that now, or not as much.

He thought about Rhonda. He thought about his uncle. And the stones. He had forgotten how important they were. Everyone working on a wall, racing to see whose end would reach the middle first. Who could lift the heaviest. People had them lining their front walks, around their flower beds. Go out an evening, stop to talk to some neighbor on the porch, and start lifting. His uncle had been great for that. Stop to visit and just start lifting. "Not bad," he'd say, picking one up. "Got a good heft to it."

"My mother-in-law found that one up by the cliffs. Had to bring it back, naturally. Rolled it all the way to the road, down to where I could get the Dodge near enough to load it in. I've never seen it to fail: the farther away they are, the more they want them." Everyone would chuckle at that.

He had brought plenty of freeze-dried food in his pack, plus there were the apples and eggs Rhonda had brought, and he could always go to the store. But he kept expecting Rhonda to stop by. Two days. Three. Four. He was up in the pasture early, as soon as he could see, working until it got dark. Then he'd walk back. Leave the tractor up there. It was more trouble than it was worth. On the fifth day there was a foil-wrapped plate of homemade muffins on the table and four mason jars of peaches. No note. Rhonda.

What does a priest know from nineteen years of listening to confessions? The homo sapien's capacity for exaggeration. Who said that? Thomas Aquinas? Cardinal Newman? No. Aristotle? He wasn't even a priest. He didn't have to listen to all that anguish and hilarity. Load the flatbed with stones, get the tractor to work, haul them as near as he could to where he was working on the wall. Then place them: that was the best part. It was like a giant puzzle and he had to keep finding the right pieces. Not this one. Here, this one.

They thought he was going to come back. Very low key. They would keep paying his salary for six months or until he found a job, whichever came first. He looked. But he was lost. It was hard to buy a pair of Levis, much less find work. They got him a job in a Catholic hospital as an orderly. Changing beds. Giving baths. Helping patients to the bathroom. Combing their old thin hair. He got himself an apartment. An Alfa Romeo that could travel a hundred and twenty miles an hour. At least that's what the speedometer had on it. And women. Afterwards, he was always reminded of a confession he'd heard from a young woman a week into her marriage: "If that's all there is to it, I've had enough." Women. They were all the same if you put a sack over their head. Who said that? Pope Pius? Rhonda? A heifer in a silk sack is what she'd said.

Where was she? It was a full week Monday. He walked down to the store after breakfast. Before, in the city, he'd had all the accoutrements. The snazzy car, the apartment, a twenty-five-dollar haircut. They weren't enough. It was more what he thought he'd missed, or what he should have missed, or what there was to miss, that kept intruding. After six months he'd had to leave again. That's when he'd tried to find the valley.

When he was a boy the store had been jammed with goods, full of the odor of apples and bacon. Now most of the shelves were empty, except for the ones behind the cash register. There was a big new refrigerator full of six-packs of beer and soda. The place smelled of dust and floor oil. He picked out the things he needed and set them on the counter. The owner sat waiting on a stool, reading a magazine. "How's business?" he asked him, for something to say.

"What business? You're the first customer I've had today, and I've been here since eight." He went on talking as he rang up. "Bought this place thinking I would semiretire. Instead I retired outright, but I didn't know that until I'd paid over the cash. The folks around here go to the county seat to shop. It's only in the winter when the roads close do I get anything. When they run out."

"Nothing's perfect, I guess."

"Except these folks. They're perfect, hear them tell it. They're peculiar people." The owner lowered his voice. "Think they own the whole country. I hawked on one of those rocks over by Chet's walk, wasn't even on his property. Must be eighty, but he took a swing at me. You never saw such a commotion. You'd think I'd spit in his face."

What an appetite he had; he was hungry all the time. He'd eaten half a package of cookies from his grocery sack and still had a mile to go before he got home. At least he knew why Rhonda wasn't around. The owner had said everyone was up at the other end of the valley shearing. No wonder she hadn't been by. He knew what he was doing. Putting all his eggs in one basket. Who said that? Old MacDonald said that. He'd thought he had all the answers. He didn't. Then he found out absolutely for sure he didn't even have the questions. Where did that leave him? With nothing. Who said that? Wish I knew, he thought.

On Thursday he didn't go up to the pasture. Instead, he puttered around the house, fixed a window screen, used a straightened-out clothes hanger to get the drain in the sink to work. He washed his clothes. Didn't hear Monte until he was in the kitchen setting down a cardboard box on the table. "I knocked but you didn't come," he said. "Rhonda sent this stuff for you."

He nodded; he was used to getting little presents from his parishioners. But he felt awkward with Monte. They both waited for the other to say something.

"How did the shearing go?"

"Not bad. We finished this morning. A lot like work," Monte said. They both managed a smile.

"You want to sit down and have some coffee?"

"No, I got to get back." He turned to go. "You know, Rhonda is my sister," he said at the door. "She went into town. To the hairdresser's again." His voice was the same as he said, "I don't want you laughing at her."

"I won't do that."

"Why did you leave your church?" Monte swung the screen door open.

"Lust," he said. "I had too many lustful thoughts to be a priest."

Monte went out laughing.

❦

She didn't come back. He'd been there almost a month. Monte came every couple of days. But not Rhonda. Monte never mentioned her. And he didn't either. They spent one whole afternoon working on the wall. Rhonda's name never came up. Chet came out one evening. The sun was going down later each day; he'd been watching it from the porch. It was getting warmer. Almost the middle of June. "More than likely get some rain tomorrow," Chet said, coming up the walk. "Here. I brought you a sack of rhubarb." He set down a brown bag. "I got so much I can't get rid of it."

Chet couldn't sit still. He'd start talking about the store owner, who he hated, then stand up and walk a few steps, then sit back down. "I see you brought some rocks down. Your uncle always left them in the pasture." He got up again and walked over to where the three watermelon-sized stones were laying against each other in a triangle. "You got these up above the creek. I recognize the stone." He bent over and lifted the smallest one. "Not bad," he said.

He got up and picked up a rock too. He lifted these all day long, but he didn't mind. Holding them long enough, you stopped feeling the weight. It was comforting. He couldn't see Chet's face in the twilight so he asked, "What do you think of when you're lifting a stone like that?"

"Let me see," Chet said, dropping the stone back in the grass. "Right now I was thinking of my mother. How she made me custard when I was sick. My wife sometimes. Even my rhubarb patch. Whatever comes to mind. It's no mystery," he said.

"I better be heading back. You stop by when you come in to the store. I got plenty more rhubarb where that came from. Say, Butch," he said at the gate. "Monte was telling me you turned out to be a Catholic priest. I got nothing against them. But why did you leave?"

"There wasn't enough money in it," he said. Chet snorted and started off down the road.

He was up in the pasture eating his lunch, his back resting against the wheel of the trailer. Chewing his last apple core, he wrote in the soft dirt with the heel of his boot, BUTCH LOVES RHONDA. Who said that, he thought. Was she his only hope? His salvation? Another person?

There was too much of a gap or space for him. It was like a blind man regaining his sight after nineteen years, all those sounds he'd connected with reality overcome by the very starkness of the actual shape of objects. He couldn't relearn, pull together reality of sound, reality of sight. He was too late. He had the emotions of a fifteen-year-old. He got up and kicked the words to pieces.

When Monte came by the next day, before he even got out of his truck he called over, "Where in the hell did Rhonda go?"

"She's acting shy, I guess. I asked her that myself. She won't come, but I'll tell her you were asking." He'd brought some spark plugs for the tractor, and they spent half the afternoon trying to get it to run.

After that they laid some stone on the wall. They did two trailer loads, almost racing to get the second one done before it got too dark. He asked Monte once, when they stopped to catch their breath, "What do you think about when you're lifting stones?"

"Nothing," Monte said. "I try not to think of anything."

They walked back down to the house. "I'll mention to Rhonda you were wondering where she was. She went into town, bought some new clothes. Took them back, then bought some more. Quit using snuff. It was tough; you can imagine."

"I was just wondering," he said. This was so silly, he kept thinking. What was he expecting? What was she expecting?

"She's shy," Monte said.

"What if I came back with you?"

"I don't think that would be a good idea. I mentioned in passing once I might invite you to dinner and you'd have thought I'd planned to bring one of the rams up to the table. You got everything you need?"

"I can't think of anything," he said. "I can always go to the store if I run out."

It turned hot the next week, in the nineties, and he tried to get up to the wall as early as he could to get a day's work in and beat the heat. No matter how many stones he picked up and put in the wall, there were always more in the pasture. The way he was going he'd never finish the wall. But it didn't matter. He couldn't think of doing anything else. He noticed the slower he worked the less his mind would drift back. As soon as he speeded up he'd start connecting the past to now, this moment. Then he'd slow down again and it would be just lifting the stones and placing them in the wall.

On the way back he stopped at the windmill tank to get a drink. The shutoff valve wasn't working. It was full, water spilling over the sides. After he fixed it he couldn't resist taking off his clothes and sliding in. He'd done this a couple of times when he was a boy, until his uncle had caught him. "The cows won't drink the water if they can taste you," he'd said. There weren't any cows anymore, and the hell with the sheep. They wouldn't come up here till late summer.

It was colder than he thought it would be, but after he got used to it, it felt good. He lay back with just his face out of the water. When he'd speeded up, building the wall, he'd been going over the time he got drunk a couple of years before he left. That was occasionally permitted by monsignor in the parish house after the housekeeper went home. Once every five years or so. He had wanted to be a parish priest, a general practitioner. Down in the trenches, as someone said. That was him; he had said that. They were playing Scrabble, watching a night baseball game, drinking beer. Who was there? Didn't matter. Looking up definitions of *purfle*, *qursh*, to see if they were really words. It struck him then: the things he couldn't define were the most important. Friendship. Not religion. Not the business of managing believers. Bingo. Propagating the faith. He tried to explain that. "You'd better go to bed," the monsignor told him. "You've had enough." Going up the beige carpeted stairs to his bedroom, he decided he'd never had a friend. Only parishioners. The other priests: he'd shared a vocation with them but nothing else. Maybe his uncle had been a friend. Taking him in.

The hot sun on his face made him sleepy. Long beards of moss floated across the surface of the water, and he couldn't see the bottom. There was such a comfort in this kind of life. Bucolic. Pastoral. Primitive. What else?

"Butch, you up here?"

He heard her voice and thought, She would come now. "I'm in the tank," he said. "Cooling off."

"I won't come near," she said. "How have you been?"

"Okay. How have you been?"

"We've been shearing sheep."

"I heard." He put just his head over the rim of the tank. "Rhonda, what do you think about when you lift the stones?"

"Sometimes about what I'm going to eat for dinner. Or what I have to do next on the ranch." She thought a minute. "Lately I've been thinking about you."

She was wearing what she always wore, except for the jacket. Her hair was combed back behind her ears, curly, like before, and tied with a red ribbon. She looked the same. She was always going to look that way. He felt relieved. "Rhonda, I want you to come in and join me." He slid back down so he couldn't see her face. She didn't answer. He didn't hear anything until she came up the steps.

"Close your eyes, Butch. Until I get under the water," she said, and then she started singing "On Top of Old Smoky."

2

Rhonda handed over her hymen like she was offering him a piece of fruit. They were in the upper pasture, sleeping out under the stars on the old mattress they'd dragged from the beat-up Airstream. It had been her idea to bring up the trailer and stay up there with the sheep. "You're sure about this?" he said. He was the one who was hesitating. She was the virgin. "You can have my cherry," she said.

By Tuesday some of the awkwardness was past. Rhonda wasn't shy; she coupled as naturally as she did everything else. When the sun was up good they'd shuck off most of their clothes and start working on the wall, lifting the stones off the flatbed and fitting them into place. He liked watching her. Sometimes she carried the heavy stones like basketballs she was going to shoot into the air.

Under the night sky in the pasture it was like lying next to another species sometimes, a giant. Not because she was half a head taller and outweighed him too. It was something else he couldn't explain to himself. He couldn't get over the uneasy feeling that seized him at odd times. This was wrong. Wrong. He tried to find a reason. When they fornicated he could see the sheep nearby; they made him self-conscious. He complained that the sheep were watching them. But he forgot about them when he measured the length of her arm, wrist to elbow, elbow to shoulder, using his thumb to the knuckle, exactly an inch, as the measure. Her leg, ankle to shin to knee to thigh. It was like part of the ceremony of lifting the stones all day.

The nineteen years he'd spent as a priest had done something to him when it came to other people. It was as if there was always that distance, that span of time that made it awkward. He was only five years older than Rhonda, but it was like she had been alive an extra twenty years. When he'd heard confession, those years before he'd left, it had been mostly old people, and not many of them, but sometimes there'd be someone from his generation in the confessional: he'd try to give them a shape on the other side of the screen, then, so he'd have one on his side.

After he left he went through a period of catch-up, chasing his whoopee dreams. He was propositioned a lot—because of or in spite of being a priest, he wasn't sure which. The women he met at the hospital where he worked as an orderly chased him like he was—what? Some kind of prize? No one had ever said she loved him, though, or gone out with him more than two or three times. But he had learned all the tricks you could find out on the old agony and groaning board, as a parishioner had called it once.

They weren't enough, though, because Rhonda, who'd had no experience in the field, had never kissed a male outside her immediate family, was already surpassing him. It was as if her weight and height gave her an advantage over his experience. She seemed to give herself over in a way that defined the act for her, as if her body were part of her ambition. When he tried to analyze why it was so different for him, he didn't know where to begin. It was as if his body had no sex memory, no ability to sustain another person.

Her brother Monte had to know what was going on. Rhonda stayed overnight now; didn't go back to her place for days. They ran half naked around the pasture building the wall, which almost reached the base of the cliffs now. One afternoon they heard Monte yelling down in front of the house, "Butch, you here? Butch? Rhonda, there's someone that wants to buy lambs; you better tend to business." He never went any farther than the house; never looked for them. Giggling behind the wall, they watched the pickup move away.

Rhonda was smiling, her eyes half closed; she'd been holding a stone while her brother was at the house. He didn't ask her what she was thinking about as she held the stone against her stomach. She would say, You.

She opened her eyes and said, "This stone is too good for the wall," and she set it aside. She put it down gently in the grass. There were plenty of stones; one more or less wouldn't make any difference. He daydreamed too much: she had almost emptied the flatbed while he watched. That woman could build a wall.

It started to drizzle that evening and they moved back into the house, driving the herd into the enclosure by the workshop. It was almost uncomfortable being inside, under a roof, behind walls. He couldn't sleep very well and woke up early. He could see from the clock on the bureau that it was just after four. He heard the sound but didn't realized it was a truck until it stopped in front of the house. Monte came through the kitchen door yelling, "Goddamn it, I had to get up in the middle of the night to see you two." He was standing at the foot of the bed. "Rhonda, sign this." He held out a check. Rhonda woke up slow, looking around her. "How are you, Butch?" Monte had what Rhonda called his big shit-eating grin on his face.

"I'm fine, Monte, and yourself?"

"Susan wants you to come down for dinner. Tonight, if you can't think of anything else to do around six P.M.," Monte said with a bigger grin. "I've already asked Chet to come out and watch the sheep."

"We'll be there," he answered. Rhonda had signed the check with the pen Monte handed her and then disappeared under the covers again.

"Rhonda, you awake? We've got to get the other flock up here; it's almost September."

"Okay, Monte," she said, still half asleep.

Monte went to the doorway and called back, "You two sex maniacs better be eating right or you're going to wither away to nothing." He went out chuckling at his own joke.

❦

It made him uncomfortable, the way Rhonda kept trying to defer to him—"You drive, Butch," but then she'd have tell him where to go. "Turn right, here. Across that cattle guard"—almost like she wanted him to be the old-fashioned male, when she was the one who was the boss, owned the flocks and about an eighth of the valley, that old house of his uncle's. He and Monte worked for her. She wanted him to drive down to Monte's for dinner. He pulled over when Chet waved them down in front of his place, holding out another sack of rhubarb from his patch. He handed it through the window. "Butch, you know what my mother always used to say? Days go by so fast it's like rhubarb passing through the hired girl." He cackled, hoisting a rock by the steps. "I'm on my way up to the sheep, Rhonda."

Rhonda lived in a double mobile home about a hundred yards

down the road from the store. They stopped there for her to change her clothes. "I gave the home place to Monte and Susan when my mother died," she said from the bedroom. "I was always going to build a house, I've got the money, but I never found the time." He waited in the kitchenette. She had shut the door to the bedroom. The whole place kind of rocked when she moved.

She came out in a dress. "What do you think?" He'd never seen her in anything but her work clothes. "You look nice." But it didn't seem like it was her anymore. Even with the big shoulders. It was some kind of cocktail dress. It was tight. Or maybe she was too big for ordinary clothes. "You don't like it, do you?" she asked.

"I like you just the way you are, Rhonda. You don't have to wear new clothes."

"What if I want to change? Maybe I don't want to be the old Rhonda." She went back into the bedroom and put on some clean jeans and a flannel shirt.

Susan had gone to a lot of trouble, tablecloth, big rack of lamb, mashed potatoes. She'd baked a cake for dessert. Rhonda made two of Susan, who wasn't more than five-four, sitting next to her at the table. The kids were going to be big, like Rhonda and Monte. Rhonda acted like she had just read a book about table etiquette, sitting straight in her chair and eating daintily with quarter forkfuls, taking small portions when the bowls were passed. "You okay?" Susan asked.

"I'm fine," Rhonda said. Monte kept cracking up. He'd gain control; then he'd start again. He poured everyone another glass of wine. "What's wrong with you?" Rhonda asked him. Monte was swallowing cackles behind his napkin. He had to stifle a snort too; it was infectious.

Finally Rhonda yelled, "What do you two think is so funny?" She put down her fork.

"Nothing," Monte said. "I'm just laughing because Butch is."

"I'm just acting silly," he said, and he put his arm around Rhonda's big shoulders. "It's a happy time; we're all together, enjoying this meal." He could feel her almost melt under his arm.

"I was just asking," she said, almost whispering. He didn't like her like this, either, when she acted diffident, trying to please him. Did two people ever work all these inconsistencies out? Two weeks together now, and it kept getting harder to remain individual, separate. But he couldn't imagine not being together.

He asked Rhonda to marry him the first week in October. She didn't answer. "I'm almost forty-one," he said, "and you're thirty-six; we're old enough." He meant it to be funny.

"It's not that," she said. "Are you sure you want to?" They were with the sheep up in the north pasture, working on that end of the wall. The grass was coming up like green needles from the last rain. He could see the sheep stretched out over the meadow as they moved like some huge mowing machine. There had been a frost in the morning and there was a cold wind now. The valley was at 5,600 feet. It didn't snow much, but it could drop down to zero easy in wintertime. "I want to marry you, Butch," she said, "but I want you to be sure what you're doing."

"I'm sure." He noticed he couldn't work and talk at the same time.

"You left bring a priest."

"That was different. The Catholic church is an institution. There weren't any regular, everyday people in the priesthood. Organized religion is a business; you can't love a corporation. But I love you, Rhonda."

"Let's wait," she said, putting a stone in its place in the wall.

She had Monte write the paychecks that came for him in his mailbox at the store every month. Seven hundred fifty dollars, the going wage for a sheep herder, plus grub and the house. They never mentioned money; he cashed the checks when he went down below and left the money in a savings account. He couldn't think of anything to buy beside some work clothes. He didn't need anything, and they didn't stint on groceries. He ran up a tab at the store, treating Rhonda to fried pies and orange soda.

It was the job that was getting to him. He couldn't always take it seriously, watching sheep. It was too easy; nothing ever happened. They were just stupid sheep. At night he drove the flock down and put them in the pen so he could sleep in the house. Rhonda would remind him of things, sometimes, and he never forgot to do those. "You always stay close to the flock." He knew that. She told him once, serious, "Sheep thrive on a shepherd's care." He didn't know about that.

He didn't always pick up one of the dogs when he went up to the herd, like Rhonda and Monte did, and when he did, he'd forget to feed it and it'd wander back home. The sheep liked him; they know better than he did what he wanted them to do. The animals were docile and would follow him once he got them moving in the right direction. They trusted him; he could almost feel it sometimes. He'd stopped having to induce them to come on with a bucket of grain. He was their friend. But the job was boring.

❦

He knew Rhonda was going to be gone the last week of the month. She was the recording secretary of the Wool Growers Association and had to attend a tri-state conference. He felt lost without her. He circled the day she was coming back on the calendar. He stayed in his uncle's house; it was too cold now for the herder's Airstream up in the pasture. The old house was cold too, but he left the electric heater on all night to keep the bedroom warm until Monte came in early one morning and saw it going. "You know what that costs?" he said. "About three hundred dollars a month. Build a goddamn fire in the stove when you get in at night, shut the house up, and wear your long johns to bed." He had forgotten what the winter was like up here. He didn't remember it being this cold, that year he'd stayed with his uncle. He'd just been happy to be there, somewhere, back then, that time his mother had dropped him off just before she married her third husband.

There'd been only a few flocks up here then; it was mostly small thirty-cow dairies, so he'd never been around sheep as a kid. He hadn't known what Monte and Rhonda were doing when they started grabbing the three-day-old lambs and cutting off their tails with a special tool. He didn't want to ask too much. Later Chet explained that was called docking and it kept the sheep cleaner and healthier. But that was nothing. The next day they grabbed the male lambs and while Rhonda held each one down Monte took out his pocketknife, slit the scrotum, then bent down and bit the testicles loose and spit them into a bucket. "Come and try," Monte called; "they taste better now, before they're cooked."

"Are you crazy?" he said.

Rhonda did it too. "This is the only way, Butch," she yelled. "These balls are too slippery to get ahold of with your fingers." He kept his distance; he had a lot to learn. Chet explained. "Rocky Mountain oysters. You can't have too many young rams in a flock. They cause trouble. You have to castrate them and sell the wethers for meat."

He woke on Sunday morning when the alarm clock rang, and it was so cold he turned on the electric heater and got back into bed. He must have fallen asleep again because the second time he woke up it was from someone yelling, "Butch, Butch." It was Rhonda. All he could think of as he put on his clothes was that she must have driven all night to get home this early. He was getting his boots on when he heard the shots, and he ran for the front door. He could see Rhonda running over the rise to the meadow. She was wearing one of her new outfits.

He didn't understand what she was doing, but he ran too. When he got to the rise he saw the dogs; they were running around the flock playing with the sheep, chasing them back and forth. Rhonda had her rifle up against her shoulder. She always kept it behind the seat in her pickup. She started firing, taking her time. He didn't know what she was shooting at until one of the dogs gave a yelp and rolled over twice, snapping his teeth at his front paws, then lay still. He watched in amazement as she shot all four dogs. Then she started running again toward the flock, which was bunched up. When he got to her he was out of breath. He was about to yell, "Why did you kill those dogs? They could have been someone's pets," when she grabbed a ewe by the back leg and dragged her clear from the flock. One of her front legs was just hanging on by the skin above the joint. Her face had been bitten and was bleeding. "Wild dogs," Rhonda said. She held the rifle out with her one hand, her arm away from her body, the muzzle in the sheep's ear, and pulled the trigger. She did the same thing to the five other sheep that were hurt. Never wasted a minute.

He noticed she'd lost her shoes. Her pantyhose were all torn at the feet. She was pushing her way through the flock, looking for more hurt sheep, and he realized how good she looked in those clothes. She'd found a style that suited her big frame: dark jackets, white blouses, and long loose skirts. Her hair was cut short now and it made her broad face look smaller. She looked feminine. Before, she'd looked like Monte's younger brother. "You look beautiful," he said. She didn't answer, just started walking back to the house.

She changed in front of him like he wasn't there, pushing her pantyhose down, yanking them off like they were resisting, letting her skirt fall to the floor. She raised her long arms to work her slip up over her head. "My Amazon," he said. While she put on her work clothes, he made coffee. "You were supposed to pen the sheep at night whenever you slept in the house," she said. She didn't sit down at the table with him to eat a bowl of puffed wheat.

"I brought them down last evening and I came inside for a minute and I forgot. They must have wandered back up to the meadow. I didn't know dogs would do that."

"They will; people let their dogs go, abandon them up here, and they form packs. They'll kill a whole flock if you give them enough time, just for fun."

"Rhonda, I'm not going to feel guilty over this."

"Butch, these are range sheep. You're getting paid to be a herder. So you have to do the work right."

He had to make her laugh. "I thought I was your love slave." She walked right out of the kitchen. He could hear her outside, hitching the flatbed to the pickup. He finished his breakfast. The hell with it, he thought, and he put everything away, swept the floor and did the dishes. Then he went up to the meadow.

Rhonda was skinning the sheep. He didn't know how and just watched. "We can sell the hides," she said. "The carcasses I'll give to the rendering plant. They'll come out to the end of the blacktop and pick them up. They can't be eaten. You don't know what the dogs might have had." She worked fast, tearing the skin back once she got a section of the hide peeled loose. When she was done skinning, they heaved the carcasses up on the flatbed. He helped load the dogs on after that. He didn't ask what she planned for them. Monte had shown up; he just looked but didn't say anything. Monte stayed with the flock while they drove down and dropped the sheep off first and then went farther until they were near the entrance to the valley. Then, every couple of miles, Rhonda got out and hung one of the dogs on the barbed wire fence. "It probably won't help, but it makes me feel better," she said.

They went back to the flock and drove the sheep down to the loading chute and he ran them through while she checked each one for bites, lifting their heads, feeling underneath. There were no more hurt sheep. When they were done, he asked her, "What would you do with another herder if it wasn't me?" He had kissed her in the truck and she had punched him on the shoulder like she always did.

"Fire him. Give him his time."

"What about Monte?"

"Monte wouldn't have done anything so dumb; he owns half the flock. And if he had, I would have docked him for the dead ewes."

"You do that to me too, then," he said. He wasn't upset.

"I was going to, Butch."

"You know, Rhonda, I don't think I like your tone."

"Butch, you didn't do your job." When they'd finished with the sheep she walked back to her pickup and drove off.

She didn't come back that night or the next day. Monte came out that morning with one of the dogs and about a hundred pounds of dry dog food. Monte went through it all again with him, the care and feeding of the flock, and the same with the dog. He tried to listen. Monte was better at it than Rhonda. "Sally's a good dog; you can trust her to let you know what's happening." Sally came up to them when she heard her name, and Monte scratched her head. Then he went over everything again with the .22. Monte had been in the army and knew all the jokes. This is your rifle, this is your gun; this one's for shooting and this one's for fun. They both thought that was hilarious.

He tried to get some order in the way he did things. He fed the dog before he took off his boots at night so he wouldn't forget. He tried to keep track of the rifle by sticking his lunch bag through the sling. He even put it over his shoulder when the sun went down behind the cliffs and he couldn't see too well, driving the sheep down to the pen. There weren't any natural predators up here. But there could be more dogs. Old Chet had told him it didn't happen very often—the last time wild dogs had killed any sheep was about nine years ago—but it did happen.

He decided he was going to be a good shepherd. The best ever. He gave Sally part of his sandwich every afternoon. She seemed to like everything but tomatoes. She ate lettuce, bread, and any kind of meat or fish. Loved mayonnaise. He had never had a pet. He had hated the monsignor's cats, who shed white fur all over the couch that his clothes picked up and pissed on the bottom window panes of the french door. It smelled so bad when you walked into the parish house your eyes watered.

He moved off from the flock to a place where he could still see them but they wouldn't get nervous and fired the extra box of shells. He used a big rock to steady his aim and hit an orange soda can at about a hundred feet easy. Then he moved back. Sally had come to watch. She looked on, approving. He started missing then and tried to remember what Monte had told him: "It's all in the breathing. Line up the front blade halfway in the middle of the peepsight, hold your breath, and use the second joint of your finger, keeping your other eye open, and squeeze the trigger. You wouldn't squeeze that hard on a woman's tit, would you? Squeeze gently; don't jerk the trigger back." Monte was more patient than Rhonda was. He started hitting the can then, again and again, until it was nothing but holes. He could learn all this if he only applied himself. He thought about Rhonda, too. It had been four days now. Three that she'd been back and hadn't stopped by, and one since Chet had walked up to tell him that both Monte and Rhonda had gone down to some kind of emergency meeting in Sacramento. Chet didn't know when they'd be back. She was mad at him. For a woman her size, her breasts weren't in proportion to the rest of her. About as big as an apple. Maybe more like large lemons. He had almost four thousand dollars in the bank. He could leave if he wanted.

He saw the camper moving down the road but didn't pay attention. It wasn't one he recognized as belonging to any of the twelve or so families who lived up here. The road coming up to the valley was a switchback heart-stopper with drop-offs of hundreds of feet, and then it deadended just past the house. Few tourists came here. The camper stopped at the house. He and Sally had just penned the sheep for the night. He walked over to the camper. Someone was getting out. "Yes sir," he said, imitating Monte, "what can I do for you?"

"My name is Kepler. I'm looking for somebody, a Father Bob Jarrell, and I was told I might find him up here."

Butch put out his hand and they shook. The other man didn't let go right away. "Brian Kepler," he said. "I wonder if you can help me. I'm doing this project, interviewing former priests, or ones that are sitting out for a while or whatever, about the lifestyles they've chosen now." Kepler let go of his hand after he finished saying that, and he went on, at his ease, confident of his audience, putting both his hands into his back pockets. "It's not a definitive study by any means. But there's a real need to understand what's occurring in the church today."

"You're with the diocese?"

"No, I'm independent. They did give me your name at the diocese, though. I'm with the Company of Jesus."

He guessed Brian was a few years older than he was. Tall and slim, with most of his hair gone from the front of his head. Glasses. He'd gone to a Jesuit high school himself and had always admired the teachers. His tennis coach and history teacher at Holy Cross had been a tough, sixty-year-old ex-Marine who'd one time punched a student bully in the stomach and then knocked him down when the bully challenged him to put on the gloves in the boxing ring. The shock troops of the church. They were always battling someone—dictators, terrorists, the pope. It took at least thirteen years to become a Jesuit; he would have never made it that long. When any of the parish priests took on the monsignor he always said, "Is that more of your Jesuitical thinking?"

"I thought I'd stop by; I'm on a kind of leave of absence myself. You know what I mean. I support myself in the manner to which I've been accustomed by doing odd jobs." He pointed to the bumper on his truck. MR FIXIT. "My colleagues always called me that, so I made it official with a vanity license plate. I have to pay my way; it's part of the deal."

"Want to stay and have dinner with me?" he said to Brian. "A neighbor sent up lamb roast cooked with red potatoes and carrots. All I have to do is heat it up." He wondered how Susan had found the time. She was watching the other flock with her kids while Monte and Rhonda were below.

"You parish priests know how to live right," Brian said.

At dinner he did most of the talking while Brian ate, explaining how he'd come back here just to see the place again because he'd been happy in the valley that time he'd stayed with his uncle. Some of the people remembered him from then; that's why he was Butch up here, not Bob. This place was isolated, no TV reception, but there were videos at the store. Radio reception was only good at night. But he wasn't lonely, he heard himself saying. "It's from keeping my expectations reasonable," he said. He didn't mention Rhonda.

At nine he was yawning; he'd tired himself out talking. "I have to get up at four," he said, covering his mouth. "I better hit the sack."

"Listen, Bob, let me offer you a proposition. I can repair almost anything, and this place could use a little work." He'd noticed Brian trying to turn the faucet off so it'd stop leaking, and when he went to the toilet he had to leave the door partly open while he peed because the switch was broken and the light wouldn't go on. "I get seven fifty an hour plus parts, which I have a good supply of, at ten percent above my cost. I can start tomorrow." He added, "If it's okay, I'll park my camper by the side of the house and run a cord to one of the outlets for juice. What do you say?"

He agreed, yawning. It couldn't hurt to have this place a little safer. He was asleep, it seemed, before his head hit the pillow. He didn't have time to even think of Rhonda like he usually did before he passed out. When the alarm went off he was up in a minute and dressed and shaved. He remembered he hadn't fed Sally last night. She was in her place under the porch, and he gave her the bone from the roast and filled her dish with dry dog food and poured warm water over the top the way she liked it. He scratched her neck while she ate. "Forgive me, Sally," he said. He went over to the pen and swung the gate back. The sheep poured out and moved toward the meadow, where the best grass was. They weren't so dumb.

That evening it was almost dark when he got back with the sheep to the pen. They were cooperating; the dog kept after them, barking short bursts to get the stragglers moving even with the rest. He knew

Brian was watching from the porch as he opened the gate for the sheep. He filled Sally's dish with fresh water and then shut the gate after all the sheep were in. "You're still a shepherd," Brian said as he came up to the porch.

"I never thought of it that way," he said. He could smell fresh baked bread as he went inside, unslinging the rifle and setting it in the corner, and it wasn't smoky in the room either. "You fixed the stove."

"I took the fire box apart and cleaned it and then I drove a sack down the smoke pipe from the roof. You should have seen the soot; I took two buckets out." Brian was moving around the place, flicking the new switches on and off, flushing the toilet in the bathroom. "I had to replace all the guts in the tank," he said. Dinner was ready, some kind of casserole. He hoped it was tuna fish, his favorite. The housekeeper used to make it every Friday. It was a parish joke that he'd eat at anyone's house if they had tuna casserole for dinner. His mother hadn't had to cook: they'd always lived in the hotels she worked in as a publicist and had eaten in the dining rooms. Brian had made chipped beef with potatoes. The table was already set.

"The place looks great. I can't get over it; everything works." He was heating the water for Sally's dinner. He tried turning the faucet at the sink on and off a couple of times to be sure.

"I could weatherstrip the place," Brian said. "Around the windows and doors, then caulk the facings outside. Put new thresholds in and insulate the attic, if you wanted to go that far. When I was first assigned to the inner city I did a lot of that. I could stick around; my camper is self-contained. I could have this place as tight as a tick in a couple of days." It sounded like a good idea.

After they'd eaten, Brian went out and got his briefcase. Gave him a questionnaire to fill out. He was tired, but he tried to remember all the dates and all the names. He had been in only two parishes, seventeen years in the first one, but there must have been more than two dozen priests who had passed through in those years. He had transferred just that once, but the second monsignor had been more of a martinet than the first. No one stayed there if they could help it. Out of his seminary graduation class of ninety, fourteen were still active in the church, the last time he'd heard. He wasn't bitter anymore about wasting nineteen years of his life. He'd found Rhonda; that was enough to make up for the time.

The form Brian gave him asked the old questions: What are your major dissatisfactions with the priesthood? He groaned. "Keep it simple, now," Brian said. He gave the same answers he always gave. Organized religion was dying, Catholicism in particular, because it wouldn't change with the times. It was almost the twenty-first century and they had a nineteenth-century pope. No one needed a middleman priest anymore. The family unit was disbanded and people sought other ways to comfort themselves. They were getting their codes, rules, and succor from each other now, or from TV and the movies, not from religion. Priests were redundant in the Age of Technology. He went on to the celibacy issue, the contraception debacle, abortion. He remembered when they used to promote the rhythm method; only a male who'd never had sex would have thought that up.

He wrote on and on but he was feeling sleepier and sleepier. He kept expecting Rhonda to show up but she didn't. He could go down to the store and phone her, but he shouldn't leave the sheep, even if Brian was here. A shepherd stays with the herd at all times, until he is properly relieved. Monte told him that. He liked to sound like a sergeant. Rhonda had mentioned once that Monte had spent eight years in the army. He asked him once, "Why did you leave? Twelve more years and you could have had a good pension." He knew of priests who went into the armed forces because of the benefits. Monte was thinking it over still and didn't answer. "Because of Susan?"

"No, I met her after I got out. It was a combination of things that accumulated and added up to me leaving. The older I got, the more I realized the army life wasn't for me. I liked the army. I was a good soldier, could give and take orders as well as anyone, but it made me uneasy. I'd catch myself thinking, This is just make-believe; I'm playing at some game here. I knew I could do the twenty years but I kept thinking, This life I'm living is *my* life, and it's the only one I'm going to get. It's hard to explain. When my enlistment was up, I left. Came back up here. I get a lot of satisfaction from my family. Running sheep."

After Brian went out to his camper he lay awake, thinking about the conversation they'd had. The changes. There was some serious talk of priests being allowed to marry, a two-tier system. You'd still have the option of celibacy, but you could be a married priest in the lower echelon. He liked that part. And the pope: Brian was funny about the pope. "A fat short Polish guy in a skirt; he's given us a lot of trouble in the Company. But he won't be there forever." Brian kept referring to the Jesuits like that, as the Company, instead of saying Society of Jesus.

He was up early and moved the sheep up near the new section of wall he and Rhonda were building. Sally drove the flock ahead of her until the sheep reached the first grass and they spread out like spilled water. He could see back to the house; there was no movement from the camper. He had left coffee on the back of the wood stove and cleaned up the place a little after making his bed and doing last night's dishes. He was developing a routine, he realized. He'd never had to make dinner for himself or clean up afterward as a priest; there was always a housekeeper.

He went to work on the wall, taking his time, fitting the stones together, overlapping the courses just a little to lock them in as tight as possible. He remembered his uncle had some kind of chisel he'd used to chip or dress a stone if he needed a perfect fit. He'd look when he went down for lunch.

He saw the camper leave about ten. It came back about an hour later as he was filling the water trough. He carried two five-gallon cans back and forth from the tank, doing it the hard way instead of using the flatbed, remembering the times last summer he and Rhonda had cooled off in the old wooden three-hundred-gallon tank. God, he missed her. Was he thinking like a teenager again? He couldn't help it when it came to emotions; he had never developed any. For love you had to act on faith, maybe, to first define yourself in some way and then yourself in light of the other person, but he had no faith in himself. Turn love into friendship, maybe? He didn't know what was next. It was easier to learn to be a brain surgeon than to understand how and why to love someone.

By lunchtime the sheep had grazed down along the road across from the house. He walked over to the porch. Brian had the front door off and was putting a new threshold down. They had soup at the table, wearing their coats and hats, it was so cold inside. He raised both shades to watch the sheep and Sally as he ate.

Brian started chuckling. "These people around here move slow. I went down to the store for some two-inch wood screws and I saw an old man standing in his yard holding a rock. When I came back from the store about five minutes later he was still in the same place with what looked like the same rock."

He wasn't going to explain, but he heard himself saying, "That was Chet. The stones are everywhere up here; you have to deal with them. For some people, it gets to be a pastime. Those stones by the front door were my uncle's favorites; he'd lift them sometimes. He'd pick one up after dinner, say, 'Got a good heft to it.' It made him feel better, I guess." He didn't know all the reasons people picked up rocks here. "It's kind of a tradition up here," he added.

"Don't you miss a little activity? Don't you feel isolated? I can see why people talk to the rocks up here."

"I have Rhonda," he said. "When she's here, I don't even notice." He had explained about her. "And I'm beginning to like the sheep. There were all dairies up here before, when I was a boy, so I have a lot to learn."

"This is a serious relationship?" Brian asked.

"Absolutely. We're going to get married."

"Sometimes, now just sometimes, with some of the former priests I've interviewed, it's been as if they had to explore their own sexuality, reassure themselves. And once they understood that part, it wasn't an issue anymore. Celibacy didn't seem like such a terrible sacrifice; didn't seem so abnormal. In fact, a few came back, decided to work as priests again after experiencing the civilian world."

"I couldn't go back," he said. "I never even think about the possibility. I have someone who loves me now." He stood up. "I've got to go."

"But Bob, we've all got someone who loves us and cares for us. Forget that," Brian said after a second. "Jesuits always have to have the last word."

He went into the workshop and looked around until he found the kind of chisel he remembered. He took a four-pound hammer too. Before he went to work on the wall he put Sally on his knees and picked out all the stickers from her fur and checked her paws for thorns. Gave her the biscuits he didn't eat for lunch. He had to look some before he found the right rock to try the stonecutter's chisel on. The lower pastures were mostly stone free now, the rocks safely in the wall that was going to extend all the way to the cliffs to keep the sheep from wandering off into the talus and breaking their legs. It might keep dogs out too. He levered a stone about the size of a five-gallon can out of the ground with his stick and rolled it clear and carefully scraped off the dirt to get an idea of the shape. He started chipping with the chisel, just to see how it worked. It wasn't easy, and when he did get some rock off it was always too much. He wasn't really trying, but one part started to look like Rhonda's forehead, and he tried to add her nose and eyes. When his back started hurting, he and Sally took a hike around the pasture and checked a wether that was limping, chasing it through the flock so he could grab him and hold him down with his knee. He couldn't find anything wrong. He went back and worked on the wall and then went back to chipping on the stone. Who said all you have to do is chip away and release what's inside? Was Rhonda inside there? He couldn't tell yet. Before he drove the sheep down he rolled the stone over near the water tank so no one would see it until he was ready.

Brian had the door back on and the fire going; it was almost warm inside. He admired the gray plastic weatherstrips around the doors. None of the window shades were moving like they used to from the cold air blowing in from the cracks. "It's tight as a drum," Brian said, "but I still need to caulk outside. I'll do that tomorrow."

He was opening a couple of boxes of macaroni and cheese when he heard a vehicle come up the road. It had to be Rhonda. No, it was Monte. He went out almost running and asked before Monte could roll down the window, "Where's Rhonda?"

"She stayed. They called this emergency meeting; she's going to have to be down there another night in Sacramento. The government is trying to raise the grazing fees on federal land. It doesn't affect us up here, but if you roll over every time they kick you, they'll never stop. Whose camper?"

"It's the handyman's. I put him to work. He's weatherproofing the place."

"That old barn?" Monte said. "He'll be there until hell freezes over." They laughed. It was good seeing Monte. He couldn't talk him into coming inside for a minute. He'd like to ask if Rhonda was still mad about the dogs getting the sheep, and if she'd mentioned him when she phoned.

He went back inside after Monte left, and Brian had the table set. After dinner they talked about the chances of ever having a pope from the United States. "That could make a major difference to us here, revitalize the church, renew the faith," Brian said. "I went to a seminary last month to visit a friend who teaches there. Thirty years ago there were a hundred and twenty in a class; now there are twenty, and ten of those are over fifty years of age. And forget the Irish; they've stopped exporting priests as their economy improves." Brian was interesting; it wasn't anything like dinner at the rectory with monsignor at the head of the table, where they ate in silence and then fled. If there was any talk there, it was on whose turn it was to go to the hospital to give communion or to hear confessions from the old nuns at the retirement home. But that didn't take long; the brides of Christ were almost nonexistent now. What is it a priest gives up, he thought, listening to Brian, and what is a priest worth?

"Let me ask you a question, Bob. What would it take for you to come back?" Brian asked. "Just off the top of your head, off the record."

He had to think. Reject the easy ones: go back to married priests, change the hierarchical control, make it more democratic; let women become priests; leave Catholic women alone, in control of their bodies. Lay off trying to influence national politics; think of the greater good. "Maybe if priests were true partners with parishioners. Do away with the altar rail. If priests could be friends instead of fathers. I don't know," he said.

"You miss the church, then?"

"I miss some of the people I liked. I don't miss the grubbing for money all the time. Wednesday bingo. Using the sacraments to raise cash. All the infighting in the diocese. When I think about it, it was like spending twenty years as a character in a comic strip that wasn't usually funny or interesting or informative or good or anything. I couldn't go back to being a caricature. Not in a million years. I feel happy now:

it's almost like my happiness has a shape, something I can pick up."

"Herding sheep?"

"No, I'm not saying it right." He heard a noise outside and listened for it again. Brian started talking. "Shhh," he said. He could hear Sally growling. He got up fast and got the flashlight and went outside, taking the rifle too. The dog was standing stiff-legged, hackles up. He walked around the sheep pen flashing the light into the darkness. There was nothing to see. The eyes of the animals were red in the flashlight ray. He walked up to the rise and then down the length of the wall to the road again. Sally, relaxed now, ran in front of him. They both peed against a fence post when they got back.

Brian was still sitting at the table, waiting for him. Before the Jesuit could speak, he asked, "What would it take for you to leave the priesthood?" He meant it to be funny. But Brian didn't answer, just got up and went out to his camper.

❧

It was almost warm in the pasture; the sun was out and some of the sheep were lying down under the shade of the wall. They were used to him now and liked to get in his way. He recognized some of them too. Monte had pointed out a ram to him by the size of its testicles. "The bigger the sack, the higher the sperm count, and the more lambs the ewe has," Monte told him. "He can produce a two-hundred-percent lamb crop from every ewe he mounts, sometimes three, and instead of servicing twenty or thirty ewes the horny bastard does fifty or sixty. I call him Ace." He asked Chet, who said it was all guesswork when it came to rams, but Ace did have a reputation.

He heard a truck and thought it must be Brian. Then he happened to look back over his shoulder and it was Rhonda, wearing her work clothes, taking long steps as if her legs were growing with every stride. He tried not to run to meet her. Her cheeks were red from the walk, and he held her by the elbows while he kissed her again and again. "I missed you," he kept saying. He couldn't keep his hands off her.

"Let's go have some lunch," she said, loosening her bear hug. "I brought you something."

Sally got the sheep moving and he slung the rifle on his shoulder and ran with his stick to head the flock down the slope. They stopped at Rhonda's truck and she took out two extra-large pizzas she'd brought from down below. They warmed them up in the oven. Brian looked surprised when he introduced him to Rhonda. They sat down, their mouths full of pizza, trying to talk. Brian was asking Rhonda questions about the place, the meeting she'd been at. "You must have known Bob had company, to buy this much pizza."

"Oh no, I could eat this much by myself," Rhonda said. He broke a burnt crust off his slice and carried it out to Sally. She liked pizza. He shooed a sheep away that was halfway under the porch. When he went back in, Rhonda was explaining she'd majored in Ag.

"Was that at UC Davis?" Brian asked.

"It was in high school," she said, taking another mouthful.

In the silence he said, "Brian is a priest with the Society of Jesus. A Jesuit," he added. He was never sure what Rhonda knew.

"Isn't that interesting," she said.

"Were there ever any churches up here?" Brian wanted to know.

"I'm not sure, but I don't think so. My grandfather was Swiss. Most of the first people up here were Swiss, so whatever religion they were, maybe they had a church. I don't remember there ever being one, though. We had an Oddfellows Club that died out. But we still use the hall. The Watch Tower people stopped coming up; gave up on us, I guess." She smiled.

When they finished Rhonda said she had to go back down below again. "We have another meeting tonight. I needed to get some papers, and I wanted to see you." They were standing outside, looking at the flock.

"I missed you more than you missed me, Rhonda." She kissed him so hard on the mouth his lips hurt, and then she got back into her truck. He kept kissing her though the open window.

"I'll be back late tomorrow or the next day," she said, backing out to the road.

"She's a real mother earth type, isn't she," Brian said later. "I don't think I've ever seen anyone eat an extra-large pizza by themself. A big nature girl."

"That's nothing," he said. "I saw her sit down at a bakery and eat a whole chocolate cream pie and then order a sugar donut. They knew her at the place." Brian laughed until he had to wipe his eyes. He hadn't meant it to be that funny.

He had time to work on the stone, which was looking less and less like Rhonda and more like himself, or his uncle—someone—before he went back to work on the wall. The chin ended up with a cleft like he had, but the nose was still hers. Just seeing Rhonda made him feel good. It was like it gave him more strength. The same thing happened when he lifted rocks all day, building the wall; it was like the stones kept getting lighter and lighter.

When he took the sheep down for the night, Brian had the rotten crawl space boards torn off and had started cutting one-by-twelves for the new ones. After dinner Brian asked him to list the best things that ever had happened to him when he was a priest. He had his notebook out. It was too much; he was tired and he stood up. "I don't remember," he told Brian. "But the best thing that ever happened in my life was finding Rhonda. I don't need anything else now. It's so much better this way, to put your faith in another person and believe in yourself because they do. It's the same feeling you get with a sunset or a big tree or a watercolor you especially like. That's my religion now."

He dreamt of Rhonda. They were building a wall with stones that had little wings on them, that flew to their place with just your hands guiding them. Sometimes the stones were playful and gave you a little ride across the pasture if you held on to them. Not far, just to the old water tank and back. Rhonda took a ride with her eyes closed because she didn't like heights, with Sally chasing, barking.

He woke up when he heard the noise, the sheep bleating, but no dog sounds. Sally would bark if there was a problem. What time was it? Only 3:40 by the clock. He got up and peed. Then he heard something again. A dog barked, but far away, Chet's dog, maybe. It was so faint the dog must be way off, chasing rabbits. He was back in bed when he thought again that he was hearing Sally bark. He got up and put on his trousers, then the rubber boots. He picked up the gun before he turned on the porch light. He could hear the dog barking better now that he was outside, but he couldn't see her. He walked toward the sheep pen and looked through the gate. The flock was bunched up to one side and there were sheep lying like rags all over the ground. He couldn't understand what was happening. Where was Sally?

He saw the big cat then; it was poised stretched out on the ground while a second cat lunged at the huddled sheep. One broke away, bleating, panicked, and the first cat pounced on the ewe's back, biting into its neck until it collapsed under him and lay still.

Then the camper door opened and Sally came charging from behind him, squeezed through the gate and was after the cats. He had the rifle up and was firing as the dog went down. Brian was yelling, "That's a protected species." He put another clip in the rifle. He had hit one of the cats and it was trying to get away, dragging itself. He kept firing until it didn't move anymore. The other cat escaped.

Sally was alive but her stomach was ripped open; her entrails looked like a mess of broken eggs. He counted the dead sheep, holding Sally's head. There were twenty-three down. He shot the dog. He thought he was going to be sick. How could this happen, he thought. He walked over to where Brian was looking down at the dead cat. He hadn't realize how big cougars got.

"I don't know what the fine is, but it could be up to five thousand dollars," Brian said.

"Why the hell did you take Sally into your camper? She would have scared them away, or at least stopped the slaughter. They're afraid of dogs."

"It was cold, and it seemed like a good idea. She wanted to come in."

"It wasn't a good idea," he said.

"Well, it wasn't a good idea to shoot this cougar either."

"Those sheep are these people's livelihood," he said. "The flock is the way they make their living."

"The cougars were here a long time before your girlfriend or any domestic animals ever were up here. They were doing what they were made to do."

"How much do I owe you, Brian?"

"Why?

"Because I want you to get the hell out of here, that's why."

He went into the house to get the two hundred forty dollars. He wanted to go back out there and punch Brian's teeth down his throat. Sanctimonious bastard. He called Rhonda nature girl. Rhonda's little toe was smarter than he was. All of a sudden he had such a hopeless feeling he didn't think he could take a step. It was like before he'd come back up here, as if his body was solidifying and he couldn't make a move to help himself. As a priest he'd failed and as a shepherd he'd failed again.

He put the money on the seat of the camper and got a shovel out of the shed and a cardboard box. He kept saying I'm sorry as he carried Sally up by the wall to bury her. He didn't hear the camper leave. The morning light was appearing as if someone were raising a window shade on the horizon. This didn't happen, it didn't, he kept saying to himself, but when he went back to the pen to let out the flock the dead sheep stayed on the ground. He tried skinning some of them, but it wasn't as easy as it looked when Rhonda did the job. He dragged a dead ram clear and recognized Ace. Oh no. No. He should walk down to Chet's and use his phone to call Monte. This was all too much for him. But he couldn't leave the sheep. Then he thought, what good was he there? He tried to convince himself it wasn't his fault; it was Brian's. The cougars'. There were never any cougars before; no one mentioned them. He gave up on skinning the dead animals and walked up to where the sheep were.

He started working on the wall but didn't have his heart in it. He didn't have a heart, period. It had withered away to nothing. He worked until he saw the green pickup stop by the house. He walked back down. "Did you shoot this?" the officer asked, touching the cougar with the toe of his boot. He wore a uniform and had a pistol in a holster on his belt.

He nodded and then added, "I did."

The warden took his clipboard and started writing something on a form. "I got a call about this," he said. He asked a few questions and went over to the sheep pen. "You have a right to shoot the animals if they kill your stock," he said.

Monte drove up and went over to the pen first, then over to where they were standing by the cat. "How many were there, Butch?"

"I saw two."

"You should have killed the other one. He'll be back."

"Who might you be?" the game warden said.

"I'm part owner of those dead sheep," Monte said.

After the warden left, taking the cat, he told Monte what happened.

"You're right it was your goddamn fault."

"I'm leaving, Monte. Tell Rhonda."

"I'm not going to tell Rhonda anything. I'm not your goddamn messenger boy. You came up here, Butch, like we owed you something because you were a priest before. You treated this job like you were doing us a favor. And you treated Rhonda like she was yours to use because she was available and willing. Some priest you must have been."

There was nothing he could say. He went back inside and shaved and washed up. Then started putting his clothes into his pack. There wasn't enough room for everything. Rhonda had given him some good wool shirts. "We only buy wool," she said, pulling up her own collar so he could see the label. He was going to have to leave half the stuff, his work clothes. He knew what a priest gave up now. His place, his identity as a person in the greater and smaller scheme of things. And what was a priest worth? Sally was more valuable than he was.

He heard Chet calling and he went out on the porch. Chet was standing by the stairs, hefting one of his uncle's stones. "I never even heard the shooting," he said. "And I never heard of any pumas up here, either. The state stopped folks hunting them, and I guess they multiplied to where there wasn't enough room for them down below and they got pushed up here."

"Chet, do me a favor, will you? Watch the sheep until Monte comes back."

Chet had to put the stone down so he could shake his hand goodbye. He couldn't face Rhonda. He stopped at the store and paid his bill. Phoned Susan. She wasn't home either, so he left a message on the answering machine. This is Butch. Chet's keeping an eye on the sheep. I'm quitting. Thank you for everything.

He started walking down the road out of town. As he walked he wondered where he was going. After only a mile a beer truck driver stopped for him. His mother had written him from Costa Rica after she'd retired down there. Come and visit me; you'll love this place. He hadn't seen her in four or five years, since she'd moved into a big retirement village of foreigners down there with her new husband. She knew he wasn't a priest anymore; he'd written her that. He wasn't anything anymore.

3

Dear Rhonda. It took him three days to get that far with the letter. He copied the words over and over as if he were practicing penmanship on the blue hotel stationery. He was waiting in San Diego for his passport. When he'd phoned his mother, she'd been happy to hear from him, insisted again that he come down to Costa Rica for a visit. Then she read off a list of things she wanted him to bring down with him. Four Michelin tires. Cosmetics. A popcorn popper. Other things that were hard to get down there. He got everything she wanted; it took an extra day, but what did time matter to someone who'd quit counting? He thought of phoning Rhonda from the airport but kept putting it off until it was too late.

When he saw Annette in the arrival lounge he remembered how the other boys at school had said, "That's your mother?" She was still striking, though she was a little over sixty, tanned, slim as a girl, in Levis and a tank top with a sun visor on her forehead. They could pass for brother and sister. He wasn't going to say it but he did: "You look great, Annette." She hugged him back. "I've got all the stuff you wanted." He kept talking as he followed her to the baggage area.

Elton was waiting near the luggage carousel, and they shook hands. It didn't seem awkward anymore. He had met all his mother's husbands, now Elton, who must be the seventh or eighth. But he'd never known his own father. He'd asked about him when he was a kid. She was always honest. Without a moment's hesitation and with perfect candor she'd replied, "I'm not sure, Bobby. He could have been any one of three boys that summer." At fourteen he'd tried to pretend it didn't make any difference. He had looked a lot like her then, but not anymore, he noticed in the mirror behind the car rental counter. His hair was thinning and turning gray, his belly hung over his belt like he had a hubcap under his shirt, and his tic was back that made his cheek flinch and his right eye squint shut. He didn't look like her brother anymore. Maybe an uncle.

Elton and Annette lived in a suburb of the capitol in a four-thousand-square-foot condominium on a golf course, the whole enclave enclosed by a twelve-foot-high stone wall you could barely see because of the shrubbery. They never mentioned what it cost, but their friends did. "Do you know what I was paying for a cook who could barely boil water?" Everyone compared the prices of things to what they'd paid in the States. He met them all: not just Americans, but an international community—people from Japan, Western Europe, Australia, New Zealand, other Central and South American countries who'd wanted to get away from the high cost of living at home. And violence, his mother added. Annette introduced him to the eligible single women in the group.

On Sunday his mother went to mass at the cathedral in downtown San Jose. She was the only Catholic in the family now. It was because of her that he'd gone to parochial school, but it had been his idea to become a priest. She had tried to talk him out of going to the seminary. "Go to a regular college for a few years first, Bobby. You can play tennis there." He had been seeded twenty-fourth nationally as a junior player. When he'd insisted he was going to be a priest, she'd backed off. "Do what you want," she said. "I always did." He drove the Mercedes, his mother next to him, Elton sitting in back. When he caught glimpses of him in the rearview mirror, Elton looked his age. Annette's grandfather. White hair with an old-fashioned pencil-line mustache like a rim of milk on his upper lip. More brown spots on his face than on the back of his hands; he wasn't as tanned as Annette, though they both played golf everyday. He must have been tall once but leaned sideways now to the left on his good hip, and for support he sometimes carried a putter for a cane.

"Don't hit those Mormons," Annette said. He hadn't noticed the boys in suits riding their ten-speeds on the side of the road. They looked so fresh-faced, as if they'd just been born, pedaling their way to heaven. Or maybe it was the wind.

"They're down here too?" he asked.

"They're everywhere. Mormons and evangelicals. They're both making a lot of converts. You know why there's always two of those Mormon missionaries?" She answered her own question. "So they won't have sex. They don't trust them back home. They report on each other."

"Poor buggers," Elton said. "Not even a cup of coffee in the morning, much less a cold beer in the afternoon. Why do religions always have to make their believers suffer?"

"Because that's how you know what you are, by what you give up, like Jews and Moslems don't eat pork or lobster," Annette said.

"When I was a kid we couldn't dance, couldn't go to the movies," Elton said.

"What denomination was that, Elton?" he asked over his shoulder.

"I don't even remember now."

He liked the rain. "A hundred inches a year in this part of Costa Rica," his mother had said. But it didn't seem to get you wet here. It never stopped anything. Golf games went on; the sun always came out. He played tennis when he could barely see the net. There was an Olympic-sized pool at the club that never had to be heated. This place was like paradise.

He never got the letter off to Rhonda. It was a postcard he finally sent. I apologize for what happened to the flock, Rhonda. It was my fault. Love, Butch.

He did miss her; that was the trouble. He kept having these sudden visions of Rhonda, her big body filling so much of the front doorway at his uncle's house that you couldn't see past her, telling him it could happen to anyone. And sex: he daydreamed being engulfed, no, merged with Rhonda. He had to think this out, consider the best way to approach the problem of going back. There was plenty of time for that.

He fit right into his mother and Elton's routine. Annette was the club's woman champion for the year, and Elton was terrible, had a handicap of twenty-two. Both played thirty-six holes a day if they could get it in. He played the first eighteen with them, early in the morning. He couldn't break a hundred no matter how many lessons Elton gave him. He liked the old guy. Elton had been married a couple of times before. Never had any children: "I was shooting blanks," he said. "Had mumps when I was a kid. And I was too busy making money anyway. I spent forty-five years accumulating a fortune, and now here I am, like a squirrel on a pile of nuts I can't eat." Elton pretended to be just another country boy who'd got lucky, but he was sharp, knew exactly what he was doing every minute.

Especially about Annette. Sometimes at night the two of them would get a golf cart and drive up and down the fairways drinking beer, stopping at certain greens so Elton could get out and walk around barefoot in circles. "It's the only way you can find out the pitch of the damn thing. I four-putted this bastard today." One night they were measuring the distance between a sand trap and the pin on the fifteenth hole, where Elton had got a double bogey. "I knew it was more than a hundred feet," he said, shaking the tape flat to roll it up. "Next time I'll know. You have to be prepared in this life, and then trust your instincts. It's the way I married your mother. I knew the minute I saw her, hadn't even talked to her yet, that Annette is an honest woman. Never mind the rest. She'll stay with me until the end. Not just for the money; I've already given her all she'll ever need. But because she said she would."

"Elton, you're going to last forever."

Elton elbowed him in the ribs. "I hope not," he said.

There were dinner dances at the country club. It was easier to go with Annette and Elton than to think up excuses. When their friends asked, "What were you in, Bobby?" Elton would answer for him, "Livestock." It was a joke between the three of them. He'd told them about his months as a sheep herder as an after-dinner story. But he'd never mentioned Rhonda.

His mother had people over for lunch, not just people from the enclave but from the city, nationals she'd met at Soroptimist Club meetings downtown. She spoke Spanish like a native. He and Elton took a conversational Spanish class four days a week, but it was slow work. "The only way I'd ever get by is with a hundred-dollar bill stuck in each ear," Elton said. After a couple of months he could understand maybe half of what was said if it was spoken slowly.

He liked the place. Costa Rica was like some imaginary country: there were more teachers here than soldiers; there was no standing army; a democracy where everyone from twenty-one to seventy voted in every election—it was compulsory. No abject poverty. A higher literacy rate than any other Central or South American country. His mother pointed all this out several times. The three of them had become a family and this was their country now. His mother wanted that. It didn't make any difference to him. He hadn't heard from Rhonda. He'd sent two more cards, one to Chet and the other to Monte and Susan. This place was as good as any. He had no real responsibilities to anyone. Living here was like being a priest, almost.

His mother must have mentioned she was inviting Marco for lunch, but he guessed he hadn't heard her, because if he had he wouldn't have showed up. Father Marco. Still in his twenties; didn't look like he was shaving yet. He was Italian-American and looked like a national but he was from Redwood City, California, Dominican order, and spoke perfect Spanish. He had been in the country two years. Why did she think he would be interested in meeting a priest?

Elton was interested. He'd started his first electronics firm in Redwood City in the 1940s, making vacuum tubes for the air force. One of Marco's brothers was working in that plant. Annette had managed the Hotel Stewart in San Francisco, and she chimed in with her personal reminiscences. They talked about the changes on the peninsula and then they talked about the changes in the church. "The older guys have told me about that, but for me that's just history," Marco was telling his mother. "I always ate meat on Friday; I never attended Latin mass or confessed through a little screen in a confessional."

"That's because you were born after Vatican II and grew up in the seventies and eighties, you infant," Annette said. "I bet you never even got slapped by a nun or yelled at by a priest."

"The ones I met were fascinating people. Dedicated. I wanted to emulate them." Marco folded his napkin in quarters.

He sat there, hating himself for staying. He didn't say anything; what was there to say? But he listened to this one just like he had listened to the Jesuit up in the valley. He remembered swapping stories with Brian, an image of the Virgin Mary that appeared on the side of a garage, a statue that cried in Pasadena, followed by a plastic dashboard Jesus that wept right in his own parish, Brian laughing until tears came. "We have some lulus in the fold," he'd got out. He had spent nineteen years going over this same ground, rehearsing these same arguments. It all came down to nothing. He excused himself, probably too abruptly, but he needed to get outside.

When the tennis pro quit, the club director asked him if he'd be interested in the job. His mother was against it. "You don't need that," she said. That was true; everything was paid for him here. His mother had even given him her gold card to use. It was easier to take the card and not use it than to reject the gift. "I never helped you much before, Bobby. Let me now," she said. "It'll make me feel better. I have all this money. Let me spend it on you."

"Mother, I'm forty-one years old now."

"What does that have to do with it?"

He had some savings left. And he'd already picked up some money at tennis when some of the members insisted on betting. He'd enjoyed playing tennis when he was first a priest until the monsignor had made some comment when he come back on a Saturday afternoon ringing wet. "If you'd spend as much energy on your duties here we'd get along just fine." He'd been a few minutes late for a prenuptial counseling appointment. He'd quit then and hadn't played in years, but it was all coming back to him. He was probably better now than when he was in his twenties. He'd lost some of his speed and wind, but he was actually thinking now, planning ahead to his next move. He wasn't trying to overpower his opponents now.

He asked Elton what he thought. He knew what the answer would be: his mother was going to have to knock it off. "Take the job; there are a lot of good-looking babes playing tennis in those little outfits. Putting those balls up under the elastic of their panties. That's an old lecher's advice, anyhow."

The job came with quarters at the club and a table in the dining room, but he mostly ate with his mother and Elton, who was taking cooking lessons from a Swiss chef. And he liked teaching; it only took four or five hours a day and gave a shape to the morning. It wasn't hard to teach tennis to beginners; just another stick and ball game. Practice makes perfect. A lot of the residents had been playing for years and just wanted to sharpen their strategy. And then there were the kids and grandchildren who came down for vacations and were looking for something to do.

After four months he got a thick letter from the States. He was afraid to open it. He couldn't tell by the handwriting, but it looked like it could be Rhonda's. The stamps he peeled off and gave to a ball boy who collected them. Two days, and then on the third he told himself grow up and slit the letter open. It was from Monte, full of news:

> *We had a good season; the shearing went well and the price of lamb held up. Old Chet had a big birthday party. He admitted to 85 anniversaries. You know him; he had to explain you only have one birthday, your first, a half dozen times. He said to say hello. Susan and the kids are fine. They're growing like weeds. Rhonda is acting silly. She tore up your card but I found it in her truck, at least part of it, with your address. She's dating a sheep buyer. He's a dud if I ever saw one, but you can't tell Rhonda anything. He's better than that Ag inspector she was seeing, I guess. The other cat came back and I got it with my 12-gauge. It was all I had; I was hunting dove with number eights in my shotgun. It didn't die easy. That priest came back up here looking for you. I told him you were gone. He'd left some of his tools, and I let him back into the house. He told me about Sally, letting her inside his camper. I don't think it would have turned out any different. Those cougars were born to kill, and that's what they're going to do. Rhonda wouldn't listen to that, either. Susan says it would have been better if you hadn't left. Then Rhonda could have got the bile out of her system. But I don't know. When I was in the army I spent 14 months down in Panama. That was before we gave it away. Jesus, what a time. I went to San Jose too. What a pretty country.*
>
> *Regards,*
> *Monte*

He read the letter four or five times; tried putting it away in the drawer of his night table, but ended reading it again and then folded it into the bill section of his wallet. For the next week he kept seeing and feeling the valley in brief still photos as if he were turning the pages of a magazine. The cliffs. Grazing sheep. Rhonda loping after a stray.

The heft of picking up a stone and just holding it, feeling strength coming and going like a current. Eating dinner, just Rhonda and him in the kitchen. How did this happen, that he was down here and she was up there?

He wrote Monte back that afternoon, just a short note that he had gotten the letter.

> *Say hello to everyone. Wish Chet a happy birthday for me. Say hello to Rhonda too; I miss her. Please ask her to write me because I'm writing her.*
>
> *Sincerely,*
> *Butch*

He spent four hours that night writing the letter to Rhonda, telling her how much he loved her. He went on and on. Just let me know there's a chance and I'll be back up there in a minute. He felt like he was throwing a bottle with a note inside out into a void. He knew now he shouldn't have left. But he always left, and he couldn't go back without an invitation.

❦

Elton was right; there were a lot of babes playing tennis. Was it a tradition that club pros were easy and available? It seemed almost expected of him to succumb to the gentlest invitation. Bedding down, that's what one called it, like they were going camping. He had to refuse; he was still waiting for Rhonda to answer. When he hadn't heard from her after a couple of months, he'd written two more letters, the last one saying, Just write me back, answer, and I'll be up there in ten hours. It felt like he was praying again to someone who didn't answer again. It was over between Rhonda and him; he could quit kidding himself.

He decided the next time a woman went trolling for him he'd consider the offer seriously. But they'd have to be over thirty, and he'd ask for their ID to be sure. A simple lustful interlude was what he was looking for. No one even tried. Had he imagined the other offers? In his own fumbling way he made a few feeble approaches, buying one woman a drink, dancing a few times with another. He not only didn't know what he was doing, there was no way he could learn. It was always the women who'd made the moves before, when he'd worked at the hospital. He had missed the whole sexual revolution and now he couldn't buy a ticket for admission. He had to find someone like Rhonda again, who hadn't participated either. He was an aardvark. No, a dork.

When he went to the condo for dinner he was surprised to see Marco and then Elton talking to a young woman. Molly gave a quick rundown on herself, as if he needed to see her passport for an introduction. She was from the East Coast, upstate New York, and did something with other people's money. She came down here to get away from the winter and her off-again on-again husband. She was a recovering Catholic, twelve years in Catholic schools and six more at Fordham to get her M.B.A.

People should be made to wear small signs like name tags declaring their subject specialties, he thought, listening. Elton's would be surviving life's peculiarities; Annette's would be the life search; Molly's was general outrage; and Marco's was spokesman for his generation as seen through the bottom of a chalice. He didn't have any specialties yet himself. He understood sheep better than he did people. He had sent for a couple of books on raising sheep. They were fascinating. He was beginning to understand what he'd been doing up in the valley for that year.

Though he and Elton went into the living room to finish their game of dominoes after dinner, they could still hear the three at the table talking loud as the argument got heated. "You're goddamn right I had an abortion. I'll have another if that's what I think is best for me.

"I'm against abortion," his mother said. "Why do you need it, anyhow, when you've got the Pill? We never had the Pill when I was young."

"According to the pope's statement on Humanae Vitae . . ." That was Marco.

"Oh Jesus," Molly yelled, "thank you very much for the enlightenment, Mr. Pope."

"I'll never understand," Elton said, drawing from the boneyard, "why people discuss religion. It doesn't do any good; it's like the weather. Wishing for sunny skies doesn't get you anywhere."

He'd had too much wine because he said, "I wish I were a ram."

Molly started beginner tennis lessons. She was going into the capitol a couple of times a week with Annette now to have lunch with Marco. Elton wasn't feeling good but he still played a round of golf each day. Annette wanted him to go to a doctor but he wouldn't. He usually stopped in at the club to say hello after his game, before he went home to take a nap. "Why did I chose a game to play that I'll never be good at?" he asked once, rattling his clubs.

"Because we all like challenges, and impossible ones are better for us."

"That sounds almost theological." They both laughed at that.

It might have been true of Molly. Each lesson was her last. But then she'd show up again the next morning, ready for more humiliation, as she called it. She wasn't coordinated, had no upper body strength, but she didn't give up. She entered a novice tournament after a couple of months and was eliminated in the first round, playing women who were ten years older than she was.

Later that afternoon she said, "I didn't know you were a priest. Annette told me last night. You don't act like one."

"What does a priest act like?"

"Well, they don't act like a sex fiend like you do." She lay back on the bed, her bra slid down around her waist like a tutu. "I'm beginning to feel very friendly toward you, Bobby."

"You're my favorite tennis student," he said.

❦

"Talk to Elton," his mother had said. "He's being foolish." So when they went riding that night down the back nine fairways, lights off on the golf cart, swigging beer out of long-necked bottles, he started out, "I'm supposed to talk to you, Elton." He didn't get a chance to go on.

"You know the worst thing in life that could happen to a man? It's not death. It's a limp dick. And that's what I'll have if I let them take out my prostate. I'd rather die."

Given his own experience, he had to laugh, because all he could come up with to say was, "Sex isn't everything."

"No, it's not, but it's not like losing a thumb or a nose, either; it's not just another digit or appendage. It's like it's your umbilical cord to your past. It's your history we're talking about here: when you're young and full of sap, and when you're old and full of pap. A limp dick doesn't keep a record. You know what I mean, Bobby?"

He wasn't sure. He kept remembering the joke in the seminary: I had a wet dream last night and I would have had another but I fell asleep. Neither he nor his dick had any record to speak of. Until Rhonda.

A lot of residents never left the enclave unless they were being driven to or from the airport. But his mother always went into the city for the big outdoor market in the plaza on Saturday, to the movies for what she called her language lesson on Friday, and of course to the cathedral on Sunday. While she and Molly went to mass, he and Elton would sit in a coffee bar reading the English-language newspapers. "Just like home," Elton said. "These funny papers still have Alley Oop; he was my favorite when I was a kid. A caveman, just like I wanted to be. Don't know how I ended up an engineer."

When mass was over they all went to breakfast. Usually Marco would join them, the three of them taking up their argument from where they left off the last time. "The church is changing," Marco insisted. "Look at liberation theology. Maybe it's dying in parts, but those that live will be stronger."

"Liberation theology, big deal," Annette said. "Is that why the Mormons and evangelicals are taking over?"

"It's a phase; the Mormons promise them jobs. It's economic; it's temporary."

Molly interrupted. "Did you read where an ecumenical committee of scholars got together and decided that the Virgin Mary wasn't a virgin after all but had consensual sex with a Roman soldier, and Jesus was the issue?"

"We're talking symbols here, Molly. You have to think how mythology works in the big picture."

"I never bought that story in the first place," Annette said.

Elton put down his fork. "Does that mean Jesus is half Jewish and half Italian? Bless me; with that combination, I can see why there's so many complications." Everyone burst out laughing except Marco.

When his mother phoned him to come over on Saturday morning he was surprised, because she and Elton usually went into town. She never yelled, but he could hear her voice through the front door: "Goddamn you, Elton, we're going back; you can't even get out of bed now." He rang the bell then. Elton was in the bedroom. He looked terrible.

"Elton," he said, trying to think of something funny. Nothing came. "Elton, you can't just not do anything to help yourself. It seems wasteful to me."

"You're going to die without the operation," Annette said.

Elton didn't answer. Wouldn't look at either of them. He turned around to leave the bedroom and Elton spoke. "I guess I can get a penile implant at the same time," he said.

Everything started moving faster after that, as if they were already back in the States where time doubled in speed. His mother had a friend with a plane and a pilot. Elton had chaired the foundation that built the clinic, so there was no problem about getting in. He had promised Elton he'd go too. But he was having second thoughts. He'd been down here for over a year now, though it seemed like a week. He'd gotten used to the place; he didn't really want to go back. This was paradise. There was no future here; all you had to do was float in the present.

He tried not to think about Rhonda. He hadn't heard from Monte or Susan in four or five months. Their kids had written after Christmas thanking him for the gifts he'd sent them. They didn't mention their aunt. When he thought of the valley now it was like he was looking at faded old photos, where you weren't absolutely sure what you were seeing was what you remembered. He could go back up there now, just for a visit. Monte was always inviting him. See Chet. It wouldn't be like when he was a kid, dumped on his uncle. Or after he'd left the priesthood, with nowhere else to go. Just for a visit, as a spectator, before he flew back to Costa Rica.

❦

He could tell the minute they passed over the border to California. Not just from the rows of houses with swimming pools, but from the feeling of energy, even at five thousand feet, like you were in the center where the needles on all the hand-held compasses pointed. "What fun," his mother said, looking out the window, holding Elton's hand. "We're back." When they landed in Santa Barbara there was an ambulance waiting.

Surgery was scheduled for the next morning. "Elton should have had this done two years ago," the doctor said. His mother was calm. "Everything is going to be all right," she kept saying. On the way to the hotel she stopped the car at the mission. Busloads of tourists milled around the steps, and a big wedding was going on inside. The pews were filled, but his mother knelt down on the tile floor in the back. He sat next to her in a folding chair as she prayed. The year he'd spent with her in Costa Rica was probably the longest they'd ever been together. Annette, the woman who happened to give birth to him, who farmed him out until he was old enough to go to boarding school, an interesting stranger he visited on holidays. But she was a good woman. Kind. He just didn't know her very well. He wished he could pray too, for Elton, for her, for himself, but it just wasn't going to work that way anymore. He thought about what Elton had said to him before they'd left the hospital. "Bobby, stick around till I get back on my feet, will you? I'd like there to be someone around to have a few laughs with in case things go wrong." It wasn't like being asked as a priest. It was like being asked as a friend. He put his arm around his mother's shoulders and held her as tight as he could.

They sat side by side in a waiting room during Elton's surgery. The doctor came out laughing: Elton had gone into the operating room with a strip of paper marked SAVE taped around his penis. The operation went well and Elton was scheduled to begin a series of radiation treatments as soon as he recovered some of his strength.

His mother rented a house, joined a study group at the Old Mission, signed up for a Spanish literature seminar and an aerobics class. Visited Elton for hours every day, reading to him or just sitting beside him, her hand on his. The treatments knocked him for a loop; he was woozy a lot of the time. He didn't look good.

He was just hanging around, driving his mother, visiting Elton. He wasn't sure what he should do next. It was like after his tenth anniversary as a priest; he kept asking himself, What am I doing here? Maybe it wasn't just habit, he'd decided back then. Maybe he could become a better priest. There was a lot of room for improvement, the monsignor would have told him. Did that mean to become another person? He'd started to work on an M.A. in counseling. Did it help? It gave him a name to put to a question, a category to put a person in. She's in denial. He's transferring. Projecting. It put him farther away, helped him distance himself, which was better.

But even after three semesters he was never sure if he was helping them anymore than before. He decided that just listening was the best and went back to that. And prayer. He prayed and prayed. For his parishioners, for himself too. Modern life was just too complicated. It got so he felt like he was being called to big highway accidents where he had to rescue people from the burning wreckage that was ready to explode. He jumped when the phone rang. "It's for you," the monsignor would yell up the stairs at two A.M. And the phone messages on the answering machine: Help. Help me. In one three-month period two parishioners committed suicide, overcome by their problems. He had been trying to help them. Then a woman he'd only talked to once shot her husband and two children and then herself. He didn't blame himself, but it was too much for him. He asked the chancellor to reassign him. At the next parish he was put in charge of the fund drive for the new hospital wing and Wednesday night bingo in addition to his regular duties. Twenty-four months of that and he quit.

He started having long talks with his mother, a first for both of them, while Elton had his radiation treatments. "I don't remember you being so solicitous of your other husbands," he said once. She was offended, but he hadn't meant to be offensive. They were in the hospital cafeteria, having a bowl of soup.

"A woman of my generation always needed a man. I thought I did, anyhow. A woman couldn't get a loan from the bank to buy a house. I could never become the director of any of the hotels I worked at, for the same reason. I married all those times because I couldn't stand the thought of just sleeping with them because I'd be a slut then. I don't think I ever seriously loved any of them. Except now, for Elton."

"How did you know it was love, then, with Elton?"

"Hindsight is the only method that really works, but that takes too much time. I don't know. Maybe you can't love someone else unless you love yourself first, and then you come to love the idea of the best part of both of you. I think it's a proof of grace that you can finally know enough, or maybe it's see enough, beyond your own self, to love another person." He had been listening open-mouthed. "Eat your soup," she said.

The next morning he woke up and decided he was going up to see Rhonda. She could ignore him if she wanted to. Just say hello. Elton seemed to be doing okay; he had five weeks of radiation left. They weren't sure they were going back to Costa Rica. "I just want him to get well," his mother kept saying. "I don't care where we live." He left a note for Elton, "I'll be back. Think only pure thoughts. Take cold showers. B."

He headed up 101 driving fast, as if he planned to get there by dinner. After five hours, cutting east now, about halfway there, he slowed down, thinking of reasons why it might be better not to go. He stopped completely around four in the afternoon, about seventy miles from the valley. He would go up there tomorrow, he promised himself. See everyone and then . . . He didn't know.

"Hello, stranger," Monte said when he answered the door. Susan gave him a hug. The kids had already left for school. They sat in the kitchen. Susan asked if he'd eaten and then cooked him a plate of bacon, eggs, and potatoes. He was hungry. No one mentioned Rhonda. "How's Chet?" he asked. He'd expected Rhonda to be there; she had an office in one of the back rooms. He told them about Costa

Rica and then Monte talked about the time he spent in Panama. Finally he asked, "Where's Rhonda?"

"She's up at your uncle's place," Monte said.

"Well," he said slapping his knee, "I think I'll go up."

"Butch," Susan said. She stopped there.

"What?" he asked.

"Things have changed," Monte said. "I don't think you ever met Larry, but he's been coming up here for years, buying. Has a place down below too. Runs sheep."

"Rhonda married him," Susan said.

All he could think of was marriage is a sacrament. Holy matrimony. Joseph and Mary. Were they married? He'd ask his mother. He was thinking foolish thoughts. They were waiting for him to say something. "How nice for her," he said. He stood up. He felt like he was turning to stone. "I guess I'll stop and see Chet, then go back down. It was good seeing you two. Tell the kids to keep writing. I really enjoy their letters." He started moving his feet toward the door.

"Butch, he was already married," Susan said. "He was married when he talked Rhonda into going over to Reno."

"What a mess," Monte said. "I'm going to break his back if he ever comes up here again. She threw him out when the other wife showed up with their four kids, and there's another one before that he never bothered to divorce either. A bigamist or something, I don't know what they call then anymore, or even if it's against the law now. Rhonda really stepped in it this time." They both walked him to his car.

As he drove up the gravel road he was thinking information highway, emotional highway, life's highway: didn't they used to say tunnel of love? Chet was sitting on his porch. When he saw who it was he got up, grinning, went to the front door to yell to someone inside, then came down with his hand out to shake but instead picked up a stone and held it against his stomach. "Damn, I've been thinking about you, Butch," he said, grinning from ear to ear. "That Indian blanket you sent was just the thing. I put it at the foot of the bed and never felt the cold last winter."

An elderly lady, Chet's niece, it turned out, brought them each a cup of coffee. Chet thanked her but held onto his stone. "No more cats, Butch. Monte got the other one. We had a good winter, hardly any snow, but a hundred and eight inches of rain."

He picked up a stone, absorbed its heaviness as Chet talked. He could see down to his uncle's place. There were sheep scattered around the pasture, in front of the house and on the road. But they didn't seem alive, moving; they looked like cutouts, props.

"Hardly any rocks came down this year. Rhonda almost caught up with them in the north pasture. You should see how far the wall goes now. I told her she'd better knock it off, in her condition. She could hurt herself." Chet put his stone down on the ground and picked up his coffee cup.

"I found those stones you were chipping on. I showed Monte. Rhonda took the one with the face inside her kitchen and put it by the stove. I never knew anyone to put one in a house. We knew you did it. Your uncle used to dress stones for the wall, but no one ever put a nose on one before."

He saw someone come out of his uncle's house. Two dogs appeared from under the porch. He dropped the stone. "I'll be back, Chet," he said. He took his time walking up the dirt road. He was in no hurry. He had all the time in the world. He stopped at the water tank for a drink. He thought of the times they'd submerged themselves in that water to cool off. Rhonda's hair floating around her face, her eyes fixed on him, oblong bubbles dripping from her lips, separating the two of them. She must be watching him cross the pasture. He could see her sitting in a lawn chair next to the old Airstream trailer.

There was a rifle leaning against the trailer door and a dog he didn't recognize was asleep under her chair. She looked the same, overalls, flannel shirt, sunburned face, curly hair shoved behind her ears. He wasn't a good judge, but she seemed six or seven months along. She held her hands cupped underneath her stomach as if she were holding up a stone. She was relaxed, half smiling, eyes almost closed, like she was drowsing. She heard him then on the path.

"Susan phoned, said you came by, that you were on your way to Chet's. I was going to walk up there, but then I thought . . . I don't know what I thought, so I came up here. I'm glad you stopped."

"I've been thinking about you, Rhonda. A lot."

"I've been busy," she said. "I managed to stop my biological clock, made the alarm go off loud." She laughed her old laugh. "And we got a good price for lambs this spring." She didn't pause. "You know what happened, if you've seen Monte. After you left I knew you weren't coming back. And I told myself I wasn't going to chase after you. So I decided if I could do it once, I could do it again. It would be that much easier. It was like entering the beauty pageant again with absolutely no chance to win. But I tried it. I flung love in every direction and hoped it would stick on someone. But love doesn't work that way, I found out. I guess a person can't be lucky in both marriage and business." She looked up at him then and dropped him a wink, and he gave her a light sock on the shoulder. "What have you been up to, Butch?"

"I was giving tennis lessons down there. I kind of liked the teaching part. I looked into it; I'm qualified to teach history if I take a few classes and get a credential. Or if I take a state test and pass it, I can substitute teach, maybe."

"You'd be good at it," Rhonda said. There was a long pause. He was watching her. "You weren't a bad sheep herder. If you'd learned to pay attention more," she added. They both laughed. "It's my turn now. I've got to concentrate on things. I even slip up, say 'my lamb' for 'my baby' sometimes. I surprised myself: this time it was me that wasn't paying attention."

"I remember how you used to say *Concentrate* all the time. I learned a lot from you Rhonda. More than I can say." Her face flushed. He put out his hand to her, and it seemed like it was a long time before he felt the warm, strong grip around his fingers.

"I'd hire you back in a minute," she said. "I need a herder. I'm suppose to be resting. I missed you, Butch."

He didn't want to let go, but he did. "There's something I have to take care of in Santa Barbara." He wanted to go on, make a declaration, a vow. But he had done that before. "I'll see you, Rhonda."

"Come back anytime, Butch."

Chet was waiting on the porch with his niece. He'd been thinking about it, coming back across the pasture. "Chet," he asked him, "can I have one of those stones by the porch?"

"Nope," Chet said.

"Let him have one over by the tree, then," Chet's niece said.

"I want those too. I've had them a long time."

"Take one off the garden wall, Butch, they're mine," the niece said. "I brought them down myself to build that wall the summer I lived up here. Cranky old man."

He took his time. There was one that was going to be easy to dress; it already had Rhonda's chin. "It's no good taking them out of the valley," Chet said. "They just get in the way. You have to keep them up here."

He hefted the rock. It felt just right. "I was planning to put another nose on this one. See if I could do it better this time. Then I'll bring it back. I promise."

Sunsinger Books
Illinois Short Fiction

Crossings
Stephen Minot

A Season for Unnatural Causes
Philip F. O'Connor

Curving Road
John Stewart

Such Waltzing Was Not Easy
Gordon Weaver

Rolling All the Time
James Ballard

Love in the Winter
Daniel Curley

To Byzantium
Andrew Fetler

Small Moments
Nancy Huddleston Packer

One More River
Lester Goldberg

The Tennis Player
Kent Nelson

A Horse of Another Color
Carolyn Osborn

The Pleasures of Manhood
Robley Wilson, Jr.

The New World
Russell Banks

The Actes and Monuments
John William Corrington

Virginia Reels
William Hoffman

Up Where I Used to Live
Max Schott

The Return of Service
Jonathan Baumbach

On the Edge of the Desert
Gladys Swan

Surviving Adverse Seasons
Barry Targan

The Gasoline Wars
Jean Thompson

Desirable Aliens
John Bovey

Naming Things
H. E. Francis

Transports and Disgraces
Robert Henson

The Calling
Mary Gray Hughes

Into the Wind
Robert Henderson

Breaking and Entering
Peter Makuck

The Four Corners of the House
Abraham Rothberg

Ladies Who Knit for a Living
Anthony E. Stockanes

Pastorale
Susan Engberg

Home Fires
David Long

The Canyons of Grace
Levi Peterson

Babaru
B. Wongar

Bodies of the Rich
John J. Clayton

Music Lesson
Martha Lacy Hall

Fetching the Dead
Scott R. Sanders

Some of the Things I Did Not Do
Janet Beeler Shaw

Honeymoon
Merrill Joan Gerber

Tentacles of Unreason
Joan Givner

The Christmas Wife
Helen Norris

Getting to Know the Weather
Pamela Painter

Birds Landing
Ernest Finney

Serious Trouble
Paul Friedman

Tigers in the Wood
Rebecca Kavaler

The Greek Generals Talk
Phillip Parotti

Singing on the Titanic
Perry Glasser

Legacies
Nancy Potter

Beyond This Bitter Air
Sarah Rossiter

Scenes from the Homefront
Sara Vogan

Tumbling
Kermit Moyer

Water into Wine
Helen Norris

The Trojan Generals Talk
Phillip Parotti

Playing with Shadows
Gloria Whelan

Man without Memory
Richard Burgin

The People Down South
Cary C. Holladay

Bodies at Sea
Erin McGraw

Falling Free
Barry Targan

Private Fame
Richard Burgin

Middle Murphy
Mark Costello

Lives of the Fathers
Steven Schwartz

Taking It Home: Stories from the Neighborhood
Tony Ardizzone

Flights in the Heavenlies
Ernest J. Finney